WHERE THE WIND
NEVER SLEEPS

A Memoir from the
High Plains of Montana

RUTH M. SHERWOOD

sweetgrassbooks
an imprint of Farcountry Press

ISBN: 978-1-59152-311-6

Cover art by Beth Loftin Studios, 406-930-1359,
bethloftinart@gmail.com, bethloftinart (Instagram)

Design by Steph Lehmann

For more information or to order extra copies of this book
call Farcountry Press toll free at (800) 821-3874
or visit www.farcountrypress.com

Produced by Sweetgrass Books
PO Box 5630, Helena, MT 59604; (800) 821-3874; www.sweetgrassbook.com

The views expressed by the author/publisher in this book do not
necessarily represent the views of, nor should they be attributed to, Sweetgrass Books.
Sweetgrass books is not responsible for the author/publisher's work.

Produced and printed in the United States of America.

26 25 24 23 22   1 2 3 4 5 6

AUTHOR'S NOTE

Ruth Helen Clark and Frank, 1920

This is the story of our family homesteading and farming in northeastern Montana. Some of the names have been created because I could not remember the names and others have been changed to protect the privacy of individuals described.

Looking at Mama's picture I can believe there is a heaven where Mama on her horse, Frank, and Papa on his horse, Sunfisher, gallop together across the vast, high plains with all cares whipped away by the eternal wind.

Beth Ann Loftin graciously gave me permission to use the cover picture she created from this photograph and other photos of Mama. She is a talented painter and sculptor who combines traditional western portraits with contemporary techniques and color work.

Loftin was born in the Osage Hills of Oklahoma, as was her mother Ruth Marie (Muller) Loftin. Beth's Muller grandfather, a German immigrant, harvested by hand stones from the Osage Hills to build their own home while homesteading and raising six children. ᏸ

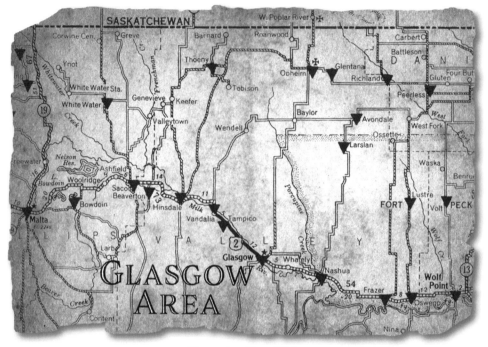

Glasgow Area Map - 1930

CONTENTS

PROLOGUE

"As sure as the sun rises in the east the wind will blow," Mama often told me. Living in northeastern Montana I found that to be true.

Mama wove stories throughout our days. Her colorful tales of living on a homestead and the neighboring homesteaders enriched my life. In 1915 when Mama was twelve she boarded a train to Montana with her divorced mother, Mrs. Clark, who claimed a homestead in the Genevieve Country. Mama and Mrs. Clark's lives changed dramatically from their life of luxury in St. Peter, Minnesota. Yet, Mrs. Clark succeeded where many men failed. Papa quoted Shakespeare to describe Mrs. Clark, "Though she be but little, she is fierce."

Mama's life changed again when she married Papa. Responsibilities and hard times exacted a toll on her. Sadness and regrets often tinged her stories of life after marriage. They lived for five years on Papa's homestead in the Barnard Community. Later, except for two interludes in Idaho, they lived on Milk River Valley farms, first near Hinsdale and later near Glasgow.

Life for me on the Milk River Valley farms proved to be of continuous interest and some fear. Our family was a team, and although we three sisters were younger than our brothers, we participated in every activity where we were allowed. Polio and WWII dominated the news, German POWs rode from their camp near Glasgow to work our sugar beets, blizzards howled in during long winters, bums who rode the Great Northern freight trains made their way to our house for food, the Milk River threatened to flood every spring, and Mama worried about the reliability of the man-made Ft. Peck Dam, since we were on the Milk River and in the Ft. Peck Lake Floodplain.

We left Montana in 1951, but Montana never left me. ◦

CHAPTER 1

BORN IN A BLIZZARD

February 27, 1940. A late-winter blizzard screamed across the northeastern Montana high plains and whipped down into the Milk River Valley town of Hinsdale. School dismissed early so students could hurry home before they could no longer find their way. Parents parked in front of the school and hastened their children and those of their neighbors into their vehicles. Blowing snow was already drifting across roads, and stinging, icy flakes thickened, making visibility difficult. Stores closed early, and every person who could sought the shelter of home.

Dr. Cockrell's nurse had cancelled afternoon appointments of those who had telephones, and, believing that nobody would venture out, Dr. Cockrell was about to close the office. His nurse answered an incoming call and informed him that Helen Sherwood, who was a maternity patient at Mrs. See's home, was in labor. He donned his sheepskin overcoat, ear-flap cap, mittens, and galoshes, grabbed his bag, and hurried into the horizontally driven snow to his car. The engine sputtered before it finally caught, then purred predictably. He had no time to lose. Mrs. Sherwood was bound to have a difficult delivery. Her narrow pelvis and fragile mental state required both his professional ability and his reassurance that she could and would make it through her labor and produce a healthy baby. She had previously delivered three healthy boys, but two other babies lay in graves in the Opheim Cemetery.

Dr. Cockrell's car roared through drifts accumulating on Hinsdale's gravel streets and stopped in front of the See's two-story house. He was grateful to Mrs. See, a nurse, for opening her home in town to some of his patients. He still made house calls in the country, but fewer of them now. He noted with satisfaction that John Sherwood's truck was parked in front. John could help to calm Helen. As he ducked his head against the wind and opened the door he could hear both the howling blizzard outside and Helen's screams from within. Mrs. See, a small, hardy lady, ushered Dr. Cockrell up the stairs into the room where Helen gripped one of John's hands while he used his other to mop the sweat from her brow. John Sherwood was no stranger to childbirth, having delivered their oldest living son, Willie, on their homestead without the help of a doctor.

Mrs. See brought steaming cups of strong coffee to John and Dr. Cockrell as several hours passed. Sensing his wife's exhaustion, John kept up his encouragement and, at the right moment, joined the doctor in urging her to push hard. At long last the baby's head crowned, and soon thereafter a strong, healthy girl wailed as Dr. Cockrell smacked her bottom.

Mrs. See cleaned and swaddled me in no time, and Papa held me as Mama smiled wanly. Then they both wept remembering another red-headed baby girl, Mabel Lillian, whom they held only briefly before she died shortly after birth. They had both wept then, but these were tears of happiness.

I was born in Montana, but my parents, Ruth Helen Clark and John Marvin Sherwood, were not. They met in northeastern Montana when Mama lived on her mother's homestead near Barr in the Genevieve Country, and Papa lived on his homestead in the Barnard Community. Throughout my childhood, they frequently spoke of their homestead years, and many of their closest friends were those they had known on the prairie, as they called all of the high plains area. Mama wove colorful stories of her homesteading days into my life and, at my request, retold those stories in her final years, so I could write them down.

"I lived, I really lived." She told me, "I was not on the outside looking in."

In 1915 when Mama was twelve, her mother, whom she always referred to as "Mrs. Clark," moved the two of them from the charming Minnesota River Valley town of St. Peter to an abandoned homestead on the northeastern Montana high plains. Alcoholism had claimed Mr. Clark, and with the loss of his job, their life of luxury in St. Peter could no longer be sustained. Caroline Watts Clark chose divorce and departure rather than life with her widowed mother and schoolmarm sister or reliance on money from her brothers.

She made that decision on her own and announced it in characteristically dramatic fashion—choosing the time and place with studied forethought.

On the day before Thanksgiving 1914, Mrs. Clark instructed Mr. Kirkpatrick, their hired man, to drive the horse and buggy to the front door of their beautiful ten-room home in St. Peter. He helped Mrs. Clark, Helen, and Elsie Sukor, Helen's governess, into the buggy for the ride to the local depot. They would travel by train to spend Thanksgiving holidays with Mrs. Clark's family, the Watts, in Minneapolis.

Mr. Clark would not be going with them. At some point in their lives, he had been a beloved father and husband that Mama and Mrs. Clark looked forward to seeing when he came home from his traveling salesman's route. Gradually, alcohol changed him into an angry, contentious man they dreaded to see come through the door. "Papa was a mean drunk," Mama told me, "and Mrs. Clark gave him an ultimatum: give up the bottle or lose his wife and daughter."

Apparently he took her seriously enough to stop drinking abruptly—either on his own or with the help of a psychiatrist or doctor. Though he survived the delirium tremens, he was left a trembling, tearful wreck with a soft mind. Mrs. Clark could neither abide his weakness nor forgive him for trading their present and future for alcohol. She wanted no part of him, and his sister took him to live with her in St. Paul.

On Thanksgiving Day the Watts family—Mrs. Clark's mother, sister, two brothers and their families, plus Mrs. Clark, Helen, and Elsie gathered at the table laden with food and set with crystal, china, and sterling silverware. As kitchen help cleared the table to make way for dessert, Mrs. Clark tapped her knife against her glass.

"I have an announcement," she said when all eyes looked toward her. "Helen and I are going to Montana—to claim a homestead!"

First puzzlement. Then shock. One would have thought the chandelier had fallen into the gravy bowl.

ৎৡ· · ◦ · · ৡৢ

They knew of Mrs. Clark's dilemma with the disintegration of Mr. Clark, but they were unprepared for her solution.

My maternal grandmother's decision, seemingly made in the blink of an eye, was unassailable. During the ensuing weeks no amount of coaxing, reasoning, begging, nor threatening from her family, caused Mrs. Clark to as much as waver. She would go. And Helen would go with her. Helen was not staying with the Watts family in Minneapolis. No, not even until Mrs. Clark could make a home for them in Montana.

Next she filed for a divorce. "Scandalous!" lamented Mrs. Watts. This further upset the Watts family's equilibrium. Their position against her breaking up the marriage did not soften until her brother Harry visited Mr. Clark and his sister. Thereafter, the family changed from assailing her for deserting her husband to promising to help her, should she agree to stay in Minnesota. Thank you, but no thank you. Mrs. Clark could and would stand on her own two feet!

Mrs. Clark moved swiftly. She had long handled all business affairs, so she readily sold some of their real estate holdings and pocketed five thousand dollars to finance her venture. She, like hundreds and hundreds of other homesteaders, was seduced by advertising, lured to Montana with rosy promises and, in some cases, outright lies. The federal government, railroads, and states waged ambitious campaigns to lure settlers west. For the past several years colorful posters in both America and Europe had advertised homesteading in the West in general and, now, in Montana in particular.

FREE LAND! Claim 160—320 Acres!
FERTILE SOIL! PLENTIFUL RAINFALL! ABUNDANT CROPS!

Mrs. Clark wheedled the Great Northern Railway agent into giving her a poster. She tacked it up on her library wall at home, to give her inspiration should her enthusiasm lag.

She corresponded with her friends, the Greers, who had left Minneapolis some years back for the sheer adventure of going west to claim a homestead and were now living in Plentywood, Montana. They offered much sound advice to Mrs. Clark as she prepared for her own adventure, including the importance of her arriving in Montana to locate a homestead before late April.

She realized by the end of January that her preparation duties precluded her continuing her social schedule. Her daily routine of mornings at her desk and on the telephone as she attended to her personal business, as well as that of various organizations to which she belonged, must change. Likewise, her luncheons, volunteer social work with poor families, helping at the hospital, committee meetings, and active participation at their Episcopal church could no longer be allowed to consume her time.

She turned over virtually all household duties to Mrs. Kirkpatrick, her housekeeper and cook, freeing up still more time for preparations for their move. Mrs. Clark spent relatively little time with her daughter at this point, having hired a governess, Elsie Sukor, to help with schoolwork, supervise piano practice, and keep her daughter company. There was no need for change in that area of her life. While it was Mrs. Clark who gave specific directions to Elsie, it was Elsie who spent time with Mama.

Although this was a well-established pattern by the time Mrs. Clark was devoting all her energies to homesteading preparations, early on she had been something of a model mother to the precious baby she had longed for. She enjoyed dressing up Helen and watching her progress as a toddler. And when precocious little Helen came down with what specialists eventually diagnosed as infantile paralysis, she stayed by her bedside and brought in the best doctors and nurses available. When the infantile paralysis passed, leaving her little girl with a decided limp, Mrs. Clark saw to it that she had the best therapy available. But Helen's immune system was weakened, and she came down with rheumatic fever. Once again Mrs. Clark had devoted herself to her daughter's care. Once the crisis had passed, she'd hired the first of a series of live-in governesses whose presence relieved her of childcare responsibilities.

With Elsie Sukor now in responsible charge of Helen's care, Mrs. Clark traveled back and forth to Minneapolis making purchases to assure both comfort and success on the homestead. Their home would be remote, so they must be as self-sufficient as possible. Toward that end she purchased books, quantities of books. They covered everything from canning tips to prevent ptomaine poisoning and botulism, to treating cattle that had eaten locoweed, to building a house. Other purchases included household, kitchen, and clothing items that would not be easily found in local stores or ordered from the *Sears and Roebuck Catalog.*

In early April she ordered Mrs. Kirkpatrick to pack minimal necessities for setting up housekeeping. Those would travel as freight on the journey west. She designated other items that were to be shipped once her house was built. Helen's beautiful Steinway piano from the Clark family in Frankfort, Kentucky, would not be going with them—not now or later. Mama said that at the time she had mixed feelings. She had been taking piano lessons for several years and practiced the piano two hours a day. She loved music but Mrs. Clark had assured her she would have more exciting things to do on the homestead.

The day of departure arrived. Elsie, who would be staying on at the Clark house with the Kirkpatricks until the school year ended, had pleaded to be able to miss classes to go to the depot with them. Mrs. Clark relented. Tears flowed as they said good-bye to Mrs. Kirkpatrick, who pressed a basket of food into Mrs. Clark's hand. Mr. Kirkpatrick helped them into the buggy for the last time. They were leaving the place that had been home to them for nine years. Yet Mrs. Clark hardly gave her lovely home and spacious grounds a backward glance.

"Don't look back," she told Mama, "We need to focus on what is ahead of us."

At the St. Peter depot Mama and Elsie cried as they parted. Mr. Kirkpatrick gave Mama and Mrs. Clark a tearful hug, then he and Elsie left for home. The Kirkpatricks would live in the house until it sold. Another job with one of Mrs. Clark's friends awaited them. When school ended Elsie would become the governess for the children of Harry Watts in Minneapolis.

The Watts family and a host of friends awaited Mrs. Clark and Mama when they arrived at the Great Northern Depot in Minneapolis. They would not board their train for Montana for several hours. In the interim, they visited as they walked around admiring the architecture of the elegant, recently completed depot that served the Great Northern Railway of James J. Hill, empire builder.

Mrs. Clark deftly fielded questions concerning her homesteading prospects, showing self-confidence, but acknowledging the risks involved in such a bold venture. "My attorney told me not to believe all the enthusiastic promotional material Mr. Hill is disseminating." Mrs. Clark laughed. "By this time in my life I have learned to trust sparingly."

Accustomed as they were to seeing Mrs. Clark in the latest fashions of the day, friends and family alike joshed her about her current outfit. She readily defended the smart twill split skirt and matching jacket she wore. "This is fashionable attire for Montana," she said. "And practical. I won't be riding side-saddle there.

Too soon the hour of departure approached, and they all walked with Mama and Mrs. Clark to the boarding area. Amid tears, hugs and admonitions to write, Mama and Mrs. Clark boarded the train, waving one last time before making their way down the aisle toward their seats—and their new life in Montana. ᏻᏇ

CHAPTER 2

320 Acres
and Fortitude

Their coal-burning train chugged west, away from familiar looking towns with trees, tidy yards, and painted houses. Cultivated farms with fences and livestock gave way to more open, unfarmed spaces. Distance between small, mostly treeless towns increased the farther west they traveled. Soft evening light cast by a setting sun dimmed the passing fields.

Mrs. Clark chose dinner time in the dining car with the ambiance of a fine restaurant to talk to her twelve-year-old daughter. Mr. Clark, Helen's once beloved Papa, was no longer the husband and father they had known. That person was gone. From now on, rather than answer questions about him, they would just say he had died. Young Helen agreed. She recognized the stigma of being the daughter of an alcoholic. Besides, she wished to remember and talk about the loving father he once was. And, another matter. Mrs. Clark said she felt and looked younger than her age. She felt like she was thirty-five.

"But, how old are you really?" Mama inquired.

Mrs. Clark laughed, "Thirty-five."

⟳ · · ○ · · ⟲

Mother and daughter looked out their train window at the Great Plains. Mid-morning sun fell on a land with no shadows. Gently rolling, vast, empty prairie stretched from horizon to horizon. Occasionally, brush or trees growing on the banks of a creek or small river cast shadows on the last of winter's snow. Large patches of snow still lay on the barren ground of the prairie. Towns and small prairie houses assumed a temporary look, as though they had been thrown together until more permanent structures could be built.

The train slowed to enter Culbertson, Montana, just inside the state's northeastern border. Mama and Mrs. Clark readied themselves to get off the train. They would visit Mrs. Clark's Minnesota friends, Amanda and Jacob Greer in nearby Plentywood before going to Hinsdale. The Greers had assured Mrs. Clark that she would learn more about finding and proving up a homestead from their experience than she would from all of her books combined. "Besides," Amanda Greer's letter had said, "We both crave a long visit with kindred spirits. Pass us by at your own peril!"

In Culbertson they caught a branch line train to Plentywood. Although the Greers had settled in Plentywood, they advised Mrs. Clark to go to Hinsdale and look for a homestead in the Genevieve Country, the area in northwestern Valley County surrounding the little town of Genevieve, where good land was still available for homesteading. Amanda, Jacob, and their five-year-old son Kevan waved from in front of a small building that served as the depot for Plentywood.

The Greers owned both a house in town and another on the 160-acre homestead they had chosen for its proximity to town. Since the homestead house was too small for company, they stayed in town overnight and traveled by wagon to their homestead. There the Greers showed them the garden plot, an orchard of small trees that would one day furnish plums and crabapples, the chicken house, barn, Hereford cattle, and the stacks of hay diminished by winter's feedings.

Jacob insisted they walk the perimeter of the twenty acres he had plowed and planted to prove up the homestead. He explained that homesteaders must cultivate and plant one-eighth of their claim. Since the 1909 Enlarged Homestead Act, Mrs. Clark could claim up to 320 acres. Should she choose the larger claim, she must cultivate forty acres. Cultivating and planting forty acres of land that had never known a plow would be a formidable undertaking. She should plan to hire neighbors. While neighbors would be hard-pressed to complete their own work, most would also be sufficiently cash-strapped to make time to help her.

The conversation during the week spent with Greers touched on Minneapolis and common friends there, but always returned to Montana and the the basics of homesteading.

"I'm confused," Mrs. Clark said to Jacob and Amanda, "Sometimes you refer to northeastern Montana as plains and sometimes you refer to it as prairie."

Jacob laughed, "It is confusing. Really northeastern Montana is part of the High Plains of the Great Plains. A prairie is actually one type of plains. Most homesteaders simply call all of the area a prairie."

As a parting gift, Amanda gave her friend Mrs. Clark a reference notebook she had compiled. It covered much of the homestead information they had discussed. Jacob gave Helen and Mrs. Clark each a small box containing a compass, and he insisted that they go outside so he could coach them on properly using a compass.

"Prairie or plains," Jacob told them, "A compass could well save your life. Many ranchers and homesteaders have been lost in the rolling hills that all look alike once you are out of sight of a building."

They both gave Mrs. Clark further warnings:

"Make friends with your neighbors. You are dependent upon them."

"Most men are decent, but lots of scalawags who couldn't make it elsewhere take to homesteading."

"There is a shortage of unwed women on the prairie and unwed women who appear to have money are particularly rare. You will be beset upon by men conniving to marry you for your money and your homestead. Beware!"

⸂⊚· · · o · · ·⊚⸃

Back on the Great Northern Railway headed to Hinsdale, Helen, who had been mulling the homestead life the Greers had shown them, dared a question, "Mama, how are you ever going to be able to do all of that work on the homestead?"

Mrs. Clark cocked her head, and gave her daughter a half-smile, "*We*, Helen, *we* are going to do all that work. Of course, we are blessed with enough money to hire men to do much of the hard labor, but there will be plenty of work for both of us! We will attack it step-by-step in order of priority. We *can* do it, and we *will* do it."

Mother and daughter stepped off the train for the last time in Hinsdale, a bustling little cow town in northeastern Montana on the stretch of the state known as the Hi-Line. The depot swarmed with potential homesteaders, many who spoke a foreign language. Mrs. Clark told Mama they would deposit their bags in their reserved room at the hotel; then find the locator Jacob Greer had recommended. The locator would take them out to look at potential homestead sites. Jacob had taken the liberty in his correspondence with the locator to tell him Mrs. Clark would pay an amount above his going rate commensurate with desirability of the site and his expediency.

⸂⊚· · · o · · ·⊚⸃

Early morning sun did not warm a piercing, cold April wind. As they traveled in the locator's buggy he extolled the virtues of the homestead site he had found for them. The 320-acre homestead had been staked and claimed, then

9

abandoned two years later. The man who'd staked the claim had found buying a one-way ticket Back East was more appealing than fulfilling the arduous requirements necessary to get a patent on his claim. The man had, however, built a typical two-room homestead shack and a few out-buildings, and he had cultivated some of the forty acres required. Best of all, the homestead boasted a spring near the house-site—a rarity in Northeastern Montana.

⋅⊚⋅ ⋅ ⋅ o ⋅ ⋅ ⋅⊚⋅

Mrs. Clark snapped up the claim as soon as they returned to Hinsdale. Their homestead, located near the Canadian border some thirty miles north of Hinsdale, was on the west side of Valley County in the Genevieve Country. Home for Mama was now the barren treeless prairie that would be burned by sun in summer and frozen by bitter winds whipping down from Canada in winter.

Mrs. Clark hired a man who had found hauling freight to and from other people's homesteads made for a better living than he could have by working his own. Once he had deposited their freight at their site, Mrs. Clark and Mama carried water from the small pond fed by the spring and set about cleaning the mouse-infested shack. At first Mama had balked at the nasty job. Mrs. Clark narrowed her eyes, "Helen, there are no princesses on homesteads!"

"He was a slob!" Mrs. Clark declared. "An absolute lazy slob. Furthermore, his building capabilities don't exceed that of a four year old. The first thing we'll do is to hire men to build our house."

Once their belongings were installed in the clean shack, Mrs. Clark and Mama spent part of many days walking several miles to get acquainted with their nearest neighbors. Three of their neighbors were bachelors who were happy to make Mrs. Clark's acquaintance and eagerly offered help. Mrs. Clark was in need of both hired hands and transportation to Hinsdale. Emmett Averial and Henry Lick would work for her as hired men part-time. Henry Lick, whose homestead bordered Mrs. Clark's on the north, would also take her to and from Hinsdale. Dutch Cable lived with his parents and worked on their homestead. He was eager to earn extra money as a part-time hired man.

Mrs. Clark's father, Grandpa Watts, had been both a successful lumber dealer and a skilled carpenter. Now Mrs. Clark critically eyed her neighbors' homestead shacks. Building was not their forte. Thankfully, she had not only bought books on building a house, but she had spent sleepless nights studying them. Additionally, she had drawn up plans for her house, and she had left a copy with the lumber company in Hinsdale. They agreed that when she notified them that she was ready, they would freight out all of the house supplies. She, not hired men, would be in charge of building her house.

Dutch Cable was kind, capable, and quiet. Mrs. Clark thought him to be knowledgeable and trustworthy. She dispatched him to buy a horse for her and one for Mama. He returned with Peggy, Mrs. Clark's horse, and a smaller horse, Teddy, Mama's horse. Their horses came with all their tack, including western saddles. Mrs. Clark was accustomed to riding side-saddle, but on the prairie she would ride astride. Dutch gave them both riding lessons and taught them how to care for their horses.

Mama said she soon developed a crush on Dutch Cable, and while she was accustomed to Mrs. Clark's flirtatious ways around men, she resented Mrs. Clark's attention to Dutch. He was nineteen—older than Mama, but much, much younger than Mrs. Clark. Mama knew she looked older than her years, and she hoped Mrs. Clark would not tell Dutch she was only twelve. Mama said that while he was not particularly good looking with his receding hair-line and pug-nose, he was well built, and he exuded warmth and kindness.

Mrs. Clark and Mama rode their horses to a neighboring homestead, La Ross's Road Ranch. They had noticed other road ranches on their trip from Hinsdale to the homestead, and La Ross's, like the others, consisted of a small building where the family lived that also served as a store and post office. For a reasonable fee one could eat meals and stay overnight. Mrs. Clark left a letter to be mailed requesting that the lumber company in Hinsdale should deliver her building supplies in two weeks.

On a sunny, windy spring day in early June Henry Lick stopped by with his team and wagon to drive Mrs. Clark and Mama to Hinsdale. They purchased groceries and a Homesteader's Outfit that included the basic supplies necessary to begin homesteading. Mrs. Clark also bought a fancy Home Comfort cook stove costing seventy-five dollars and bags of coal to be delivered to the homestead. Before leaving Hinsdale, she checked at the lumber yard. Yes, they had received her letter, and all of her building supplies would soon be delivered. ॐ

CHAPTER 3

SCALAWAG

A few nice homes dotted the prairie, but most were constructed from kits called homestead shacks. Lumber companies sold the one-room and two-room kits containing all materials necessary for their building, including tar paper to cover the shack making it more weather-proof. Homesteaders assembled the kits with varying degrees of skill. The treeless prairie did not come with lumber for buildings. Homesteaders who could not afford the price of the kit used whatever they could find, and their shacks often gave the appearance of having been thrown together with questionable materials and covered with tar paper.

Mrs. Clark told Mama that they should both be thankful they could afford to build a "real house." She chose a site close to the spring. Equipped with her house plans, knowledge, and high expectations, Mrs. Clark supervised the building of her house. She hired Dutch Cable, Henry Lick, and a carpenter from Hinsdale, Mr. Worsell. He often stayed over in an empty building that had once served as a barn.

Mrs. Clark anticipated resistance from men unwilling to accept that a woman might know more than they did in any area other than domestic affairs. Dutch Cable and Henry Lick, who were both working on their own homesteads, arrived mid-morning and left mid-afternoon. When Dutch and Henry were not there, Mrs. Clark talked with Mr. Worsell of her expectations, and she often helped him when he worked long hours alone.

Mama said she doubted that Dutch Cable would have minded taking directions from a woman, but it was clear that Henry Lick, in spite of his own poorly built homestead shack, thought he knew more about the building than even Mr. Worsell. In fact, he seemed to feel he knew more about almost everything. Mrs. Clark flattered Henry Lick with smiles and attentiveness as long as his erroneous, and sometimes outlandish, ideas did not affect her goals. Yet, she stood firm when his ideas collided with hers. After all, she controlled the purse strings.

Henry Lick was a good-looking man of medium build with brown hair and blue eyes. Mama said that Mrs. Clark openly flirted with Henry Lick.

Mama suspected that he was much younger than Mrs. Clark, but he clearly enjoyed her attention. Discussions of Henry Lick at La Ross's Road Ranch included a rumor that he left his German relatives back in Minnesota because he was so ornery they didn't want him. Though she was young, Mama remembered the Greers' warning about scalawags. Could Henry Lick be one of the scalawags planning to separate Mrs. Clark from her money? That was a worry Mama kept to herself. Mrs. Clark would not have appreciated having her judgment called into question.

The house was finished by mid-July. After camping in the miserable little shack, their house looked charming. The outside was painted white with dark green trim, and light creamy yellow calcimine brightened the interior. Downstairs consisted of a combined kitchen and front room, Mrs. Clark's bedroom, and a porch. Stairs led to Mama's bedroom and a storage area. A large heating stove in which they could burn coal or dried cow chips stood in the front room, and, as the Greer's had advised, the coal-burning Home Comfort cook stove served the kitchen.

Dutch Cable had cultivated the garden area in late May, and Mama and Mrs. Clark had planted it. Now Dutch worked on a way to pipe water to the garden and Henry Lick built a fence around the garden, chicken pen, and barnyard. They bought laying hens from their neighbors, the Dicksons, and ordered chicks from a poultry catalog. Emmott Averial, a self-contained loner, continued to spend his time fencing Mrs. Clark's homestead. Mrs. Clark planned to build up a herd of cattle, and she did not want neighbors' cattle grazing on her land, nor did she want her cattle to stray from her property. "Fences make for good neighbors." Jacob Greer had advised her.

Dutch located six large work horses for Mrs. Clark's team. A wagon and farm implements were delivered from Hinsdale. With abundant pasture and the spring-fed pond for water, Mrs. Clark purchased a small herd of Hereford cattle. Henry Lick sold Mrs. Clark two of his Guernsey milk cows with their young calves, and he taught Mrs. Clark and Mama to milk the cows.

As long as Mrs. Clark was nearby, Henry Lick was kind to Mama, but as soon as he was alone with her, he criticized her, gave her orders, and scolded her for no reason. Mama told him that he was not her father, and she did not take orders from him. She also complained to Mrs. Clark, who spoke to Henry Lick. Each time his behavior improved temporarily, but soon he returned to his old ways. Mrs. Clark told Mama that he wanted to be in charge of the homestead, and since she was not about to relinquish her authority, he was taking his resentment out on Mama.

Mrs. Clark and Mama had arrived in Montana unaccustomed to physical labor. After a summer of morning to night work they both wore an unladylike tan, and they developed muscles they didn't know they had. Mrs. Clark, healthy and strong, could do a surprising amount of work. Since Mama's health was somewhat compromised from having had polio and rheumatic fever when she was younger, Mrs. Clark kept her busy, but her work required less strength than that which Mrs. Clark did.

Mama remembered that first summer on their homestead as the best. She and Mrs. Clark worked hard, but they worked as a team. The only time Mrs. Clark had spent so much time with Mama previously was when Mama had been sick. Now, together, they learned to garden, care for their livestock and poultry, milk cows, gather eggs, and cook. Growing up in a house with servants, Mama had never cooked, and Mrs. Clark's previous cooking experience, as she told Mama, "consisted of a few short funny stories."

Mrs. La Ross taught both Mama and Mrs. Clark how to cook the kind of hearty, basic food that men like. Mrs. La Ross, herself a mail-order bride, told them that in the catalogs advertising mail-order brides one of the most popular phrases was, "Makes good gravy." She assured them that they could cook biscuits, gravy, potatoes, salt pork, and pies three times a day and satisfy most men.

When fall came Mama saddled Teddy each morning and rode four miles to the Barr School. Most of the building was below ground level with the back dug into a slight rise. The front and part of two sides were clear, but the roof was dirt and students could walk on it. The dugout had two windows and a door in the front. Actually, it turned out that on the prairie a dugout was a good idea. The teacher, Miss Kingsley, kept a fire going in the coal stove during cold weather and the dugout stayed nice and warm. It was more comfortable than the homestead shacks most students came from.

Mama found attending school in a dugout to be a "frontier adventure" after attending the proper schools in Minneapolis. An incident that still brought her laughter happened during one of the many visits of their teacher's boyfriend. Boyfriend was one of the bachelors from a homestead near Genevieve. When he rode his bay quarter horse to see Miss Kingsley during classes she would send the students out to recess and lock the door. If the weather was pleasant, the extra recesses were fun, but many winter days were far from pleasant.

One day when it was twenty below zero and the little ones were crying, Arthur, the largest boy, walked up the dugout roof and sat on the chimney. When smoke filled the dugout Miss Kingsley and Boyfriend came out coughing. Boyfriend rode away, and Miss Kingsley and students went in as soon as most of the smoke cleared.

❧· · · ◦ · · ·❧

A few weeks after school started Mrs. Clark told Mama that Henry Lick would move into the original homestead shack, which he and Dutch Cable had improved and converted to a bunk house. He would be eating his meals with Mama and Mrs. Clark. This would give him more time to work on both homesteads. Up until then, Mrs. Clark was still engaging Mama in conversation at mealtime, but Henry Lick directed his attention solely to Mrs. Clark, and he sought to engage her in conversations that excluded Mama. Mrs. Clark seemed not to notice, so Mama didn't mention it to her.

Not long before Thanksgiving, Mrs. Clark announced that from now on Henry Lick would sleep in their house on a day bed in the front room. Emmott Averial stayed in the bunk house part of the time, and he and Henry Lick did not get along. Mrs. Clark surmised that Henry Lick wanted to be in charge of Emmott, and Emmott was having none of it. Mama objected to Henry Lick's moving into their house, but to no avail.

Mama was not the only one to object. When Mrs. Dickson learned about the arrangement, she came to visit, saying that she and other neighbors were shocked that Mrs. Clark would allow a man who was not her husband to live with her. This was not "that kind" of community! Besides, what kind of example was she setting for Helen? Mrs. Dickson's twins, Buel and Buela, would not be allowed to visit Helen as long as Henry Lick slept in the house.

The next day at school Buela told Mama about her mother's visit with Mrs. Clark. "Your mother lives with a man she isn't married to. And she told my mother to mind her own business. I don't think you and I should be friends any longer."

❧· · · ◦ · · ·❧

Mrs. Clark supported the homestead with money she brought to Montana with her, most of it from the sale of property in St. Peter. She paid the hired men well, believing that this helped to assure both their loyalty and their production.

She did not want to siphon money from investments. Since Barr School only held classes through seventh grade, Mrs. Clark decided that Mama would finish eighth grade and high school in Glasgow. Rather than Mama's boarding with a family as most students did, Mrs. Clark and Mama would live together in Glasgow during the school year and live on the homestead in the summer. Mrs. Clark would get a job in Glasgow to help support the homestead.

Mama said that living in Glasgow with Mrs. Clark was a good time in their relationship. Mrs. Clark asked Mama about her classes, her teachers, and her friends. They walked to school activities at the North Side High School, attended local theater productions, and ice skated on the Great Northern Pond.

With renewed opportunity for one-to-one conversations, Mama talked to Mrs. Clark about Henry Lick and why she did not like him. Mrs. Clark told Mama that she was sorry his living with them caused Mama to be embarrassed, but the reason she had not married Henry Lick was that she did not trust him. Additionally, marriage would legally give him the "upper hand," and he would be over-bearing, perhaps even mean. He was a hard worker, and, thus far, as her hired hand, he had no choice but to comply with Mrs. Clark's wishes. Mrs. Clark pointed out that the homestead required much hard labor that neither she nor Mama could do. Besides, in a few years Mama would leave the homestead to live her own life.

Summers during Mama's school years in Glasgow, she and Mrs. Clark returned to the homestead where Mama spent much of her time herding their cattle—often with Henry Lick who was even more disagreeable. Mama told Mrs. Clark that Henry Lick's strategy was to "divide and conquer." Mrs. Clark agreed that he was jealous of her relationship with Mama, but she reminded Mama that she would soon finish high school and be free of his aggravating presence.

In spite of Mrs. Clark's reservations, she married Henry Lick in May of 1919 when Mama was sixteen. Mrs. Clark, knowing that Mama would not approve of her marrying him, did not tell Mama they were married until later. Indeed, Mama did not try to conceal her disappointment with Mrs. Clark and her anger toward both of them. Henry Lick had won, and, perhaps because he saw Mama as less of a threat to his goal of controlling the ranch, he was more civil to Mama. After all, in his mind, he had divided and conquered.

When Mama finished high school, Mrs. Clark encouraged her to enroll in the School of Nursing at the Deaconess Hospital in Glasgow. It was a year around program that would keep Mama away from the homestead.

This pleased Mama, but while she found nursing to be highly interesting, it proved to be harder for her physically than the work she did on the homestead. Nursing meant long hours of grueling work. In addition to classes and patient care, nurses were required to help with most housekeeping and janitorial chores. They mopped floors, filled coal bins, changed and washed the bedding. . . . Nursing required the total commitment that Mama had and a strong constitution that Mama did not have. She left nursing school after eighteen months and returned to the homestead for a short time.

Riding and herding in the open air helped to restore Mama's health, but Henry Lick was once again cantankerous. Mama felt this change was due to the obvious tension in the marriage. While Mrs. Clark seemed happy to have Mama home, Henry Lick did not. Mrs. Clark confided to Mama that he had apparently believed, mistakenly, that marrying her gave him total control of the ranch and access to her money. She had not added his name to any of her financial holdings; therefore, she still could control most of the decisions about the ranch, but she also must keep in mind that she needed his help to succeed.

༺ · · o · · ༻

Mrs. Clark, believing that Mama needed to further her education, arranged for Mama to attend the University of Minnesota Twin Cities School of Agriculture. Mama said that she thrived at the university. No physical work was expected of her. She earned money by typing papers for other students and helping professors with research. She participated in extra-curricular activities. She was a member of the swim team, she sang in the girl's quartet, and, best of all for Mama, she joined the drama club. Her favorite activity during college was performing in plays. That cinched her goal for her future—she wanted to be an actress. Mrs. Clark thought otherwise. She informed Mama that in no way was she paying for Mama's education for Mama to be an actress.

Mama was graduated from the university in 1925 with a degree in agriculture. She did not go on stage as an actress, rather she returned to the ranch. Mrs. Clark, having been granted a patent on her 320 acres and having acquired a large herd of Herefords, now called her homestead a ranch. She recognized that while Mama was capable resource for information about horticulture and animal husbandry, she did not have the physical stamina required for a life of ranch work.

Mrs. Clark encouraged Mama to attend the Montana State Normal School in Dillon, Montana, to get a certificate to teach school. Their certification program required one school year consisting of three quarters of study and passing a state exam. Mama completed the requirements in two quarters and passed the exam. Once certified she was asked to teach in the one-room school in the Barnard Community. Two of her students, Edna and Lester Sherwood, were children of Aubrey Sherwood, John Sherwood's brother.

Mama had heard about John Sherwood before teaching at Barnard. Her girlfriends were abuzz about the handsome bachelor in the Barnard Community who was determined to stay single. Most bachelors on homesteads actively sought a wife, but not John. Mama said that, even though she always had beaus, her curiosity about John Sherwood was piqued. ◦〜

CHAPTER 4

TO A TAR PAPER SHACK

Mama met John Sherwood at a Saturday night dance at the Barnard School in the fall of 1926. Dances on the sparsely settled prairie were highlights of the homesteaders' social life. They came on horseback, in buggies and wagons, and, in winter, they came in bobsleds. Those whose homes were too far away to return that night, stayed with acquaintances, or rolled out robes and blankets and spent the night in the school.

Barnard School where Mama taught was over twenty miles from Mrs. Clark's ranch. Mama boarded with the Madison family during the week and returned to Mrs. Clark's ranch on weekends to work. When a Saturday night dance was held in Barnard, Mama spent the weekend with the Madisons. Dance nights the girls all met at the house of the girl who lived closest to where the dance was held. Mrs. Madison told Mama she could invite her girlfriends to stay at their house when the dances were at Barnard. They came early to dress, put on make-up, style their hair, and ride their horses to the dance together. The laughed and talked of the men who might show up at the dance. After the dance they all spent the night, often visiting until the early morning hours.

Talented and untalented musicians played an assortment of instruments, dancing couples filled the middle of the floor, observers visited, and children darted in and out among all the adults. Mama, who the school board had already chastised for "kicking her heels too high at the dances," danced every dance.

She noticed John Sherwood, who visited with spectators throughout the evening. He never danced, nor did he appear to notice Mama. She was not accustomed to going unnoticed. When the musicians finally put away their instruments, Mama walked directly over to John Sherwood and asked him to help her saddle her horse. This began their courtship on horseback. On their third date John surprised Mama by asking her to marry him, if Mrs. Clark would give her permission. He told her that she needed someone to take care of her. He also told her that she was the most interesting woman he had ever dated.

The next week Mrs. Clark sent a letter to John requesting that he come to visit for the weekend and stay over in the bunkhouse. She must get acquainted with the man who wished to marry her daughter. Friday after school John rode with Mama to Mrs. Clark's ranch. Mama wondered if Mrs. Clark would approve of John. She had not previously approved of any of Mama's many beaus as suitable husbands. Mrs. Clark had even flirted with some, saying later to Mama that any man who would respond positively to her flirting was absolutely not husband material.

John Sherwood was different. He did not call Mrs. Clark by her given name as she requested, rather he called her "Mrs. Lick" to establish boundaries. When John was present at mealtimes Mama was not excluded from the conversation. Mrs. Clark, Mama, and John talked of books they had read, people and places, history, current events, and ideas. They learned that John had a college education and that he was a WWI veteran who had fought on the Western Front in Europe. Henry Lick attempted to turn the conversation to himself and his activities on the ranch. But this time his monopolizing Mrs. Clark with his mundane conversation was without success. He sulked at the table and left as soon as he cleaned his plate.

Mrs. Clark approved of John Sherwood. He was intelligent, educated, interesting, well-mannered, and soft spoken. As much as Mrs. Clark approved of Papa, Henry Lick disapproved. Henry Lick and Papa were about the same age, but Papa was everything Henry Lick was not. Henry Lick, uneducated and with limited conversational abilities, was a rough-hewn, hard-working farmer. He sought to bolster his ego by enlarging his holdings of land and cattle. Mama believed that he married Mrs. Clark to further the realization of his ambitions.

Mama, who had always worked on the ranch weekends and summers, now contributed her teaching salary as well. Mama knew that one reason Henry Lick opposed her marriage was that she was a dependable, unpaid ranch hand and her teaching salary, though small, helped to buy cattle.

On Mama and John's fourth date, another dance, Mama told John she would marry him, in spite of Henry Lick's objections. When time came to leave the dance and saddle their horses, Mama surprised John by swinging her saddle up on her horse and cinching it down faster than he could. Saddling her horse would not be one of the ways he would take care of her.

Mrs. Clark fully supported Mama's marrying John in June when the school year ended. Mrs. Clark began plans for an elaborate community wedding.

Grandma Watts' unexpected death in the spring saddened Mrs. Clark and Mama, and out of respect for her passing, they planned a small wedding at Mrs. Clark's ranch. Only a few close neighbors were invited.

John rode his horse fifty miles to Glasgow to get the wedding certificate at the Valley County Court House. Since Mama was finishing her school year, she did not go, and John, who was not bothered by details, reported both Mama's age and their wedding date incorrectly.

Henry Lick continued to object to the wedding; finally, he went as far as to say he would not allow it. That was too far. Mrs. Clark, who usually catered to Henry Lick and fluffed his ego, told him in no uncertain terms that this was her ranch, her money, her daughter, and he had no say in the matter. And, if he could not be pleasant, he could stay in the bunkhouse.

The day of the wedding, June 17, 1927, Mama wore her rose silk crepe graduation dress. Mrs. Clark had insisted that Mama looked lovely in it, and nothing she could buy before the wedding would look better. Reverend Kuller arrived to perform the ceremony. Their Belgian neighbors, Mike and Germaine De Walshe and Ernest Van Lant Schoot came. Henry Lick hardly spoke; he was surly and drinking.

John, whose homestead was twenty miles away, arrived last with his horses and wagon. Henry Lick watched as John cared for his horses. When he saw John approaching the porch he hurried to meet him. As John entered the porch door Henry told John that he forbade him to marry his daughter, and he tried to push John out. John did not feel like being pushed out. A lively fight ensued.

A large wrench lay on a shelf close enough for John to reach. He grabbed it and whacked Henry on the head. Henry sank to the porch floor. John straightened his tie, stepped over Henry Lick, came into the house, and met Reverend Kuller and the guests. None of the neighbors liked Henry Lick, and they all agreed it was high time somebody put him in his place.

Reverend Kuller conducted the wedding ceremony without the stepfather of the bride in attendance. During the ceremony they heard him gallop away on his horse. Mama said that from time to time she shook slightly with suppressed laughter as she thought of Henry Lick's whack on the head. She hoped the others would think her shaking to be wedding jitters.

Mrs. Clark had cooked for two days to prepare a festive wedding dinner, but Mama said that Mrs. Clark's good intentions exceeded her cooking skills. Mrs. Clark's fancy wedding cake fell. Nonetheless, dinner was a resounding success. In Henry Lick's absence, all were in good spirits as they drank liberally to toasts and recounted funny stories about Mama. Mike told how he had met Germaine, and they all talked of good times past on the prairie that would return with the rain.

ᏹᎧ· · ◦ · · Ꭶ

Late afternoon sun edged ever nearer to the western horizon with a show of orange and pink. Mama and John Sherwood, my Papa, would travel to his homestead under a ceiling of bright stars in the chill prairie night. Mama had already packed her clothes—attractive, high quality clothes mostly selected and purchased by Mrs. Clark—into a trunk. Another trunk held linens and lovely items Mama had collected for the home she would have one day. Two others held miscellaneous items. Wooden apple crates held some of Mama's books. Papa loaded Mama's trunks and books into his wagon. Mama would ride her beloved horse Frank, purchased after Teddy died, alongside Papa's wagon. She strapped on her holster that held her Iver Johnson pistol and readied to mount Frank.

Papa hesitated, "Are you sure it's safe to leave your mother alone to deal with Henry Lick when he returns?"

Mama laughed, "She's been dealing with Henry Lick for years. She will lock him out of the house, and he'll stay in the bunkhouse until he regains some manners. If he tries to break in, she'll fire her pistol, and, if he breaks in, well, he's dead. It would be good riddance to bad rubbish."

"Oh!" was all Papa could manage.

Mama rode away from Mrs. Clark's charming four-room white house to share Papa's typical homestead shack—two rooms covered by tar paper. Mama surveyed her new home, a home below the standard of anything she had yet lived in. Many of her friends lived in homes no better than Papa's shack. Well, if they could, she could, but now she understood why many mail-order-brides took one look at their new home and fled "Back East."

Mama, who had longed to be "the lady of the house" in charge of her domain, told me that she had no idea how ill-prepared she was to do so. Mrs. Clark ran her household and her ranch. Mama lived and worked there, but she did not make the decisions, any decisions, she now realized. Mrs. Clark even made the grocery list and purchased groceries. Papa, thirteen years older than Mama, had been batching for seven years. He took charge. And, Mama told me, he never passed the reins to her. She said that at first she was relieved, but later she resented his control as she had resented Mrs. Clark's control. "Never," she advised me, "Marry an older man."

⌘ · · ○ · · ⌘

Papa remembered his seven years of batching on his homestead as the best years of his life. He had followed his brothers from Missouri to Montana and had claimed his homestead in 1917 when he was twenty-six. The following year he returned to Missouri and enlisted in the army to help America win The Great War. In 1919, after the horrors of the war, all Papa wanted was the quiet peace of the prairie. There, the whistling sounds were caused by prairie winds, instead of incoming German shells.

Papa and his brothers—Don, Aubrey, Henry, Ben, Guy, and Fred—had all settled adjoining claims. They worked together and played together. They planted, harvested, branded cattle, butchered, and drove cattle to the railroad stockyards in Hinsdale. They also picnicked, held their own rodeos, hunted, and brewed beer.

Once married, Mama and Papa must forge a life together. Papa was still in his own kingdom, and, initially, not much changed for him, but Mama was obliged to create a new life. The school board policy prohibited married women from teaching, but this proved no hardship for Mama. She said that she and Papa, who had taught at the Barnard school for a while before she did, both intensely disliked teaching.

Mama worked on their homestead, gardening, canning, cooking, caring for poultry, and, when Papa was late in the field, she milked their two cows. They still found time to socialize with family and neighbors and to attend an occasional dance. Mama knew some of Papa's neighbors from teaching in the Barnard school. Many afternoons when her work was caught up, she saddled her horse and went riding or visiting neighbors. Other afternoons she read from Papa's library. Evenings she and Papa often read and visited until bedtime.

Papa owned a Bible. For all the books Mrs. Clark had collected, none was a Bible. Papa, whose mother died a few days after his birth, was raised by his Grandfather Bagby and his Aunt Jenny. They were devout Methodists. Every evening after supper Papa read to Mama—first a short passage from his Bible, then a prayer from his prayer book. She found this to be interesting. Mrs. Clark had been very active in the Episcopal Church in St. Peter, but she told Mama that "religion was a crutch."

Sundays were best of all. Mama and Papa did not go to church, but every Sunday was revered as the Sabbath and only necessary work was done. Sometimes they visited with family or neighbors, but mostly, fearless and unfettered, they rode across the prairie trailing laughter in the wind. ৵

CHAPTER 5

DEATH AND SURVIVAL

In the summer of 1928, Mama realized that she was pregnant. Mama told me that she grew up longing for siblings, and now she wanted her own family of at least three children. She believed that Mrs. Clark had not proved to be a dependable mother figure for her. In St. Peter, social work had consumed Mrs. Clark. Mama was left with governesses and the household help. Later, Mrs. Clark allowed Henry Lick to distance her from Mama.

Papa, too, wanted a family, but money was tight. The dry years that Papa previously believed to be an anomaly began to seem a harbinger of the future. No longer were his fields of flax sky-blue with blossoms, no longer did wheat heads hang heavy on their stalk, no longer could the fields of hay produce enough to feed his cattle. …

One by one, Papa's brothers were leaving the dusty, barren, drought-stricken prairie. Fred had long since moved to Canada, Don and Henry chose northern Idaho, Aubrey moved to Oregon, Ben relocated to Stillwater County, Montana, and Guy drifted from one place to another. Still, Papa stayed, hoping and praying for the return of the rains. Mama called Papa "The Eternal Optimist."

Papa now leased land vacated by his brothers for a total of 520 acres that he grazed and farmed. He worked harder for longer hours. Mama milked the cows more frequently, because Papa had not returned from the fields. Their long pleasant evenings grew shorter, and their Sundays were not always free. Mama wondered to Papa if they should join the exodus from the prairie. Papa wanted to hold on a little longer. Surly, the rains would come.

Other neighbors had left the prairie. Those who stayed worked and worried together. Should they stay, or should they go? Could they hold out financially?

In February 1929 when Mama's time for delivery neared, Mama and Papa talked of what would be best for her delivery. They lived too far from Opheim to travel by horse and bobsled once labor pains began. Short on money, Papa wasn't sure how they would pay the doctor and for Mama's boarding in Opheim as she waited to deliver. Many homestead wives stayed at home and a neighbor lady, who served as a midwife, came to assist with the delivery.

In the end, Papa insisted that Mama go to Opheim to board and have a doctor present for delivery. They would work out payments.

On a cold February day Mama took one last look around their home to be sure that all was ready for their baby. The tiny, soft clothes and diapers she had sewn for the layette and the beautiful bassinette, Mrs. Clark's gift, awaited their homecoming. Papa helped Mama into the bobsled, and they rode across the snowy, frozen prairie filled with anticipation and twinges of anxiety.

Once Mama settled into Mrs. Rowland's boarding house, Papa returned home to attend his livestock and farm chores. A friend at the lumber company would ride out to notify Papa when Mama's labor pains began. Papa would then notify a neighbor who would take care of Papa's chores while he was gone. They had decided not to notify Mrs. Clark, lest she drive her new automobile the thirty miles to Opheim on roads that could drift over in a matter of minutes, leaving her stranded.

Mama spent several uncomfortable days waddling around in Mrs. Rowland's small boarding house. The walls of the few rooms Mrs. Rowland rented out were paper-thin, and sounds from the two adjoining rooms drifted clearly through them. Mama listened to another homestead lady scream through her baby's birth. Later Mama admired a perfect, precious baby girl. Mama longed to hold her own baby.

When Mama's labor pains began, Papa was not present. He had not been notified as planned. Labor pains began in the afternoon, continued through the night, and into the next day when Dr. Hoffman and his nurse arrived. Mama, suffering and spent, began to fade from time to time. Evening approached, Dr. Hoffman paced the floor, and his nurse threatened to leave if the baby was not delivered by supper-time. The baby was ready to be pushed out, but Mama was too tired to help much, and Dr. Hoffman delivered the baby with forceps.

Mama heard a baby crying from a great distance before she lost consciousness. Later when she tried to awaken she heard a baby crying—a shrill crying that never seemed to stop. Papa hovered over her praying and stroking her hair. When she had enough strength she asked to see her baby, a boy she was told. She wanted to comfort him and stop his crying. "You are too weak to hold your baby," the nurse said. And so, for most of two days, Mama floated in and out of consciousness, and always the baby cried.

Finally, she awoke to see Papa, his head down on her comforter crying, but she did not hear her baby. He was dead. John Bright Sherwood was buried in Opheim the next day, February 26, 1929. Papa must go back to the home-stead to care of his livestock, but Mama was too weak, so she stayed at the boarding house.

⁂ · · · o · · ·⁂

When Mama recovered sufficiently, Dr. Hoffman drove her home in his car. Papa hurried out to the car, lifted Mama into his arms, and carried her into the house. Papa had wrapped up the bassinette and layette in a blanket and put them away in the barn, but the pain and emptiness that enveloped Mama were not so easily put away.

Wan and listless, Mama passed much of the rest of the winter of 1929 in bed. Mrs. Clark came from time to time with help, food, advice, and finally, when nothing else worked, a good tongue-lashing. She lambasted Mama for her selfishness. Couldn't she see that John was grieving too? Yet, he must do all of his work, plus come in and do Mama's work. And, he must listen to her indulgence in self-pity.

Whether it was the tongue-lashing or warm spring winds, Mama wasn't sure, but she rallied. She planted the garden Papa had tilled, she took over the kitchen again, and she rode her horse across the prairie.

By mid-summer, Mama realized she was once again pregnant. She was gripped with hope one day and fear the next. Would this baby live? Papa continued to pray to his God and rest his case with a power that had brought him home from The Great War against all odds. Didn't he still have his wool great-coat with a hole in the collar where a German artillery shell had passed through it when his head was pressed into a frozen rut? Hadn't Aunt Jenny received notice of his death from the Spanish Flu? Didn't he still carry shrapnel in his elbow?

Summer advanced as the wind carried away dry topsoil. God did not answer all prayers. As if the drought that marched south across the Great Plains was not enough, the bottom dropped out of America's economy on October 29, 1929. Blessedly, Papa had not borrowed money for a tractor and other machinery as so many homesteaders had. Dr. Hoffman's bill was paid by Papa's granting him a percentage of the mineral rights to his homestead.

Somehow, Papa managed to buy an automobile. When Mama believed it was time for this baby, he would drive her to Opheim and stay with her. She expected her baby in early April, perhaps on her birthday, April 9. When

Papa came in for dinner on March 10, he found Mama walking the floor, timing labor pains. There was no time to go to Opheim; there was not even time enough to go for the midwife. Papa delivered Marvin William Sherwood March 10, 1930, without a hitch. This beautiful strong, healthy baby cried lustily. Papa immediately placed the baby in Mama's arms. This boy would not be kept from her and left to wail and die.

Initially, Mama was joyful. Yet, an unreasonable fear assailed her, even though her baby appeared to be perfectly healthy. What if Baby Willie should die? Without him, she knew she could no longer find the will to live. She gave him most of the basic care he needed, but she realized only much later on, that she withheld her love, lest he die and leave her shattered once again. Too often Papa was the one to bathe Baby Willie, hold him, and sing to him. Mama gave him her breast, but withheld her heart.

Papa wished for Mrs. Clark to help with Mama, but Mrs. Clark was spending more and more time with friends back in Minneapolis. Finally, fearing Mama would descend to an emotional depth too far to return, Papa sent for her. She arrived at the homestead, none too happy to have been called home. Once again she took charge cajoling and advising Mama until she lost her patience and exploded.

"This baby needs a mother, and he doesn't have one! So, you say you can't love him, because he might die. That is rubbish, and you know it! Even if he were going to die, he deserves to be loved and cared for properly in the meantime. What kind of mother are you to neglect your own baby?"

Again, Mama rallied. Was it the verbal flaying or the fact that Mama sensed she was pregnant again? She had no choice but to carry on.

Mama found the strength to care for Willie, but their world was closing in on them. The drought persisted, and when winter came Papa once more considered whether they should leave while they still could. Henry and Don urged Papa to come to Idaho where life was better, but Papa decided to give Montana one more year. If it was another dry year, they would leave. Surely, surely, the rains would return.

Timing for Mama's third baby was perfect. Papa drove her to Opheim as soon as her labor pains started. After another excruciating, protracted labor, Mama delivered a red-headed baby girl, but Dr. Hoffman could not conceal his concern from the new parents. This time at least the nurse gave the baby to them to hold, yet Mabel Lillian Sherwood died in their arms. They mourned.

Again, Mama was too weak to attend her baby's graveside service, but Papa reported that, as before, several of the Opheim women had attended the service to offer emotional support.

Papa brought Mama home on a sunny June day in 1931, when puffy white clouds scudded across the rainless blue sky. Mama, already in depression, scarcely noticed Baby Willie. Mama lost expression and often stared unmindful into space. Papa sent for Mrs. Clark. Mrs. Clark whipped the messy house into shape, cooked meals, laundered, and lavished care on Baby Willie who was only seventeen months old. She prodded Mama.

"Helen," she asked, "Have you seen how many babies' graves are in the cemetery in Opheim? You are not the only one who has lost babies. Not only are there too many babies' graves, but too many graves of young mothers also. You are here. You have a healthy little boy. You need to snap out of it!"

"What if I am never able to have another baby that lives? What if I only have one baby?" Mama sighed.

"Sometimes," Mrs. Clark was sharp, "You should just be thankful that you can have one."

"You can't understand," Mama sniffled, "What it's like to lose two babies."

Mrs. Clark turned on Mama with eyes narrowed to a slit and a fury Mama had seen before, but that had never before been directed at Mama. "I can't understand? Why do you think you are my only child? I had three miscarriages and two babies stillborn. And you have the unmitigated gall to say I don't understand?"

Mama gasped, "I never knew."

"That," Mrs. Clark grimaced, "Is because I did not make a life of wallowing in my sorrow!"

❧ · · · ◦ · · · ❧

The improvement in Mama's mental health that began during Mrs. Clark's visit continued. Still, there were sleepless nights when prairie winds whipping around the shack carried a baby's high-pitched cries. One such night Mama sat at the table in the dark, so as not to disturb Papa and Baby Willie, who slept in the bedroom.

Mama became aware that the wind carried another sound—music. A soft light penetrated the darkness. Beautiful music, unlike any Mama had ever heard, moved toward Mama and a gentle glow of light illuminated the kitchen.

A cloud slid through the outside wall as it floated past Mama. Two babies played on the cloud. Mama knew instantly that they were John and Mabel. She thought she had died and gone to heaven. She called to her babies, but they couldn't hear her. The cloud moved on through the shack and disappeared.

As the light and music began to fade, Papa stepped from the bedroom. "Do you hear music?" he asked. He was confused. Mama lighted a lamp and told Papa what she had seen. Mama told me Papa believed her, only because he had heard the music and seen the light.

"I saw heaven," Mama later told me, "And for the first time in my life, I believed in the God that your father worshipped."

Shortly after Mama's glimpse of heaven, Mama and Papa decided to move to Idaho. Papa believed that Mama's grip on sanity was tenuous. Idaho held no ghosts for her. Perhaps, she would heal sooner there. And even Papa, had to admit that the good years on the prairie were gone, and they were never coming back. Before it was too late, and all hope was blown away, Papa, Mama, and Baby Willie left Montana in a swirl of dust. ૭૦

CHAPTER 6

An Idaho Interlude

Mama and Papa bought what seemed to them a small sixty-acre farm near Sandpoint in Idaho's northern panhandle. The panhandle was lush and green from thirty-three inches of annual precipitation. Evergreen trees covered all but natural meadows and the fields where farmers had cleared the land. Sandpoint, with a population of 3,300, was located on the shores of 43-mile-long, beautiful, pristine Lake Pend Oreille. The scenic area was surrounded by the Selkirk, Cabinet, and Bitterroot mountain ranges in the Rockies. Idaho's panhandle was everything northeastern Montana was not.

Evergreen trees covered much of their farm and blended with those covering the adjacent foothills of the Rocky Mountains. Bears, mountain lions, and deer wandered down from the mountains to roam the farm. A crystal clear, icy stream flowed beneath a stone milk house and rippled past their snug four-room log cabin.

Mama said they recognized that northern Idaho looked like Paradise, but after long years on the prairie, Idaho did not feel like home. Now, hemmed in by mountains and trees, they could no longer look out to a vast sky above a seemingly endless prairie. Precipitation that greened Idaho fell from clouds that often concealed the bright sunlight they were accustomed to seeing most days. Without the various melodies of unceasing winds, silence seemed uncomfortable. "Yet," Mama smiled remembering, "We grew to love Idaho."

Many of the evergreen trees on the farm must be felled and the stumps dynamited before Papa could make a living there. In the meantime, Papa found additional income at the new airport under construction in Sandpoint. Weekday mornings he milked their three cows in the darkness, hitched his team to his wagon, and traveled to the airport. Once there, he unhitched his wagon and hitched his team to his "slip," a large flat-bottomed open bucket that he left at the airport. Papa's job was to move dirt with his slip.

Weekends, Papa cut trees and dynamited stumps to clear their farm. Mondays, Papa again traveled back and forth to the airport. Exhausted from hard work and too little sleep, he often slept in his wagon on the way home. The horses found their way without his help.

Initially, the only source of income for the farm was an established apple orchard. Thanks to the education in agriculture that Mama had received at Mrs. Clark's insistence, Mama recognized that their mostly sandy soil was only good for certain crops. One of those crops was strawberries. The first fall in Idaho they planted rows and rows of different kinds of strawberries that would ripen next summer at different times to provide for maximum production.

Idaho's winter brought heavy, wet snow totally unlike the light, fluffy, low-moisture snow that blew in horizontally across Montana's high plains and whipped up drifts at every opportunity. Mama stopped helping to shovel paths through the snow when she realized she was pregnant once again. At times apprehension gripped her, but she had gained emotional footing in Idaho, and her pregnancy was filled with more hope than fear.

Most Idaho farms were small, so neighbors lived nearby. Mama said she had not thought about the distance between neighbors' homes on the prairie, because that was the life she knew. Now the close proximity of neighbors brought her comfort and the social contact she so much enjoyed. Neighbor women travelled frequently to visit one another sharing coffee, cookies, gossip, their laughter, and their problems. A problem a few of them had in common was rheumatism.

While Mama's mental health had improved, the rheumatism that had caused some pain in Montana now became more aggressive with the humid climate in Idaho. Dorothy Bowen, a neighbor, recommended that Mama see a specialist in Spokane. She was given a diagnosis of rheumatoid arthritis when she visited him. It was believed that her having had rheumatic fever as a child significantly increased her chances of having rheumatoid arthritis as an adult. She returned home with medication and cautious optimism.

In addition to visiting and household chores, Mama planned their truck garden. She would use the farm's sandy soil advantageously. She determined which vegetables to plant, where to plant them, and the best time for planting. Mama felt ownership in her truck garden project, and come spring, she helped plant the tilled soil. Throughout summer, she continued to feel well enough to help with the garden. They sold strawberries, tomatoes, and vegetables for cash and traded them at the general store for credit.

Sherman was born in late August 1932. When Papa brought Mama and Sherman home from Sandpoint, two-year old Willie's face registered disappointment when he looked at Sherman, "Oh!" he lamented, "You could have brought me a little white dog instead."

Even so, Willie soon appointed himself as Sherman's care-taker, and by the time Sherman was crawling and walking Willie was his constant companion.

"He seemed to have decided I was not a good enough mother," Mama recalled. "At times I was swept with the fear that one of them would die, and I seemed incapable of showing them the love they deserved. But, I did have a better handle on reality." Mama pulled a wry face as she remembered her relief that Papa did not need to send for Mrs. Clark, "I sure didn't want her coming to sort me out and boss me around again! She thought everyone should have her iron constitution and steely resolve. Besides, she was spending more time in Minneapolis. I could only assume that all was not well on her ranch."

Willie still wanted a dog. Papa bought an Airedale terrier that Willie named Curly, and Willy, Sherman, and Curly became a threesome. One night Papa heard Curly barking and barking as Curly sometimes did when mountain lions or bears were in the area. Since none had ever come to the house or barn thus far, Papa let Curly bark. In early morning darkness when Papa went to the barn to milk the cows he found that a mountain lion had killed Curly. The barn cat was part way up a tree near Curly meowing piteously. Papa climbed up the tree to rescue the cat, but the terrified cat would not release its claws. He left it there knowing that eventually the cat would come down on its own. Burying Curly was like burying a family member.

꘎ꙮ· · 0 · · ꙮ꘎

Papa's brothers, Henry and Don, both lived near Sandpoint. Henry was a successful farmer, and he gave Papa many helpful suggestions about farming in Idaho. Mama, Papa and the boys visited back and forth regularly with Henry, his wife Ada, and their children Bob and Virginia who were a few years older than Willie and Sherman. Don, who was single once again, often joined them. He had decided there must be a better way than farming to earn a living; now he was in demand as a professional paperhanger and painter. Don gave Papa many helpful, from Don's perspective, suggestions about marriage and how to treat women. Mama hardly thought Don, who spent his evenings in the bars in Sandpoint and whose wife had divorced him, to be in any position to dispense marital advice.

Additionally, Mama fully believed her brother-in-law Don to be bereft of sound judgment, even when he was stone sober. Her favorite story to illustrate this point was Don's attempt to capture a bear cub. He owned a new car, and he liked to take Mama, Papa, Willie, and Sherman for a ride after Sunday dinner. On one Sunday they turned a corner to find a sow and two cubs on the road in front of them. When the bears saw the oncoming car the sow and one cub ran off the road on one side. The other cub ran off the road on the opposite side and promptly climbed a tree. Don slammed on the brakes and jumped out of the car, declaring he was going to get a cub for Willie and Sherman to keep for a pet.

Papa told Don he was a fool, because the sow could reappear at any moment to get her cub. Don whipped off his Sunday dress jacket and tied the sleeves around his waist as he continued to the tree. He managed to get a grip on a limb and swing up into the tree where he proceeded to shinny upwards. Once near the cub, he untied his jacket and managed to get it partially around the cub.

Papa looked apprehensively in the direction the sow had disappeared as he paced beside the car and swore about Don's stupidity. Mama said Papa seldom swore, but Don could definitely bring him to it.

Suddenly all they could hear was Don's yelling as he and the cub toppled to the ground. The cub chewed and clawed on Don as they fell, and once on the ground the cub ran off. Papa helped Don to his feet berating him with every breath. He managed to get Don in the back seat with the boys, and Papa drove home. Before going into the house, Don retrieved a bottle of whiskey from under the car seat. Once home, Mama dressed Don's wounds as he alternately swigged whiskey and groaned.

⤸ • • ○ • • ⤹

Mama's ideal of a perfect sized family was three children. Her arthritis had eased somewhat, Willie and Sherman were healthy, and with Willie's self-appointed guardianship of Sherman, Mama decided it was time for her third baby. At first she did not become pregnant, and she worried that, like Mrs. Clark, she might not be able to have more children, but Nathan was born in December of 1935, after Sherman's third birthday. When Nathan proved to be a sickly, fretful baby, Mama bogged down emotionally with understandable, but unfounded, worry that he might die. Nathan and Mama were both much too thin, and now even with her medicine, her rheumatoid arthritis plagued her.

Jenny Hernvall, one of Mama's friends, decided that goat milk would put both Mama and Nathan on the road to health. They must visit the Goat

Lady and buy some goats. The Goat Lady lived up the mountain over a nearly impassable, rock-strewn road. It was commonly believed that drinking goat milk was a path to health, and many found their way to the Goat Lady, in spite of the road.

Jenny told Mama the story about a city man who had stopped at their house asking directions to the Goat Lady. Jenny said he was a pale, spindly looking man who did not look capable of walking up the mountain, and she told him that his car could never make it. Besides, it was autumn and the first snows were due. The Goat Lady's road was never cleared, and once up the mountain, if snows came, one stayed until spring. He said he must go, anyway. The snows came the next day, and the next, and the next. . . . During the long winter Jenny wondered what happened to the city man.

Come spring, a man Jenny did not immediately recognize knocked on her door. It was the city man looking hale and hearty. Yes, he had spent the winter on the mountain with the Goat Lady. As Jenny had predicted, he had not driven far before his car hung up on rocks, so he walked the rest of the way. Now his car would not start, and he needed a ride into Sandpoint.

On a cool, sunny summer morning Papa hooked his team to the wagon and helped Mama, Willie, Sherman, and Baby Nathan into the wagon. Once on the rough, rocky road, Papa knew his old truck could never have traversed it to the Goat Lady's farm. Mama said she had expected to see a hard-looking older woman. Not so! The Goat Lady was a handsome, interesting woman who was probably in her forties.

They visited, ate goat cheese and bread, and left the Goat Lady's tidy farm with three goats. Mama told Papa it was no wonder the city man's health improved so much after spending the winter there!

Mama and Nathan both gained weight from drinking the rich goat milk, and Nathan's health improved significantly. What did not improve was Mama's rheumatoid arthritis. Northern Idaho's damp climate was crippling her; the doctor in Sandpoint recommended that Mama should move to a dry climate.

They weighed their options. The sandy soil on their farm minimized production for income. The only time their farming efforts were profitable was while they sold strawberries, produce from their truck farm, and apples in the fall. Papa found work during the winter months doing various jobs, but it was becoming clear that financially they must make a change. Mama and Papa talked of moving back to Montana with its dry climate. The decision would be up to Mama.

Before Mama and Papa moved to Idaho from their homestead, they had had the option of having the Federal Government buy their homestead. This would be in exchange for fewer acres of land in the Milk River Valley where they could irrigate. The goal of the Milk River Project of the Resettlement Administration was to help dry land farmers and ranchers who were unable to survive financially, because of the drought of the 1920s and 1930s and the depression of the 1930s. Mama and Papa fell into that category, but they chose to move to Idaho believing that a totally new environment would help Mama regain her mental stability.

Sure enough with the passing of time and three healthy children Mama was stronger emotionally. She wished to return to Montana for some relief for her arthritis. Papa corresponded with the Resettlement Administration and found they still qualified for a resettlement farm on the Milk River near Hinsdale.

In preparation for their move, Papa bought a new robin's-egg blue 1937 one-and-a-half-ton Chevrolet truck. Gus Hernvall bought their beautiful farm and helped them load their belongings into the truck. Emotions were mixed, but hopes were high, as they left behind their snug log home with its crystal clear, icy mountain stream rippling past it. ❧

CHAPTER 7

MY HOME'S IN MONTANA

In 1937, after six years in Idaho, Mama, Papa, and the boys arrived in Hinsdale, Montana. Resettlement farms like the one they had been assigned bordered the muddy-looking Milk River, and farm pumps delivered sulfurous water. The rainfall would be scant, the winters bitter, and the winds continuous, yet they felt as though they had come home.

During their early married years on the homestead, trips into Hinsdale had been highlights for them. They would spend nights at a roadhouse, the Northern Hotel, or with friends. Now many of their friends from that period lived in or near Hinsdale on Resettlement farms. Some of the families Mama spoke of from the Genevieve–Barr Country, where Mrs. Clark's homestead was located and where Mama first attended school, were the Amestoys, Riggins, Hattons, Dartmans, and Schulers. Some they knew from the Thoeny–Barnard Community were the Franzens, Sorensons, and Mungers.

The government had divided the land along the Milk River designated for resettlement into approximately 150-acre plots. Papa's plot was seven miles northwest of Hinsdale. Since the house on their farm was not livable, a new house had to be built before winter. In the meantime, they rented a house from the Fewer family on the south edge of town.

It was too late for Papa to plant crops, and, besides, the irrigation system necessary to water the crops was not yet in place. So Papa began working days for John Frisch to earn money, and he spent his evenings and weekends preparing his farm for irrigation. He also earned money for the first two years on the resettlement farm by using his truck to haul men, tools, and small equipment as needed for the Reclamation Project. The purpose of the Reclamation Project in Valley County was to bring irrigation to farmers who lived in areas where irrigation would make farm land profitable. Toward that end, dams, canals, and ditches were built.

Their new house on the farm was ready to move into by October. The house looked nice, but it was not built for Montana winters. On days of high winds, Mama's curtains waltzed gently in drafts that pushed through cracks around the window frames, and unwelcome cold air pressed in around the doors. As the weather grew colder, Mama and Papa used table knives to poke rags into the cracks. Papa stacked straw against the exterior foundation and covered it with canvas tarps. All of this helped, but when the coldest weather came, Mama and Papa moved the boys into their bedroom and closed off the boys' bedroom to conserve heat. They missed their snug log house in Idaho.

༄ · · ० · · ༄

Part of the Resettlement farm package was a loan from the Farm Security Administration. Before spring, Papa used proceeds from his loan to buy additional farm equipment and more pigs and cows and to make general improvements on the farm—especially to the irrigation system. And, "providentially," as Mama liked to say, Lew Balky came into their lives. A short stocky man with a large mustache twisted on the ends, Lew was a bachelor in his forties who was adrift in life with no home of his own. He worked one place and then another. Lew and Papa were mildly acquainted from having met in the Barnard Community when Lew worked for a rancher on a large spread west of Opheim. Mama and Papa thought him to be a bit odd, but he was amiable, hard-working, and honest.

Papa and Lew modified the old, basically unlivable house that came with the farm into a comfortable bunk house for Lew, and Lew ate most of the meals with the family. Together, Papa and Lew accomplished twice as much work as Papa working alone, and sometimes more. Cutting wood for winter was a perpetual task. Over time, they planted a Russian olive windbreak and winterized the new house. They made significant improvements to the irrigation system. An orchard designed by Mama was set out under her supervision. Fields were seeded with alfalfa hay, corn, potatoes, and sugar beets. Sugar beets were labor intensive, but they paid in two ways—cows ate the trimmed tops, and the beets brought a good price.

༄ · · ० · · ༄

Mama and Mrs. Clark corresponded regularly, but Mama was surprised to receive a letter the summer of 1939 saying that Mrs. Clark was coming from Minneapolis to visit! She had been living and working in Minneapolis for some time now. Mama and Papa had wondered if she was divorced from Henry Lick, but Mrs. Clark did not welcome questions about her personal life. Mama had seen Henry Lick a few months earlier in a grocery store in Hinsdale, but Mama said she refused to acknowledge him, much less engage him in conversation. She had heard that he was still bent upon building an empire of land and cattle. Mama was convinced that Mrs. Clark had unwittingly helped him to get his start. From the outset he had been after Mrs. Clark's fine ranch with its spring. Mama said that Mrs. Clark's vanity had overruled her judgment and by finally giving in and marrying him she had played right into Henry Lick's hand. And whatever the current state of their relationship, that marriage had, in effect, given him legal rights to Mrs. Clark's land and the spring.

Mama and Papa met Mrs. Clark at the Hinsdale depot on a rainy summer day, and they drove to the farm. She would be staying in the boys' bedroom, and all three of them—Willie, Sherman, and Nathan—would be staying in the bunkhouse with Lew. This arrangement pleased the boys more than Lew. Mama suspected this was because Lew guarded his privacy and the boys were nosy. Additionally, she believed that Lew's surreptitious nipping on his whiskey during the day was probably indulged on a larger scale in the evenings. The boys seemed not to mind his habits, and they never tired of Lew's stories of derring-do during his younger cowpuncher days. "A man who herds cattle is a 'cowboy' in movies and books written by people who don't know what they are talking about." He was fond of repeating, "But a man who herds cattle is a cowpuncher."

One morning before Lew showed up for breakfast Willie came into the kitchen and reported that Lew looked at women modeling undergarments in the *Sears & Roebuck Catalog.* Papa told Willie to mind his own business and that he would not tolerate Willie's spying on Lew. That day Mama laughed to herself off and on as she made a curtain from a sheet and hung it in the bunkhouse so Lew would have more privacy.

Mrs. Clark brought gifts: books and games for the boys, a beautiful dress for Mama, and a dress shirt and tie for Papa. She had learned in letters from Mama that Lew liked his whiskey, and she brought a bottle of fine Scotch to him. Lew was both touched by her thinking of him and embarrassed that she might think he "drank." To ease his embarrassment, Mrs. Clark insisted that she and he both have a shot immediately. They laughingly agreed that it "would do in a pinch!"

Mrs. Clark's expensive jewelry and clothes, her make-up and perfume set her apart. But using a silver cigarette holder to smoke put her in a class by herself. The boys had seen Papa smoke, but he never, ever used a cigarette holder.

Mrs. Clark busied herself during her ten-day visit. She spent two of the days at a hotel in Hinsdale while she met with old friends. While on the farm she engaged the boys with conversation about their lives and watched as they did their chores. Seeing that one of their most time-consuming chores was pumping water for the cattle, she ordered a Briggs and Stratton motor that would pump the water for them, and she told them that now they had more time for reading and homework.

All in all, the boys found Mrs. Clark to be fascinating; Mama found her to be bossy. In the course of helping with the housework, she decided Mama could save time by being more organized. Toward that end, she reorganized the cupboards and pantry for efficiency—with no thought for Mama's reasons for the previous arrangement. In fairness, Mama had never really organized things for herself. One thing became clear. After seeing how much work Mama did, Mrs. Clark decided that Papa had his much-needed hired man to help him, and Mama needed a hired girl to help her. Mama not only cooked and did laundry for her family, but for Lew as well. When Mrs. Clark suggested getting a hired girl to Mama, Mama told her that Papa would never allow it, but, when pressed, Mama admitted she had never brought up the issue. After Mrs. Clark talked to Papa, he announced that Mama would have a hired girl. Mama knew exactly who she would ask—Dorothy Christensen—whose parents, the Ray Christensens, were friends.

Mrs. Clark had advice for Papa, too. The two of them rode around the farm in the truck as he showed her the progress they were making. She asked why he had not bought a tractor yet. Papa explained that he wanted to be sure he did not borrow more money than he could pay back. After she pointed out how he could, indeed, make more money with a tractor, Papa agreed to think about it.

The day before Mrs. Clark left to return to Minneapolis Mama worked up the courage to ask about Henry Lick. "He turned out to be the bastard I feared he might be when I had saner moments." Their marriage? "Divorced." Then Mama asked about her ranch. "Gone, all gone."

The answers were short and to the point. When Mama tried to talk about the invaluable spring, Mrs. Clark closed the topic with familiar words, "Remember, Helen, never look back. You can't move forward and look back at the same time."

Dorothy helped Mama, and Lew helped Papa. The boys did their chores and learned the basics of raising crops and livestock. With continued hard work, the farm prospered. Crops planted in the rich river valley soil flourished with irrigation. Papa sold cream and eggs that he hauled to Hinsdale several time a week, and, when they were sufficiently mature, he sold calves and pigs. Mrs. Clark's advice had its effect, and before the next beet harvest Papa bought a new Farmall F12 tractor with iron lug wheels. When the tractor was started it said, "Putt, putt, putt, putt . . .. It was quickly named Putt-Putt.

Lew worked hard and took pride in the success of the farm. He was totally dependable, and in the late summer when Papa was away hauling wheat from the dryland farms to the elevators, Lew assumed full responsibility for the farm. Monday through Saturday he worked from dawn to dusk, but Saturday beginning at six in the evening until Monday morning was Lew's time off. By seven o'clock Saturday evening, Lew was cleaned up and dressed up, and he clattered off to Hinsdale in his old Chevrolet car. Mama and Papa knew he made his rounds at the bars, his favorite being the Northern Bar.

Even after a late Saturday night, Lew seldom missed Mama's big Sunday breakfast. He enjoyed sharing news of people he saw and local gossip. One Sunday Lew missed breakfast, even though his car was parked by the bunk-house. He did arrive for Sunday dinner, but he did not look like Lew. He looked like his face had been used as a punching bag—his lips were fat and bloody and one eye was swollen almost shut. Papa gave the boys a look that said, "Don't ask Lew any questions." But they stared wide-eyed. Mama and Papa tried to carry on a normal conversation. Finally, Lew put down his fork.

"I suppose you're wondering what happened?" Neither Mama nor Papa said a word. "Well," Lew continued through his fat lips, "I was dancing with this pretty lady, and a man, a big man, told me that I had his woman. I told him to show me his receipt for her. Let's just say that what followed wasn't to my advantage."

Mama suppressed a smile, "Could we say that he was Goliath, and you were David without a slingshot and a rock? Why don't you let me doctor your face after dinner?"

While Papa and the boys took care of the dishes, Lew allowed himself to be patched up. Once again, Mama's nurse's training was put to good use.

ᥫᦱ· · ◦ · · ·ᦱᥫ

Dorothy Christensen was a godsend to Mama. Her health was the best it had been in many years, though rheumatoid arthritis still pained her, it was no longer disabling as it had been in Idaho. Then, in August of 1939, Mama learned she was pregnant again. She already had the three children she had wanted, and she and Papa had not planned to have another baby. As the reality of her situation set in, she regressed emotionally—what if the baby died? She felt she simply could not carry another baby that would become so much a part of her yet might not survive. Dr. Cockrell insisted that her fears were groundless assuring her that when her time of delivery neared she could stay at Mrs. See's maternity hospital just blocks from his office. And, as Papa reminded her, they had three sons and no daughters. Perhaps, this baby would be a girl.

The boys debated the pros and cons of having a new brother or sister. Sherman believed that all babies are a lot of work. Papa agreed, and he told them they would all help more, so Mama would have time to take care of the baby. Willie thought a brother would be better than having a sister. "Girls," he declared, "Can be a real nuisance." Nathan always agreed with Willie.

Sure enough, I was born in Hinsdale February 27, 1940, at Mrs. See's home during a late winter blizzard. Although Mama was only called Helen, I was given her first name, Ruth. Dorothy's help and unfailing cheerfulness speeded Mama's recovery.

At first the boys were skeptical about the new baby—and a girl at that. Soon, however, one of them hurried to pick me up when I cried, and often asked to hold me when I was awake. Mama told me that Willie had a maternal streak, because, in spite of not wanting a baby sister, it was he who bonded with me first. She said that Willie was like a third parent to us younger siblings. Dorothy, hoping for a family of her own one day, held me when she had a break. Mama said that I spent much of my first year in somebody's arms. Even Lew Balky would reach over and touch my cheek when Mama held me at the table.

⟨⟩· · ◦ · · ⟨⟩

As Election Day of November 5, 1940, approached, Mama and Papa had lively discussions about who would make the better president—President Franklin Roosevelt, the Democratic candidate who was running for his third term or Wendell Willkie, the Republican candidate, who had never run for public office. Papa was a staunch Democrat, while Mama was a sometime Republican. Mama said they should just stay home, since they usually cancelled each other's vote. But, they took the privilege of voting seriously.

On Election Day after Willie and Sherman left for school Mama, Papa, Nathan, and I rode to Hinsdale in our truck, so Mama and Papa could vote. They began their errands after voting. Papa backed his truck up to the loading dock of the Farmer's Union store and went inside to purchase feed for the livestock. Mama held me while she and Nathan waited in the truck. The truck faced the railroad track where men worked repairing the track. It was a chilly day with high winds, and the men wore jackets and caps for protection from the cold.

Mama recognized some of the workers. One, whose family Mama had known when homesteading in the Genevieve Country, was young Jack Dartman. The Dartmans now lived a few miles from Mama and Papa.

Mama heard a train whistle as it approached. At first with their winter caps and the high winds the workers seemed not to hear it, but soon they started moving from the track not noticing that Jack was still working. The train continued whistling as it approached, and the men yelled at Jack to move. His back was to them, and, with his earflaps down, he did not hear. Mama sat frozen in horror as the train bore down on him. Too late brakes screeched and Jack looked up.

Men raced into the Farmer's Union, raced back with a door for a stretcher, and placed Jack on the door. By this time Mama had handed me to Nathan and hurried to Jack to see if she could help. One look at Jack's blood loss and mangled body, and Mama knew he was dying, and there was nothing she or anyone could do. She walked beside Jack as the men moved him to the back of a pickup to take him to Dr. Cockrell's office.

Jack looked up at mama, "Don't cry, Mrs. Sherwood, I'll be all right." ❧

CHAPTER 8

PEARL HARBOR AND SKIN CANCER

News in rural areas spread not only by newspapers and radio, but also by traveling salesmen. The morning of December 8th, 1941, the Watkins salesman who sold spices and condiments called on Mama. Had she heard that America was at war? Mama and Papa typically listened to the evening news on their battery-operated radio, but the night of December 7 they had not. The Watkins salesman told Mama that by not hearing the news last night they had missed President Roosevelt's message to America when he proclaimed that the Japanese bombing of Pearl Harbor would be "a day which will live in infamy."

When Dorothy arrived, Mama dispatched her to the field where Papa and Lew were feeding cattle, so she could tell them the news. Dorothy, Lew, Papa, and Mama sat around the kitchen table drinking coffee in stunned silence as they listened to the radio. Finally, Papa broke the silence. A veteran of The Great War, he had never forgiven Germany for the atrocities he witnessed in Europe. Now he announced that he wanted to join the army to help defeat Germany again. Mama turned on Papa with uncustomary vehemence and told him that he would do no such thing. She reminded Papa that they were raising three boys and me, not quite two years old. Additionally, she was nine months pregnant! Papa knew full well that Willie, at eleven years old, was too much of a handful for Mama to manage. Papa assured her this would never happen—the army did not accept fifty-one-year-old men.

Over the next week Dorothy served pots of coffee and plates of cookies to neighbors who dropped by to discuss the war. Some admitted they had mistakenly believed that giving Hitler a free hand in Europe, Japan a free hand in Asia, and having oceans between us, would assure America's safety. Others had feared, as had President Roosevelt, that Hitler would endeavor to conquer America as soon as he wrapped up Europe. Nobody had foreseen Japan's bombing of Pearl Harbor.

Grace, a beautiful baby with dark hair, blue eyes, and Mama's light olive complexion, was born at Mrs. See's home on December 21, 1941, into a world at war. Mama said in later years that while another child was not planned, Papa had spoiled me so rotten that it was a good thing for me to have had a younger sibling.

President Roosevelt's Christmas address to the nation encouraged Americans to carry on their lives as normally as possible and celebrate the holiday season. While listening to news of the war became a consistent evening activity, day to day life and labors on the farm must continue. Once Mama and Papa recovered from the shock of the war, they determined to be as optimistic as possible. They prayed for an Allied victory soon, but kept their focus on farm and family.

During the workday Lew or Papa sometimes came into the house for a cup of coffee and a short visit. Lew, like so many of the bachelors Mama had known on the prairie, took a keen interest in babies and small children. Such men didn't want any themselves, but they seemed fascinated with them. When Lew came in for a break, Mama brought Grace to sit on her lap at the table as Lew drank his coffee. He would reach out and touch Grace's chubby cheek gently with his finger. A few times he embarrassed himself by talking baby-talk to her.

Mama wondered why Lew had never married. She and Dorothy conspired to find out. One day when Lew came in for a cup of coffee, Mama engaged Dorothy in conversation and asked why she had never married. Dorothy told Mama that the right man hadn't shown up yet.

Then Mama turned to Lew. "Lew, why haven't you ever married?"
Lew swirled the coffee in his cup. He shifted uncomfortably in his chair. Mama raised her eyebrows, looked at Lew, and waited. Dorothy offered Lew more cookies. And waited.

Finally, Lew looked at the ceiling, "Well, I almost did once." Mama winked at Dorothy.

"I had one of those catalogs for mail-order brides. I saw the prettiest little lady in there. So, I wrote to her. One thing led to another, and before I knew what was happening she was going to catch the train out here to marry me. I hadn't really planned to marry. Writing letters to her and reading her letters helped pass lonely nights. That was all I meant to do.

"I couldn't seem to write and tell her to call off her plans. Writing to her was a danged-fool idea anyway. I wasn't proud of myself. My letters sounded more like a Wild West movie than like my life really was.

"Rather than tell her not to come, I met the train. Some ladies got off, but none looked like her. I stood around for a while, and this lady comes up to me and asks if I am Lew Balky. I would be kind to say she wasn't little, and she wasn't pretty. But, I reminded myself that I didn't look like any prize either. I was in a pickle, because once a woman comes out to marry you, it is a cowpuncher's code of honor that he marries her. I loaded her trunks into my wagon. All six of them! There wasn't going to be room in my little shack to hold the contents of six trunks! When I asked what she had in them she just laughed and said that she knew a bachelor's home would need to be decorated.

"I didn't rush into a wedding as some cowpunchers did. She had a right to know what she was getting into. I showed her around Hinsdale. She made it clear that she didn't think much of Hinsdale. Next, I took her out to the ranch where I worked. She didn't like the treeless prairie either. When I showed her the shack where we would live, she started crying. She cried all the way back to town. I don't save much money, but I had enough to buy her a ticket Back East. It was the best money I ever spent!"

⟳· · ◦ · ·⟲

The war intruded into the daily life of Americans. Young men that Mama and Papa knew from neighboring farms and in Hinsdale went off to war. Willie, Sherman, and Nathan gathered materials that could be recycled and used for the war efforts. The school encouraged students and their parents to bring in paper, cardboard, tin cans, metal scraps, old tools, equipment, and tires. In June of 1942, Japan surprised America again by invading and occupying two of Alaska's Aleutian Islands. They used this vantage point to launch air strikes against two American military bases nearer the Alaska mainland.

Residents of western states, including Montana, feared a Japanese attack. Papa's robin's-egg-blue truck was highly visible on moonlight nights. He painted it an ugly black. Evenings when lamps were lighted the widows were covered so that no light was visible from the outside.

Although, farmers had been successfully raising sugar beets in the Milk River Valley since the early 1900s, they now became a highly valuable crop to America. While Americans had used sugar produced from both sugar beets and sugar cane, the sugar from sugar cane was preferred for cooking. Most of it had come from the sugar cane fields of the Philippine Islands. When Japan occupied the islands, they cut off America's sugar. The government encouraged farmers to grow more sugar beets, and sugar became the first food product to be rationed. Papa diverted more acreage to the growing of sugar beets. He knew he could count on a few teenagers and a few men who did not qualify for the draft to help as needed. Horrific as the war was, with the soldiers need for food and sugar, our farm prospered.

⊷· · o · · ·⊶

Mama and Papa's attention was redirected from the catastrophic tragedies of the war to a looming problem in their personal lives—skin cancer. It had plagued Papa's brothers. Their fair, freckled skin could not hold up under Montana's relentless sunshine. Papa's skin was no exception. Dr. Cockrell treated the sores on Papa's face and neck with different salves, but he developed a sore on his lip that would not be healed. Dr. Cockrell sent Papa to see a doctor in Glasgow who diagnosed skin cancer. The specialist Papa needed to see practiced in Spokane, Washington.

After the sugar beet harvest, Papa boarded the train and traveled to Spokane. The dermatologist told Papa that northeastern Montana's dry, windy climate of sunny summers and extremely cold winters was the worst possible place for him to farm. He treated Papa's lip and face by burning off places and sending him home with a salve to help clear up his sores. He direly predicted that if Papa's lip did not heal, he would need surgery to cut off part of it. He told Papa to move to a different climate to avoid this happening. At best Papa must have six-month check-ups in Spokane.

Once he was home, Mama and Papa talked about their options. The dermatologist had said that some skin cancers could metastasize. Papa's brothers who had left ranching in northeastern Montana had found that a different climate did, indeed, reduce their cancerous and pre-cancerous skin sores. Mama decided that while the rheumatoid arthritis that had plagued her in Idaho was debilitating, it was not immediately fatal, as she feared Papa's cancer could become. They felt their only option was to move back to Idaho with its climate of humidity, low wind, and mild, often cloudy, summers and winters.

But winter was upon them, and Mama was pregnant again. The season, their faith in Dr. Cockrell, and their worry about Mama's difficult deliveries meant they would not move until the boys were out of school in the spring. That winter was particularly long, cold, sad, and depressing. The world war was not going well, and Mama and Papa's personal war with fate was bitter.

50

They had worked so hard, and they had established a farm that now rewarded them for their labor. March brought more hours of daylight, milder weather, and Mama and Papa's grudging acceptance of the idea of moving from their beloved farm. They tried to bolster each other's spirits by talking of the good things about living in Idaho. They both agreed that, most importantly, Papa must be close to his doctor in Spokane.

Mary Louise was born at home on Mama's birthday in the spring of 1943. When Mama looked at Mary with her blonde hair and big blue eyes, she pronounced her to be their "Little Dolly." The name stuck. One of the neighbor ladies who came to visit looked at Dolly's blonde hair and round face. "If this child did not have John's droopy eyelids, I would say you have been going down the road to visit the Swede bachelor!"

⎐· · ◦ · ·⎐

Mama's recovery from Dolly's birth was slow. Dorothy stayed over with us in the boys' bedroom, so she could be of more help to Mama. And, the fact that I was every bit as much trouble as the boys had initially feared I would be did not help matters. One afternoon when Dorothy was busy on the back porch doing laundry, and Mama, Baby Dolly, Grace and I were in the bedroom to take a nap, I found the opportunity to carry out my plan.

Papa had bought a new clock for the kitchen. It ticked loudly, and I wanted to know how it ticked. First, I had pulled a chair over to the kitchen counter and taken the clock down to see what made it tick. Mama rescued the clock and slapped my hands. She told Papa to make a shelf to place the clock on, so I could not reach it from the chair. I was not to be deterred. Once Mama, Baby Dolly, and Grace were asleep I slipped down from the bed and hurried out to where I often played under the Russian olive trees in our windbreak by the house. There I picked up one of the sticks under the trees and took it back to the kitchen. I pulled a chair over and used the stick to knock the clock off the shelf. Grabbing the clock I raced to the windbreak to take it apart.

As I busied myself trying to take the clock apart, I felt myself being snatched from under the trees. Dorothy was not happy. She administered the spanking she had been telling Mama was long overdue. Then holding tightly to my neck, she directed me back to the house and told me to get back to bed without a sound. I did. Although the clock had a big crack across the glass, it lasted several more years.

With a new baby and moving preparations Mama and Dorothy were unusually busy. More and more Nathan was in charge of my care. Nathan found my tagging along to be a nuisance to him. Bertie Payne, a neighbor girl, who was Nathan's age, came over from time to time to play. Previously, I would stay in the house and Dorothy and Mama would keep track of me while Nathan and Bertie played; however, they did not have time to watch me now. Nathan, Bertie, and I were a threesome, and neither Nathan nor Bertie liked this arrangement.

One day Nathan and Bertie suggested that we all inspect the chicken house. Some hens squawked and flew off the nest, but others hens just eyed us curiously. The hen nests were wooden boxes supported with 2 x 4s and filled with straw. They were higher than my head. Nathan picked an empty nest in the farthest corner from the door and asked if I would like to sit in it. I could pretend to be a hen. This sounded good to me. He and Bertie placed me in the nest then bolted out the door and closed it. The chicken house was dark inside, very dark. I screamed in terror and outrage until they returned and rescued me. Nathan did not want Dorothy to find out what he had done. He finally accepted that I would be his cross to bear.

૯ఄ· · · o · · ·ఄૅ

June of 1943, after six years in Montana, Mama and Papa were almost prepared to move. Papa asked Lew to go with us, but he said that he said he could not live hemmed in by mountains. Mama and Papa both cried when Lew said good-bye and clattered off in his old car with his few belongings.

Willie, 13, and Sherman, 11, helped Papa pack everything they could into the back of our '37 Chevrolet truck. Nathan, 7, took care of me, and sometimes he helped with Grace who was now eighteen months old. A farm sale was held to sell all else except the tractor, Putt-Putt—named for the way it sounded—and equipment for the tractor. That which did not sell stayed with Dorothy Christensen and Esmond Vanderhoef, who were buying our farm. Dorothy, who had spent so much time with us, married Esmond who had helped Papa with several sugar beet harvests. Mama and Papa's only consolation about leaving the farm was that Vanderhoefs would live there. They were fine, hard-working people.

Gus Hernvall had driven his truck from Idaho to haul the tractor and its farm equipment back to Idaho. Willie rode with Gus. Sherman and Nathan rode in the back of our truck in a snug area next to the cab. Grace and I squeezed into the middle of the cab between Papa and Mama, who held three-month old Baby Dolly. When Mama and Papa had left Montana in 1931, they'd felt certain they were moving to a better life. Now they left Montana with deep regret.

. . . o . .

When we arrived in Idaho, Papa learned that the farm he had arranged to buy through correspondence with the owner had been sold out from under him. Fortunately, there was a farm to rent near where their first Idaho farm was located in the Sandpoint area. We moved to the rental farm where an icy, clear mountain stream flowed down from the Rocky Mountain foothills and passed in front of our house. We arrived in Idaho too late to plant crops, and Papa decided to buy only two cows for milk until he found a suitable farm. While he looked for a farm, he must generate an income. Few farmers had tractors, and Papa found work using his Farmall F12 tractor to clear farmers' land of trees and stumps.

Most of the neighbors our family had known when living in Idaho previously still lived there. With only two cows, no irrigation chores, and no other livestock to tend, Willie found he had time on his hands. He hunted and visited neighbors. He shot his 30.06 rifle at targets until he could withstand the rifle's kick without missing the bull's-eye.

A neighbor told Willie that the logging company was looking for a man to work nights guarding their horses from mountain lions. Trained horses were critical to the logging operation; even though the horses were corralled at night, the presence of a mountain lion could spook them. Willie was only thirteen, but he was stout, a crack shot, and gutsy. He pleaded with Papa to let him ask for the job. Mama and Papa discussed the pros and cons. Since Willie had announced one day that he thought he would hitch-hike eight miles into Sandpoint, they both had decided Willie did not need idle time on his hands. Perhaps, this job was their answer.

Papa went with Willie to the logging camp. Willie was hired on the spot. He liked being in the logging camp, because he was treated like a man. He slept as he wished during the day and filled up with delicious logging-camp fare. Every night held the exciting prospect of shooting a mountain lion.

When fall came Willie protested leaving the logging camp before they closed for winter. After all, he hadn't shot a mountain lion yet. Papa thought school to be more important, and Willie, Sherman, and Nathan were all enrolled in a country school in Colburn.

The lighter work load of winter gave Mama and Papa more time to visit with neighbors and family. Sunday dinners resumed with Uncle Henry's family and, sometimes, Uncle Don. Uncle Henry and Aunt Ada had two children, Virginia and Bob, both older than Willie. Bob drove Uncle Henry's car, and sometimes he came by to pick up Willie and Sherman, and they rode around the Sandpoint area.

Don still lived alone year round on a house boat in Dover and made a living by painting and papering houses. Uncle Henry said that Uncle Don was not only very good at what he did, but he was very fast, and he could always find work. Uncle Don's weakness was that he often visited the bars in Sandpoint at night. Henry said that now that Bob could drive, Bob would be sent to pick up Uncle Don and take him home when somebody at the bar called saying Don was too rowdy.

When Don joined us for dinner, he walked with a cane that he called "The Missouri Headache." He claimed that, even though he was no longer young, he could hold his own with the help of The Missouri Headache. He showed us how he had drilled a hole up from the bottom of the cane and filled it with melted lead that he let harden. The cane was deceptively heavy and potentially deadly.

A constant topic with both family and neighbors was the continuing war. The quick victory that had been hoped for had not happened. Mama and Papa knew fewer young men in Idaho who served in the military than they had in Hinsdale, so they heard fewer personal stories. Robert Hernvall, Gus and Jenny's son, as well as two of Papa's nephews, Lester Sherwood and young Fred Sherwood, had joined the service.

Winter brought Mama's rheumatoid arthritis back with a vengeance. Papa's pre-cancerous sores, and the one on his lip in particular, improved. On Papa's mid-winter visit to his doctor in Spokane, the doctor announced that a new salve had just been made available, and it should help Papa significantly. Papa explained about Mama's arthritis and questioned the doctor about moving back to Montana. Papa was told that he would need to return in a few months. Why not wait until then to talk of moving?

Papa was doing so well physically that he no longer pursued looking for a farm, and he and Mama made plans to move back to Montana. Indeed, when Papa returned to the doctor, he was told that, given Mama's deteriorating health, they should move to a drier climate. He stressed that Papa must wear a hat to protect his face and neck from the sun, he must use his salve daily, and he must get six-month check-ups. If, they were going back to northeastern Montana, the doctor recommended Dr. Agneberg in Glasgow for his doctor.

Mama and Papa decided as soon as the boys finished the school year they would move to Glasgow with its population of 3,800, rather than Hinsdale with a population of only a few hundred. Hinsdale was 29 miles from Glasgow, and they wanted to be closer to Dr. Agneberg and more medical and other services than were available in Hinsdale.

This time Papa was taking no chances. He corresponded with real estate agents in Glasgow to line up several farms to look at before we moved. Papa boarded the train in Sandpoint and traveled to Glasgow. This time he would have binding paperwork drawn up before returning home to Idaho.

Papa returned from Glasgow with an enthusiastic report about the farm he had chosen. It required much work, but Willie and Sherman would be able to help him restore it to a productive farm. After only one year in Idaho, our truck, named Old Shiny Eyes by Grace for the way its light shone when Papa drove home after dark, was loaded again. Once again, Mama, Papa, Grace, Dolly, and I rode in front, and Sherman and Nathan rode in back behind the cab. Gus Hernvall and Willie followed in Gus's truck with the tractor and equipment.

When night came Mama, Papa, and we girls stayed in a motel, but the boys and Gus slept in the trucks to prevent theft. One of the motels we stayed in had an electric light on the ceiling of the room. While we girls had seen electric lights in town, we had never spent a night in a room with an electric light. Papa showed us how the amazing light could be turned on and off by pulling a string hanging down from it; then he held each of us up, so we could turn the light on and off.

We drove away from beautiful Idaho with its mild winters, adequate precipitation, mountains, clear, icy streams, and evergreen trees onto a vast, empty prairie that stretched to a distant horizon. Only occasional river valleys relieved the endless monotony of the prairie. But, Mama and Papa were glad. Montana was home. ❧

CHAPTER 9

Through Fields
of Clover

Finally, Papa drove into Glasgow in northeastern Montana. Glasgow was located in the green, irrigated Milk River Valley. While the town looked better than many of the smaller barren towns we had passed through, compared to rain-washed Sandpoint, Glasgow looked harsh, bare, and gritty.

We stopped in town long enough for Mama and Papa to sign the final paperwork for the McColly farm. Then Papa headed west out of Glasgow on a gravel road bordering the Great Northern Railroad tracks. Gus Hernvall and Willie followed in Gus's truck loaded with the tractor and equipment. Three miles from town, and a half mile after we crossed the truss bridge over Milk River, Papa turned onto a dirt road that led to a railroad underpass. Mama who feared railroad crossings said that it was providential that we, unlike the neighboring farms, would go under the railroad, rather than over a railroad crossing. We drove through the underpass with willow sprouts growing thickly along both sides of the railroad. Coming out of the willows we could see the house and buildings less than a quarter mile distant. A narrow, hard, dirt road through fields of blooming yellow clover led to the house.

The McCollys, an elderly couple, greeted us warmly, as if we were long awaited relatives. Indeed, Mama and Papa had known them in homestead days. We girls and Mama stayed in the house and visited with Mrs. McColly while Papa, Sherman, and Nathan toured the farm with Mr. McColly. Mrs. McColly served Mama and us girls hot drinks. Since tea and cocoa were unavailable due to the war, she served Postum, a hot drink made from grains and molasses, to Mama and a combination of hot water with some milk and honey in it to us girls. Mrs. McColly and Mama talked of old friends and days past. She was small, thin, and fragile-looking with a shrunken mouth. She laughed often, and when she did I could see her gums that held no teeth. I tried not to stare.

Later I asked Mama why Mrs. McColly did not get false teeth. Mama laughed, "Oh, her mother wore false teeth, and she didn't like her mother, so she won't wear false teeth. That is called 'biting off your nose to spite your face!'"

Putt-Putt on Gus's truck had been too high to go through the underpass, so he and Willie had stayed by the town road to begin unloading the tractor. Nathan returned to the house. He asked Mama if he could go to see how Willie and Gus were doing. Grace and I begged to go with Nathan, and we promised to stay out of the way. Willie and Gus had just finished unloading the tractor, and Willie readied to drive it to the house. Laughing and shouting, Nathan, Grace, and I ran behind Willie and the tractor on the lane that was bordered with yellow clover higher than our heads.

⁓ · · · o · · · ⁓

The McCollys had already purchased a house in Glasgow and moved almost everything they did not plan to leave behind for us. They were merely camping in the farm house until we arrived. We spent the night in a motel room in Glasgow, and the next day Papa, Gus, and the boys finished loading the McColly's few belongings into Gus's truck that had been emptied of equipment. Gus would help the McCollys unload their belongings in town, and then he would head back to Idaho. Papa, Willie, and Sherman began unloading our truck while Mama directed where items should be placed. Nathan took care of Dolly, Grace, and me.

When Mama said it was time for dinner, we picnicked under a large cottonwood tree on the west side of the house. Papa spread a tarp on the ground under the tree; then he helped Mama bring out food.

"This will have to do until the kitchen is set up for cooking." Mama said of the egg sandwiches, pickles, and canned peaches.

Sherman concluded that this cottonwood was the biggest tree on the farm. We decided to name it "The Big Tree."

After dinner we children walked with Mama and Papa as we checked out the buildings. We started east of the house. These buildings lay in a line next to the big irrigation ditch on the south and approximately one hundred fifty feet from the riverbank on the north. A row of chokecherry trees grew directly behind the cellar to the back of the chicken house. Mama told us that we would be able to eat all the chokecherries we wanted and still have plenty to make syrup and jam.

Farthest east was the chicken house, a snug, sturdy building banked with dirt and made of railroad ties. Mama believed it would be warm enough to keep the hens laying eggs all winter. Light-reddish-gold Buff Orpington hens

Papa had bought from the McCollys pecked and scratched in the chicken pen. Just east of the chicken house was a small orchard. Mama identified the trees—a few crabapple trees, a few plum trees, and a small raspberry patch.

Nearer to the house we peered into the darkness of the granary. Papa told the boys that they needed to clean up the floor, because they would sleep there all summer. The McColly's cozy two-room house was acceptable for two people; five would squeeze in this summer, but not eight. Papa planned to buy a house and have it moved onto the farm before winter. He noted that there was a perfect place for another house between the root cellar and the McColly house.

The root cellar was next. A big door on a mound of raised ground opened to steps leading down to the cellar. Two lizards raced to hide when we came down. "Izzy and Lizzy!" Mama laughed. Rows of shelves for canned goods and two bins for holding root vegetables had been built against the dirt walls. The temperature in the cellar stayed consistently more moderate than the outdoor temperature, making it cooler in summer and warmer in winter. The McCollys claimed it never froze, no matter how cold the winter.

Coming up from the root cellar we walked west past the house and The Big Tree toward the barn. On the trail to the barn we passed a small pond with brownish water and green algae around the edges. Mama declared it was unclean and we were never to go into it. The barn was the only building west of the house. It was separated from the riverbank by only fifty feet, which was much too close, because a flood could render the bank unstable. Still there was enough room for a row of chokecherry trees between the barn and the riverbank. A pole corral surrounded the other three sides. The barn's thatched roof worried Mama and Papa. Wouldn't a flat thatched-roof leak? But the barn was nice sized with a row of stanchions across the west end and enough room for cows to stay inside during the coldest winter days. Papa had paid Mr. McColly for his three cows, and now all three stared at us curiously from the nearby pasture.

⁂

On Sunday Sherman carried Dolly, Willie carried Grace part of the time, and we children followed Mama and Papa on a walk around the fields, woods, and perimeter of our farm. The sixty-five acres lay in a narrow strip with the long north side bordered by the Milk River and the south side bordered by the Great Northern Railroad. The river curved around the east end, and a dirt road led past the west end. Over fifty acres of the rich river-bottom soil could be irrigated. About half of the arable land supported an abundant hay crop. A system of irrigation ditches ran through the farm, and the ditches needed only minor repair.

Deciduous trees, mostly large cottonwoods, formed a wood along the east end of the property. Papa noted that the trees could supply fuel for our wood stoves. Large cottonwood trees grew on both sides of the river banks. We stood on the river bank behind the house and looked, what seemed a long way, down to the river. Papa said that his only problem with the farm concerned high water and flooding. He pointed to the sharp cuts in the river bank where it had caved off from the erosive power of rapidly flowing high water.

"One day," Papa predicted, "This river will reach a flood stage so high that most of this farm will be under water."

⋅⊙⋅ ⋅ ⋅ o ⋅ ⋅ ⋅⊙⋅

Of more immediacy was the pressing problem of food, especially meat. As farmers we were accustomed to eating lots of meat. The continuation of WWII called for more and more sacrifice by Americans at home. Food rationing was in full force so adequate food could be sent to our fighting soldiers. Sugar, canned milk, butter, coffee, some meats, and some canned and processed foods were limited or required ration stamps to purchase.

Before summer ended, we would be producing much of our own food, but, in the meantime, we ate eggs, lots of eggs. Mama churned butter and made clabber cheese. Willie and Sherman caught fish from the river to supplement the meat Papa could purchase at the store. Sugar must be saved for the jams and preserves Mama would can from the rows of chokecherry trees and the small orchard of crabapple and plum trees. Papa bought a five-gallon can of honey for sweetening hot drinks, for some cooking, and to be used in place of jam on bread. We spooned Karo syrup onto our hot oatmeal porridge.

Papa bought a bull and five more milk cows of mixed breeds. The cows gave us milk for our own use, cream to sell, and skimmed milk to feed to the pigs. He bought three Chester White sows with their piglets. Before winter the piglets would be large enough for Papa to butcher two of them. Mama ordered chicks from the *Murray Mc Murray Hatchery* catalog. The cockerels grow more quickly, and in a few months, they could provide food; the smaller pullets would be saved for laying eggs. Willie and Sherman helped Mama and Papa plant a large garden—large enough to provide vegetables for our table by mid to late summer and a surplus to can for winter.

Many products besides food were rationed, but most, such as electrical appliances, did not apply to us. We lived simply, and electricity had not come to our rural area. The popular WWII slogan, "Use it up, wear it out, make it do, or do without" may have impacted those who were accustomed to being less frugal than we, but to Mama and Papa who came from the homestead, frugality was a way of life.

When Willie, Sherman, and Nathan started school in Glasgow they contributed to the scrap drives that were organized to recycle materials that could be used by our soldiers. McColly farm, like so many others, had some dump piles that the boys searched for items to bring to the collection. Discarded metal and rubber articles were about all they could find that was accepted— farmers, as a rule, discarded very little. Part of the goal with the drives was to help Americans feel a part of the war effort, and for Willie, Sherman, and Nathan this was accomplished.

ლ഻ · · ○ · · ·ல

The summer of 1944, Mama and Papa still listened to news of the war daily and discussed it with the boys and with neighbors who dropped by. I was only four and unable to process objectively what they said. I often feared that the Germans or Japanese might attack us. One July night I awoke in the darkness to crashes, a pounding on the roof, and blinding flashes of light. Were we being attacked? I lay whimpering in terror until Papa lifted me out of bed. No, it was not the Germans or Japanese, it was a thunder storm. Mama stood near the open south door holding Grace. Dolly slept. Papa pulled two chairs close enough to see out the door, and we four sat watching the storm. Lightning illuminated hail slamming into the ground, bouncing up, and rolling a short way. Soon the hail stopped and sheets of rain fell and danced on the ground. And, all the time thunder roared, first up close; then rumbling into the distance. Now that I felt safe, I was mesmerized.

When the boys came to breakfast, Mama asked what they thought of the storm.

Willie shrugged his shoulders, smirked, and raised his eyebrows in mock surprise. "Was there a storm?"

Sherman was more forthright, "It scared the hell out of us! It was all we could do to keep Nathan from trying to run to the house!"

"We can be thankful that at least the hail wasn't bad enough to damage the garden," Papa said.

જ્⊙· · · o · · ·⊙ૐ

When Papa could line out jobs for Willie and Sherman to do on the farm without his help, he worked with Putt-Putt and the slip to move dirt to form a mound for the new house. He had already located and purchased a well-built two-room house and a long narrow building that had served as a house. He arranged for both to be moved when he finished building the mound of dirt on which to place them. He and Mama agreed with Papa's initial idea of locating the new house between the McColly house and the cellar.

Papa created a pond on the south side of the main irrigation ditch by excavating dirt with Putt-Putt and his slip. He brought the dirt across the ditch bridge and built a large flat mound on which to place the houses. They would be connected by an entryway-closet area once they were in place. When he felt certain that the packed mound of dirt was high enough that it would not be reached by flood waters, he would notify the men to bring the houses.

As Papa had predicted, we were able to move into New House before cold weather, and the boys moved from the granary into one room of Old House. The other room was kept for food storage. New House with only three rooms—front room, kitchen and long bedroom—felt spacious.

Papa wrapped the entire outside of the house with tarpaper, a homestead staple, and banked the foundations with dirt for warmth. He planned to add an artificial brick siding paper over the tarpaper, but that must wait. Winter was approaching and his work load was overwhelming. One of the tasks with which Willie and Sherman proved to be a big help was to repair irrigation ditches, so next year's crops could be irrigated. The continuing war increased the demand for sugar beets, so Papa would plant sugar beets as he had in Hinsdale. Sugar beets require very precise irrigating. Under-irrigating causes stress and reduces the yield, while over-irrigating, especially near harvest time, lowers the sugar content.

The boys began school in early September, but on weekends and some evenings Willie and Sherman helped Papa haul and stack the last of the hay and cut wood for winter. With four stoves that burned wood—two heating stoves and Mama's Monarch cook stove in New House, plus a heating stove in Old House, the demand for winter wood would be relentless.

As he had during the summer, Nathan took care of us girls when he was not in school. Papa often helped Mama, but, still, her workload of canning, in addition to all the cooking, laundry, etc. required for a family of eight, was too much to do with three little girls to care for. Nathan's caring for us and Willie and Sherman's helping Papa became a pattern that was not to Nathan's liking. He wanted to be with the men. Mama told Nathan to think of his job as herding—he was herding us girls. This did not make him feel any better.

A short way beyond the truss bridge on our way to Glasgow we passed a sign near the road and a railroad overpass. The post and sign background were painted white, and the lettering and picture were red. The top line said, BIDDLES, a silhouette of a hog was in the middle, and the bottom line, said DUROC HOGS. Mr. and Mrs. Royce Biddle, owners of the sign whose land lay directly across the river on the east, had come over to welcome us to the neighborhood and now came to visit from time to time. Their son who served in the military was fighting overseas. The grown-ups talked about the war, and we children listened. They were all worried because the Allies had not prevailed sooner.

One afternoon when they visited and talk turned to the war Willie and Sherman became much more attentive when Mr. Biddle spoke of the Glasgow Army Air Field located northeast of Glasgow. This was a satellite airfield with a bomber squadron stationed there. He said airmen flew B-17 bombers, and there were bombing and gunnery training sites. Mr. Biddle knew Papa planned to grow sugar beets. He said he heard that a German prisoner of war camp was being moved onto the airfield site in December. It was rumored that the German prisoners of war would be helping farmers who raised sugar beets.

After the Biddles had left, Mama and Papa spoke hopefully of the possibility of help with sugar beets from the German prisoners of war. Papa said that before time for spring planting he would find out for certain. In the meantime, anticipating help, he would prepare more acreage for next summer's sugar beet fields.

"The extra income from more sugar beets would be a godsend," Mama declared. ૭ꙭꙅ

GERMAN PRISONERS OF WAR

The presidential election of 1944 brought lively discussions between Mama and Papa at supper time; Mama was a Republican, and Papa was a Democrat. Mama had voted for Republican Wendell Willkie in 1940, and now she threatened to vote for Republican Thomas E. Dewey. Papa was adamant that with the war going more favorably for the Allies, it was not time for America to change presidents.

Mama admired Eleanor Roosevelt, President Roosevelt's wife. Papa reluctantly admitted she was an asset to the President, but she was "a woman who didn't know her place."

"That," Mama told Papa, "is exactly why I like her!"

A few days after Election Day Mama finally told Papa that she had not voted for Dewey, but rather for President Roosevelt—really for Eleanor. "I just wanted to 'get your goat'!"

When Mama looked at pictures of President Roosevelt, Churchill, and Stalin at the February 1945 Yalta Conference in *Life Magazine* and other periodicals, she commented on how much President Roosevelt and Churchill had declined—especially President Roosevelt.

"President Roosevelt is a man in very poor health," she pronounced.

She studied one picture further, "Stalin still looks good. You couldn't kill him with a club!"

Still, when the radio carried news of President Roosevelt's death on April 12, 1945, we were all stunned. President Roosevelt had traveled to his Little White House in Warm Springs, Georgia, for much needed relaxation. While there he died suddenly of a stroke. He was sixty-three years old, only eight years older than Papa.

"I never saw him, but I feel like I have lost a friend." Papa expressed how much of America felt about Roosevelt's untimely death.

For several days the talk at meals focused on President Roosevelt. Mama and Papa talked of the unimaginable mental and physical challenge he had experienced during his presidency. He entered office in 1933 facing the economically devastating Great Depression and the drought on the Great Plains—the nation's worst natural disaster. By the end of 1941, under President Roosevelt's leadership, America was embroiled in World War II. "President Roosevelt carried the weight of the world on his shoulders, and it was too much," Papa believed.

Mama and Papa agreed with an editorial reprinted from *New York Times*, "Men will thank God on their knees a hundred years from now that Franklin D. Roosevelt was in the White House." With a lesser president, the United States could be faring much worse in the war.

Vice-President Harry S. Truman was now America's president. Roosevelt, always in the forefront, had given America little chance to know Vice President Truman. Unlike President Roosevelt whose broad shoulders and projection of self-assurance inspired confidence in Americans, President Truman was short and slight of stature. President Truman did not possess President Roosevelt's resonant voice that had quelled Americans' fears as they gathered around their radios to listen to his Fireside Chats. Who was this little man that would now lead America in this critical time of war?

"Well, he can't be all bad. He is a fellow Missourian!" Papa laughed; then added seriously, "Let's pray for President Truman and give him a chance.

⁊⁊· · · ◦ · · ·◌⁊

We all gathered around the big table in the front room at mealtime to share Mama's good food and our family's lively conversation. After Papa's prayer of thanksgiving, we discussed news brought to us on our battery-operated radio and read in the newspaper and magazines. We also talked of family and farm activities. Mealtime was leisurely, but still, never long enough.

Many of the farm activities were family activities. We girls wanted to tag along whenever we were allowed to do so. Nathan's primary job was to see that we stayed out of the way of the work. Papa, Willie, and Sherman had followed Mama's advice when they added fruit trees, mostly various kinds of plums and crabapples, to our orchard. They planted a strawberry patch and a larger raspberry patch.

Papa planted fields of sugar beets, and Willie and Sherman made final repairs to our irrigation system of ditches. Mr. Biddle's news of the German prisoner of war camp was true. German prisoners would be helping farmers who raised sugar beets.

The night of May 8, 1945, our radio carried the news of Victory in Europe Day, V-E Day! The Allies accepted Germany's unconditional surrender. The mood at our supper table was jubilant. Even I was relieved. Maybe, my nightmares of German's dropping bombs from their planes as they flew over would stop.

"Who is going to help us with the sugar beets now?" Sherman wondered.

Papa worried. He had planted many more acres of sugar beets than he and the boys could possibly tend; further he counted heavily on the income from the sugar beet crop. When Papa checked with officials they assured him that repatriation of German prisoners would not happen any time soon.

Fortunately, the school year ended before the sugar beets had to be weeded and thinned. German prisoners would help with this, but their coming significantly increased the work load for Papa, Mama, Willie, and Sherman. Nathan, too, had no break in his job of herding us girls. Papa's entire day would be spent with the German prisoners from his trip to pick them up until he delivered them back to the POW camp in the evening. Willie and Sherman must do their work and the work Papa would have done. Mama would do all household work, plus cooking for us and preparing lunch for the German prisoners. While the German prisoners were sent with a light lunch, Mama and Papa both believed that hard working young men needed more food.

The Big Ben alarm clock jangled in the darkness before morning's light to wake Mama and Papa. Mama cooked a big breakfast of meat, eggs, cereal, and pancakes or biscuits. Papa ate hurriedly, so he could make the thirty mile drive to the German prisoners of war Camp located on the Glasgow Army Air Field. He had built benches around the inside perimeter of the truck bed to prepare it to haul the German prisoners and their guards to our farm. Once the prisoners boarded the truck they must be seated on the benches. An interpreter and a guard with an automatic carbine stood watch over the prisoners. Another guard with an automatic carbine rode up front with Papa.

While Papa was making his round-trip to the POW Camp, Sherman and Willie milked the cows and completed the livestock chores. When they carried foamy pails of milk into the kitchen, Mama served them a big breakfast.

While they ate Nathan stood on a wooden box that gave him the height needed to turn the handle of the De Laval cream separator. Mama saved out whole milk for us to drink. The separator sent skimmed milk out one spout and cream out the other spout into buckets that had been set in place. Willie poured the cream into a five-gallon cream can. He then carried the whole milk and the cream to the cellar to stay cool, and Sherman took the skim milk to the pigs.

At seven o'clock Mama let us girls get out of bed and helped us dress. She was too busy to have us underfoot any earlier. Once we were in the kitchen, she served breakfast to Nathan and us three girls. When we finished breakfast Nathan began his "herding" duties while Mama began preparing big pots of stew and homemade bread for our family and the POWs.

Mama and Papa often spoke of how much they missed Lew Balky and Dorothy Christensen. "They were not only a tremendous help, but they were great companions," Mama sighed

Papa spoke hopefully, "This farm is capable of producing enough income to pay a hired girl to help you. Willie and Sherman will be able to assume more responsibility helping me as they grow older. All in good time."

When the German prisoners finished thinning and weeding our sugar beets, they moved on to another farm. Life on our farm settled back to a, still busy, but less intense routine. Papa helped Mama with breakfast while Sherman and Willie continued doing the morning chores. During the day Willie and Sherman helped Papa with farm work. Mama gave Nathan breaks from his "herding" job now that she was not cooking the huge quantities of food for the German prisoners.

Neighbors, who were also busy on their farms, stopped by occasionally for short visits. When a car or truck appeared on our dirt road after passing through the underpass, we all gathered to listen to the talk. While crops and some local news were discussed, the talk always turned to the war. It was personal. Every family had one or more members in the military or knew others who did.

As more news was broadcast daily giving additional information of the concentration camps established by the Germans, neighbors discussed it in shocked tones. It was as though by discussing it, some of the horror would dissipate. Some transferred their anger toward the German prisoners of war. Papa maintained that most of the German people and probably none of the German prisoners knew anything about Hitler's concentration camps.

"Nonetheless," Mr. Biddle told us, "They are showing films of the concentration camp carnage to the POWs at the camps."

Papa told of conversations with the interpreter for the POWs. "Most of them are just boys conscripted into the military. They tell the interpreter that they now realize that much of what they heard in Germany was propaganda with no basis. They like Americans, and they frequently mention how much better off they are here than they would be in Germany at this time."

Mr. Biddle arrived one day with more disturbing news about the Japanese. Mama and Papa were never sure of his sources, because he often learned information before they heard it on the news broadcasts or read it in printed material. Mr. Biddle's son was in the military, and one of his friends operated a short-wave radio. Perhaps his information came from one of them.

The Japanese were launching hundreds, if not thousands, of balloon bombs. We already knew of a balloon bomb landing in Oregon. A minister and his wife had taken five children who attended their Sunday school class on a picnic. The minister parked their car while his wife and the children explored the picnic area in Oregon's beautiful mountains. He heard an explosion and raced to find them. They had come close enough to a Japanese balloon bomb to set off its explosives. The fiery explosion killed all six of them. I shivered in horror when Mama told the story. I rationalized that Oregon was far away and closer to Japan.

Mr. Biddle explained that the government now knew that the Japanese had launched balloon bombs that could be carried on air currents as far as the Midwestern states. The government did not want to disseminate this information, because of the panic it might cause.

This information did cause panic—Mama's panic. She warned us many times, "Don't ever, ever go close to any balloon you see. One could land any place on our farm. If you go near to it, you will be burned terribly and blown to bits!"

Every time we went out to play we expected to see a balloon bomb. What if one landed on our house?

The Japanese now stood alone against the Allies, but they were tenacious. The Allied victory in Europe only intensified the Japanese efforts to prevail. America, with British naval support, was dominating the land and sea battles in the Pacific. America's bombing of Tokyo stepped up, and the United States army and marine forces finally won the long, bloody Battle of Okinawa. Occupation of Okinawa put Japanese mainland only four-hundred miles away. A ground invasion of Japan looked possible.

The neighbors visiting us were apprehensive about our soldiers invading Japan. So many Americans had already died in the war. It was believed that

Japan could not win. If only they would surrender, so further bloodshed could be avoided. But Mama, Papa, and those neighbors who had read about the Japanese culture concluded that the Japanese, to a man, would prefer death to surrender. Invasion would be a blood bath.

President Harry Truman, the little man from Missouri, chose a way to save America's military men and women. Japanese deaths were inevitable, but more American deaths could be prevented. August 6, 1945, the United States dropped the atomic bomb on Hiroshima. Within hours President Truman called on Japan to surrender or "expect a rain of ruin from the air, the like of which has never been seen on this earth." ๛

CHAPTER 11

VICTORY AND LOSS

America waited with bated breath to see if Japan would surrender. President Truman stood firm in his decision that far too many American lives had been lost in a war we did not start. The onus would be on Japan. They started the war. They could surrender and avoid more Japanese deaths, or they could suffer "a rain of ruin from the air."

Minutes ticked by; then hours passed. Hours became days—August 7, 8. . . . President Truman waited with diminishing hopes and patience. No surrender from Japan. Perhaps, they erroneously thought President Truman was bluffing. If so, they could not have been more mistaken. A few hours after midnight on August 9 America dropped another atomic bomb, this time on the Japanese city of Nagasaki.

Even America's second rain of hell did not bring immediate surrender. Again, days passed; finally, August 15, 1945, Imperial Japan announced its surrender. Due to time zone differences the announcement was made in America on August 14. The official document of surrender was signed aboard the USS *Missouri* on September 2, 1945. President Truman called this date the official Victory over Japan Day, V-J Day.

After all the anger, all the fear, and all the wartime deprivation, America's mood turned jubilant. In cities people took to the streets on foot and in cars. They danced, sang, shouted, and honked horns. They praised President Truman.

America was safe. The men and women who still served overseas would be coming home. Families we knew wept. Some wept with happiness because those they loved were spared, and others wept because those they loved had not been spared.

The day after we learned that World War II had ended, our family celebrated. Papa and the boys stopped work early. They went to town to buy ice and rock salt for making ice cream while we girls stayed with Mama. Laughing and chattering we watched as Mama mixed cream, eggs, sugar, and vanilla in a big bowl. When Mama was satisfied with the taste, she asked me to get three spoons, and she spooned a little into a small bowl for each of us.

She told us that we could give her mixture a taste test. We assured her that it was delicious!

When Papa and the boys returned from town, we all gathered under The Big Tree by The Old House. The boys brought the hand-cranked ice cream maker and a jar of Mama's canned strawberries. The ice cream mix and strawberries were added to the canister. Ice was packed into the wooden bucket, and salt was added. Sherman and Willie took turns cranking the ice cream until Mama pronounced it ready to eat. We ate slowly savoring every bite of our celebration treat.

Papa sighed, "If only President Roosevelt could have lived to see the war end."

◦ ◦ ◦ o ◦ ◦ ◦

German Prisoners-of-War stayed at their POW camp waiting for their official release. They would work sugar beets this fall. Once again Papa would leave in early morning darkness to pick them up and bring them to our farm. Activity on our farm would go into high gear as always when they came to work in the beets. In the spring they had thinned and hoed, and they had returned in the summer to weed and hoe the beets. All were back-breaking jobs using short-handled hoes. They were given a short break at the end of each row. This gave them time to straighten up and limber up their backs.

The Milk River Valley in Northeastern Montana proved to be a perfect place for growing sugar beets. The alluvial soil of the flood plain of the Milk River was rich and rock-free, and the irrigation was timed to maximize beet production. Summer's long, sunny days with temperatures mostly 60 to 80 degrees and cool nights of 40 to 50 degrees increased the sugar content.

"It looks like a bumper crop," Papa told Mama in early September when he returned from irrigating one of the beet fields.

Sugar beet harvest began in late September, because sugar beets stop growing with the first hard freeze. Fall harvest put more strain on Mama and Papa, because the boys were back in school.

One of Nathan's primary jobs when he was home and POWs were on our farm was to keep us girls out of sight of the prisoners. Farmers were told that German Prisoners had not seen women in a long time, and that all females were to be kept out of sight. Mama and Papa's real concern was that a little girl could be easily snatched and used as a hostage for an escaping prisoner. They warned us repeatedly of the danger of us girls being near the prisoners. Just to make sure their message was heeded, Mama told us that the prisoners would "chop us up into little pieces and eat us with salt and pepper!" We stayed away. When Nathan was in school we spent much of our time in the house until he came home to take us outside. We girls looked forward to the POWs going to another farm to work.

It was always a concern that one or more prisoners would try to escape. Once the prisoners arrived in the field they were not allowed to leave the field for any reason. The two guards with their automatic carbines stood watch, and so did Papa with his .45 Colt pistol. During harvest another guard was added, because Papa was too busy to help guard POWs. He must drive the tractor in the field; then stop and drive the truck to town every time a load was ready.

Harvesting was demanding and precise work. First Papa drove our tractor, Putt-Putt, the Farmall F12, pulling a beet lifter that lifted the beets and loosened their central root. German Prisoners designated as pickers followed the lifter and yanked the beets out of the ground. This was not easy, because sugar beets can have a root that is five to eight feet long! Once the pickers pulled the beets out of the ground, they stacked them in neat piles.

Another group of POWs known as toppers used long knives to slice the tops off the beets at the crown. Topping was critical, and topping thousands of beets required much expertise. A farmer's beets were inspected when they were brought in to sell. If toppers cut too far below the crown, the beets lost sugar-bearing material, and the farmer's price was cut.

POWs called loaders followed the toppers to load the topped beets into the truck bed. When the truck bed was full Papa drove the truck to town to have the beets inspected and then to the beet dump by the railroad in Glasgow. Getting the beets to the beet dump as soon as possible was imperative, because, once topped, they began to lose sugar content.

Willie begged to stay home from school to help with the harvest. He could drive the tractor pulling the lifter while Papa took beets to the dump. This would speed up the process. Finally, Papa relented. He did need Willie's help, and Willie hated to go to school.

One evening when Papa was taking the POW's, their guards, and the interpreter back to camp the truck stopped right in front of our house. Even though the truck with POWs drove past twice a day, it had never stopped in front of our house. We girls, who often peeked over the window sill when Mama was not looking, now stood staring as one of the POWs and the interpreter jumped down from the back of the truck. When the POW and the interpreter turned toward the house, we girls bolted for the bed, and all three of us crawled under the same one.

We heard a knock on the door. We heard Mama opening the door and a man's voice speaking German to her. Mrs. Clark had insisted that Mama learn to speak German when they lived in St. Peter, and now Mama could converse in German with the POW. After a brief conversation, we heard the door close and the truck drive off. Only then did we emerge from under the bed. We were awed. Mama had spoken to a German prisoner and lived to tell about it. She was, though, a grown up, and it was little girls that they cut into pieces and ate with salt and pepper.

"He was only a boy," Mama shook her head sadly in answer to my question about what the prisoner wanted, "Not much older than Willie. The prisoners noticed our chickens, and they're hungry for fresh chickens to eat. The boy was sent as their spokesperson. He said they would trade fatigue clothes and combat boots for some chickens. John and the boys could sure use the clothes —especially the boots. We made a trade. They will have chicken for supper tomorrow night!"

Mama readily agreed to such a good deal, because footwear was rationed during the war, and buying new clothes was discouraged.

That night as we sat around the table eating supper, Mama and Papa discussed the German prisoners.

"They're all just homesick boys," Papa said. "After the Great War the return-ing German soldiers were triumphant, because, although they lost the war, they kept their homeland safe. After the Germans' laying waste to much of Europe they were able to return to a country untouched by the war. This time will be much, much different. It's going to be tough on these boys to go home. They lost the war, and their homeland has been devastated. They have a food shortage, like much of the rest of Europe. Many will have lost civilian family members in the bombing raids. What they did to others has been done to them."

Now that the war had ended Mama and Papa discussed how long they thought it would take, before the rationing ended. Even with the rationing, America was so much better off than Europe where food shortages were critical. And, we, as farmers, were so much better off than Americans living in cities. Our farm produced in abundance many of the rationed foods, and we were able to purchase more sugar, because we raised sugar beets.

What Papa did need and looked forward to buying was new tires for the truck. Tires were rationed, because the Japanese had seized control of most of the rubber fields that shipped rubber to the United States. A red **T** sticker on the windshield of the truck designated it as being a farm truck, so Papa was able to buy more gas than for non-farm vehicles. The reverse side of the **T** sticker faced the driver; on it was written "To Save Tires Drive Under **35**. Is this Trip **really** necessary?" Thirty-five miles an hour was called the "Victory Speed."

Neighbors who stopped by to visit speculated on when rationing would be terminated, and they discussed President Truman's use of atomic bombs to end our war with Japan. More news about the ensuing devastation was becoming available daily. As with the concentration camps established and controlled by Germany, discussing the long-term tragedy caused by the bombs seemed to help people grapple with the horror.

The difference was that all were repulsed by the concentration camps for which America was in no way responsible. All were repulsed by the human suffering caused by the bomb, and this time America was responsible. Should the atomic bombs have been dropped? Most neighbors said President Truman did the right thing. Others thought America had worn Japan down to where we could have invaded and conquered Japan without much loss of life. Papa thought the latter to be ill-informed.

One thing upon which all agreed was their desire for America to "get back to normal."

After one neighbor drove away Mama said, "What is normal? Before the war, we came through the Great Depression and America's worst drought ever. What's next?" ல

CHAPTER 12

THE MYSTERIOUS MRS. CLARK

Mama and Papa believed that the sugar rationing would continue until countries could reclaim and restore the cane sugar fields. This could well take a couple of years. Part of our sugar shortage was solved by the Bee Tree, a cottonwood tree growing east of the house on the river bank near the cow trail. The Bee Tree trunk was exceptionally large and slightly twisted. During warm weather bees flew in and out of a hole in the trunk that was about eight feet above the ground. When the weather grew cold the bees stopped all activity. It was then that Papa "robbed" the Bee Tree.

When Papa announced at dinner that this was the night they would rob the Bee Tree, we girls begged to go. Papa reasoned that we were not old enough to be out that long on such a cold night, and he and the boys would be too busy to take care of us. We begged. Grace was almost four years old and I was five years old. I knew that she and I were not the problem. Dolly was only two, but she was not about to be left out of any activity that Grace and I were allowed. Mama solved the dilemma. If Dolly stayed at the house with her they would make mint candies and Dolly would get to eat some.

Papa and the boys gathered buckets; a long wide bladed knife we called a corn knife; a large long-handled ladle; and flash lights. Mama helped Grace and supervised me as we pulled on coats, bonnets, and mittens. Temperatures dropped on early November nights. She said she did not want us to catch our death of cold as we stood around watching Papa and the boys.

We followed the cow trail east beside the Milk River bank lined with cottonwood trees. In the growing darkness we could see the irrigation ditch and sugar beet fields south of us. A few stars twinkled, and great horned owls hooted from large cottonwood trees farther down along the river bank. The trees had lost their leaves, and now, with black, naked limbs and branches they looked eerie.

Last year before they harvested the honey, Papa had cut a hole in the tree above the level of the bee's honeycombs. Once he had harvested honey for us and left enough to see the bees through the winter, he had covered the hole with a piece of wood and screwed it down. Now he reopened the hole and cut the honeycomb with the corn knife. Next he ladled honey, comb and all, into the buckets.

Darkness replaced dusk, the temperature dropped, our feet grew cold from standing, and Grace fussed. Before they finished Papa told Willie to take Grace and me back to the house so Mama could get us to bed. Grace and I walked beside Willie who carried a pail of honey with one hand and shined the flashlight on the trail with the other hand. A train whistled at Biddle's crossing and thundered west toward our farm. We could see the train's light approaching as it clickety-clacked into sight. It was a passenger train with the cars lighted. Just as we reached the house the train rumbled out of sight.

Willie returned to the Bee Tree as Grace and I pulled off our winter gear. Dolly was already asleep. Mama made some hot milk for Grace and me and spooned some honey from the bucket into our mugs. Then she spooned out a bit of honeycomb onto a saucer for each of us. Grace and I agreed that robbing the Bee Tree was great fun!

৵৶· · • ○ • · ·৻৶৸

The next week Mama received a letter from Mrs. Clark who had moved to Seattle during the war to manage a hotel. Now that the war had ended Mrs. Clark was moving back to Minneapolis. She would be passing through Glasgow on the train, and she would stay for several days in a hotel while she visited us and friends. She planned to spend Thanksgiving with us.

Thanksgiving was only two weeks away. Mama went into a tail-spin. She told Papa that Mrs. Clark would not approve of anything Mama did or how she did it.

And, Mama said, "Unless this house gets a top-to-bottom cleaning, Mrs. Clark will ask why we are living in a pigsty."

"Has she ever said that?" Papa asked. Well, no, but none-the-less Mama maintained that was what Mrs. Clark would be thinking.

Papa helped Mama, the boys helped Mama, and the house was scrubbed from top to bottom.

Two days before Thanksgiving Mama, Papa, and we girls rode in the truck on snowy roads to the train depot to pick up Mrs. Clark. We girls wanted to arrive well before the train, so we could see the Black conductors step off the train and assist the passengers as they came off. We pulled up to the depot as the train slowed to a stop. Off stepped the conductor from the train car in front of us. He looked splendid in his maroon colored uniform. We could see the flash of his white teeth as he smiled and talked to the departing passengers.

Mrs. Clark stepped from the train wearing a fur coat, fur hat, leather gloves, and fancy overshoes. Mama and Papa hurried to greet her with hugs while we girls waited in the truck. I decided she was the best dressed passenger.

After Papa had loaded Mrs. Clark's suitcases into the back of the truck, he opened the door and helped Mama and Mrs. Clark into the cab. Grace sat on Mama's lap, Dolly sat on Mrs. Clark's lap, and I squeezed between them. Mrs. Clark turned to give each of us girls a kiss on the cheek. The fragrance of perfume clung to her and soon permeated the truck cab.

Mrs. Clark asked us girls if we would like to come into the Rundle Hotel dining room for a treat after Papa carried her suitcases to her room. We all three chimed yes, almost before she finished her question. We had driven past the Rundle Hotel, but we had never expected to go in.

The Rundle Hotel interior looked unlike anything we had ever seen. Mrs. Clark explained that the architecture was Spanish, and that was why it looked different. We three sat subdued by such grand surroundings as we nibbled at lightly sweetened buns we had been served. Mrs. Clark, Mama, and Papa caught up on news in their lives. We left with the promise to pick her up at the hotel Thanksgiving morning.

The day before Thanksgiving saw a light snowfall and a major flurry of activity as Mama and Papa prepared much of Thanksgiving dinner. We did not have turkeys, but a fat goose was killed, dressed, and hung in the cold pantry-kitchen of The Old House. Willie was allowed to stay home from school to chop wood and do many of the chores Papa completed while the boys were in school. I supervised Dolly and Grace in the front room at the big table as we colored and played games.

On Thanksgiving morning we girls rode with Papa to pick up Mrs. Clark. I had heard Mama tell Papa that she needed us "out of her hair." She helped us into our winter clothes mid-morning, and we raced to the truck that Papa was warming for us. Mama stayed home to continue our dinner preparation. Willie and Sherman worked at necessary outdoor chores, and Nathan stayed in the house to help Mama in any way he could.

Mrs. Clark walked out of the lobby when Papa stopped the truck in front of the hotel. She was dressed up, just as she had been when she stepped off the train. She carried her purse, but she also carried a bag with her. We girls wondered what was in the bag, but we knew we dared not ask. That would be rude, and Mama and Papa did not tolerate rude. Again, she gave each of us a peck on the cheek and the soft fragrance of her perfume enveloped us.

Once home Mrs. Clark greeted Mama with a hug and each of the boys with a handshake. She was barely out of her coat and overshoes when she asked Mama to get an apron for her. She was going to help with last minute dinner preparations.

She turned to Mama as she tied her apron, "Helen, you are worn out! You sit here at the kitchen table and visit with me while John and the boys help me get dinner on the table." She made a cup of hot Postum and honey for Mama. She instructed Nathan to help us girls back into our outdoor clothes and see to it that we ran off some energy. Willie was to fill the wood box. Sherman was to set the table. She stoked the fire in the kitchen range, mashed potatoes, made gravy, and summoned Papa to take the goose out of the oven.

When we were called for dinner we girls and Nathan tumbled into the entry laughing and exhausted. Mrs. Clark directed us to the wash basin to wash up, and then sent us to the table where everybody else was seated. Papa said a prayer of Thanksgiving and a prayer for all those who still suffered from food deprivation caused by the war. We looked at our table that was laden with so much good food—almost all of it from our farm.

"We are richly blessed," Mama spoke for each of us and began passing food around the table.

Before Mrs. Clark engaged Mama and Papa in dinner table conversation, she took time to talk to each of us six children. She asked the boys about school in general, their teachers, their friends, their interests, and their work on the farm. She asked us girls about games we played, whether we preferred living in Idaho or Montana, what we did during the long winters. . ..

When Mrs. Clark turned her attention to Mama and Papa she wanted to know how the war had impacted them. She was especially interested in the German prisoners. After being told of the story about the exchange of chickens for boots, she laughed.

"Now, Helen, aren't you glad you learned to speak German?" She paused, "I do believe that were it not for Winston Churchill, and, of course, President Roosevelt, we would all be learning to speak German, involuntarily!"

We all wanted to know what Seattle was like during the war. Mrs. Clark loved managing the hotel, but she worked hard and put in long days. She said it was a middle class hotel, but, due to war time, lots of shady business went on there.

Willie asked for some specific explanation of shady business. Mrs. Clark tilted her chin up and laughed. "Willie, let's just say this. I was shocked, and I am not easily shocked!"

"Imagine what would go on in a city roaming with military on leave and transient workers from the airplane and ship building factories. Most were fine, upstanding people, but there are always some rotten apples in the barrel."

Additionally, she volunteered at the USO, United Service Organizations. She explained that it was like a club for military men and women. They spent time on their leave just relaxing and visiting, and writing letters home. They drank free coffee, watched movies, listened to music, and danced. It was a "sort of" second home for them.

She told of the underlying fear that Seattle might be bombed by the Japanese. It was one of the most important war time cities in America. At night cars were not allowed to drive with lights on and all homes must have windows covered so no light showed. Businesses that failed to darken their stores had the windows broken out by irate citizens.

"The saddest part of living in Seattle was the round-up of Japanese and their being sent to Internment Camps. I treated cattle more respectfully. They were a hard-working group of people who contributed to the success of Seattle. They were Americans, for god's sake. Many of their husbands and sons served in our military." Mrs. Clark shook her head.

"Why are you moving back to Minneapolis?" Sherman wondered.

"Oh, there was a small exodus beginning in Seattle after V-J Day. Itinerant workers were being laid off and leaving. Women who had joined the work force due to a shortage of men were returning to their homes. And, I decided it was time for me to leave. Hotel business was dropping off. Minneapolis will be a more stable place right now."

After we finished our dessert of Mama's home-made mincemeat pie and squash pie, Mrs. Clark asked the boys to help her clear the table. She insisted that Mama and Papa stay seated. Once the table was cleared and wiped clean, Mrs. Clark asked if we wondered what was in the bag. Even the boys joined us girls in saying, "Yes!"

"Willie, please bring the bag and my purse."

Mrs. Clark stood and picked up the bag. Before opening it, she explained that due to limited suitcase room, she could only bring small items. She took out three little boxes and gave one to each of us girls. She watched smiling while we opened them. We all had a heart locket that she showed us how to open. She had cut out a tiny picture of each of us and put it in one side of our locket.

"That way you can tell them apart!" She beamed at us.

Next she took out a somewhat larger box for each of the three boys. When they opened them they exclaimed "Barlow knives! Real Barlow knives!" She showed them where their knife had each boy's initial engraved on it.

Mama was next. Mrs. Clark unwrapped the paper and showed Mama two beautiful lustrous pieces of silk material and a pattern. One piece of silk was navy and the other piece had tiny navy and yellow stripes. She slid her hand gently over the soft, smooth fabric before handing it to Mama.

"Silk," Mrs. Clark said, "was very hard to come by." She laughed, "Fortunately, I knew some low people in high places!'

"And, John," Mrs. Clark pulled out four packs of cigarettes. Papa liked to smoke, but cigarettes were given first to those serving in the military, and Papa had not smoked for several months.

We all clapped and thanked Mrs. Clark. She smiled, "You are most welcome. I had fun finding just the right gifts."

She sat down and produced her silver cigarette holder from her purse. "Shall we?" she asked Papa. ๑๑

CHAPTER 13

WILLIE'S CARING AND DARING

Mama and Mrs. Clark corresponded frequently after Mrs. Clark returned to Minneapolis. She now worked as a concierge at a hotel, but she felt restless. With both her mother and her sister The Aunt Grace deceased, she said she rattled around in the Watts' large family home she had inherited "like one pea in a pod meant for many." Her brothers, Charles and Harry, were busy with their own lives. Many of her friends had moved on—to their graves or Back East to their childhood cities.

In January of 1947 Mama received a letter from Mrs. Clark. She had placed the Watts' house up for sale. She would move to Glasgow when the weather grew warmer! I overheard Mama telling Papa that Mrs. Clark would be trying to "run her life again, as she always did."

Mama brought up the Thanksgiving Mrs. Clark spent with us when she was on her way back to Minneapolis, "She treats me like a child!"

"You are her child," Papa reasoned. "She was just trying to help you."

"And," Mama added, "She takes over my kitchen the minute she walks in!"

"You have always made it clear that you resent having to spend your life in the kitchen. I would think that your mother's help would be welcome." Papa pointed out.

"It's the way she does it!" Mama would not be pacified.

The subject came up again at supper. We children looked forward to Mrs. Clark's return, but, seeing Mama's irritation, we said nothing.

"Why does she want to come to Glasgow?" Mama wondered. "She always liked big cities."

Sherman said, "Well, maybe, since you are her only child and we are her only grandchildren, she wants to live where she can visit us. And, you have said that she has lots of friends in the Glasgow and Hinsdale area."

Mama made a wry face, "I think her reasoning is more like, so she can boss me around."

Then Mama laughed, "I remember when the men were building our house on the homestead." Mama chuckled, "Mrs. Clark had studied books on building houses. She concluded that neither Henry Lick nor Dutch Cable knew how to properly build a house. She hired a carpenter, Mr. Worsell, from Hinsdale to help build and to supervise. I was sweeping up after the men one day when Mrs. Clark inspected a door frame Mr. Worsell had built. It was not built to her satisfaction. She asked him to tear it out and do it right. She turned to walk away and Mr. Worsell said something rude about her bossing everything. He didn't intend that she heard, but she did. She whirled around, flew back to Mr. Worsell, and gave him a verbal dressing down that embarrassed not only him, but Henry and Dutch. Later I asked what he had said, but she wouldn't tell me. She only said that it was language I did not need to hear. Since Mrs. Clark's language could get pretty salty, I wondered what he could have said that I hadn't already heard."

"Though she be but little, she is fierce!" Papa quoted.

"Yes," Mama said, "But, you do know that if you plant a little tree by a big tree the little tree will not grow."

Letters from Mrs. Clark throughout the winter apprised us of the progress she was making toward her move to Glasgow in the spring.

৩৯০· · · ০ · · ·৩৯৵

The longest part of Montana winters is after the holidays when nights are long and days are short. The great horned owls were nocturnal, so we seldom saw one during the day, but by late afternoons as dusk settled they became active, and we could hear them hooting from cottonwood trees along the river bank.

Early mornings, Willie and Sherman hauled hay from the stacks to feed our cows before daylight. They commented about how many more owls they seemed to be hearing this winter. Although, I heard the owls in the evenings when we girls walked to the barn to watch Papa and the boys milk our cows, I wanted to hear the owls in early morning.

"That is before seven, and you are not allowed to get up before seven," Mama reminded me.

Grace and Dolly both chimed in. They wanted to listen to the owls in the morning, also. I knew this doomed my chance of going. Mama certainly did not have time to get us all up and dressed for outdoors and still have breakfast ready when Papa and the boys came in from chores.

That evening when Mama came into the bedroom to supervise our getting ready to go to bed, she was able to whisper to me without Grace and Dolly hearing. She would wake me early in the morning, and Willie would come to the house to get me when he finished feeding hay to the cows. If Grace or Dolly woke up, I wouldn't be able to go.

I lay awake after story time, almost too excited to sleep. The next I knew Mama was gently shaking my shoulder and motioning for me to follow her to the kitchen. She had gathered my clothes and was warming my underwear shirt and pants in the open oven.

By the time we heard Willie stomping snow from his boots in the entry-way, I was ready.

"John said that it is almost twenty below this morning." Mama told him, "Don't keep Ruth out too long."

I followed Willie's trail through crunchy snow to the haystacks. We did not need a flashlight. The reflection of soft light from a quarter-moon shining on the snow lighted our way. Willie boosted me up onto the haystack from which they had been forking hay. Together we crawled to the higher undis-turbed part of the stack. This made a perfect back rest for us to sit against. Once I sat down, Willie pulled hay over my legs and feet to help me stay warm. Willie motioned for me to be quiet. The owls were not quiet—I had never heard so many owls calling at one time. "Hoo hoodoo hooo hoo," some called. Others answered, "Ho hoo hoo hohoo hoododo."

We listened in the magic of early morning until cold seeped under the hay and through my warm winter clothes.

Willie stirred, "It's time to go to the house,"

He lifted me down from the haystack. He must have been cold, too. When we turned to walk east to the house we could see the horizon was tinged with a faint pink of growing daylight. Grace and Dolly were still in bed when we returned. I decided not to tell them of my owl adventure.

⟡ · · • ○ • · · ⟡

By March days were long and snow melted a little on most days. Willie celebrated his seventeenth birthday in March. All he asked for on his birthday was to be able to quit school. His grades were poor, but letters from school and meetings with his teachers all assured that he was perfectly capable of doing better, but that he chose not to. Mama and Papa knew this. Papa had not spared the strap in his efforts to get Willie to study. Nothing had worked thus far.

Results Willie had wished for happened after another letter came in the mail from school requesting yet another meeting. Willie was to attend with

Mama and Papa. They were to meet with the Superintendent and one of Willie's teachers. It seems that Willie had been disruptive in class, so his teacher, Miss Karr, had shut him in the coat closet. He had used his time in the closet to take out his pocket knife and unscrew all the screws holding the door knob. When Miss Karr jerked the door knob to open the door and let Willie out, she staggered backward as the knob came off in her hand. Willie's classmates had roared with laughter. Miss Karr saw nothing even slightly amusing about the incident, and she was still furious.

Willie told us girls, Sherman, and Nathan later about the meeting. It seems that Miss Karr's face turned red and her eyes bugged out as she recounted the incident to Mama and Papa.

Papa explained to all of us at supper that Willie would not be going back to school, but the rest of his life would be more difficult, because he would not be educated.

✿ · · ○ · · ✿

One Sunday afternoon when most of the snow had melted Willie, Sherman, and Nathan planned to walk through the woods looking for magpie nests that they would later rob of eggs. They agreed to take us girls with them. They wanted to spot old nests before the trees had leaves. The magpies using old nests would lay eggs sooner than the magpies that built new nests.

The boys were able to make a small amount of money each spring from magpies. They were paid for the heads of magpies they shot and for the eggs gathered from magpie nests, because no bird in Montana was so despised by farmers and ranchers as the magnificent looking magpie. The black-billed magpie was mostly black with a white underbelly, graceful white markings on the upper part of wings, and flashing white patches on the ends of the wings when flying. Besides the striking black and white pattern of the magpie, the black on the wings and tail shone an iridescent metallic blue and green.

The handsome magpies did help farmers and ranchers by eating, mice, grasshoppers, flies, and other insects. This was not enough to make up for their being responsible for the deaths of cattle, horses, and sheep. Magpies pecked at any open sore on an animal until it became infected. This included fresh brands on cattle, saddle sores on horses, and shearing wounds on sheep.

We began with Willie carrying Dolly as we walked from the northern part of the woods to the southern part of the woods. The boys focused on which trees had nests so they could find the nests again after the magpies laid

86

eggs. Each egg was worth ten cents. We walked slowly crisscrossing through the woods until we reached the southeast corner where the Great Northern Railroad Bridge spanned the Milk River and its banks.

We looked up at the bridge. Papa had told us that the bridge was about two-hundred feet long and about thirty feet above the river. The extra length and height were necessary, so the bridge would be higher than Milk River's highest water at flood stage.

Willie suggested that we go up the embankment to the tracks. He wanted to show us something. He was going to walk across the bridge. We did not know he meant that he would walk across the top of the foot-wide metal horizontal ledge above the bridge's vertical metal panels. There was absolutely nothing for him to grab hold of should he lose his balance. We watched spell-bound and horrified as he made his way across the ledge above the river covered with ice. My heart pounded in fear. What if he fell? He would die, I was certain. What if a train came?

Once he reached the east side of the river, he jumped down and walked back across the ledge on the other side. When he reached us he laughed and held up his hands. "Easy!" We had a sober walk back to the house. I decided I would never come to the bridge with Willie again. I did not want to watch him die. None of us ever mentioned the incident to Mama or Papa.

Later I asked Nathan what he thought about Willie's walking across the bridge ledge. I was relieved when he told me that he would never do that. But, he added, Willie had shown him a daring stunt on the bridge. There was a five-foot space between each of the vertical metal panels under the ledge. Willie showed Nathan how they could hold onto the ledge and stand between the panels with their backs to the train as it passed. By holding onto the ledge they would not fall backward onto the tracks or forward into the river. Nathan said that was easy. But, he added, it did scare the hell out of him.

⚬ · · ○ · · ⚬

Every spring when the river ice began breaking up, loud cracks like rifle shots could be heard from the river. Water from melting snow upstream caused the river to rise. Ice tore loose and floated downstream until chunks of ice filled the swollen river. Sometimes the icebergs floated placidly; other times the pieces violently churned and ground against each other. Occasionally, a large chunk of ice would get pushed under another only to pop up somewhere further down the river.

One Sunday we children stood watching the river ice in fascination. Even though we were forbidden to get close to the flooding river, Willie talked

Sherman into walking on icebergs across the river to Mr. Combs' farm. Willie picked up a long pole telling Sherman that he would maneuver the icebergs with it. They stepped out onto an iceberg as other icebergs shoved it toward the shore. Nathan stood rooted to the spot he stood on, but I tore off to the house to tell Papa. Willie and Sherman were both going to die.

"Willie and Sherman are on the river ice!" I screamed.

Papa rose from his chair with a look of disbelief that turned to fear. He reached above the doorway and grabbed his rifle. I ran behind him as he raced to the river.

Papa yelled to Willie and Sherman in a terrible voice. At first they did not hear above the noise of rushing water and grinding ice. When they did hear, they turned to look at Papa holding his rifle.

"Get back here right now!" Papa ordered, "You will die crossing the river!"

Sherman turned toward our bank, but Willie hesitated.

"Willie!" Papa yelled. "Get back here or I'll shoot you, because you're going to die anyway!"

Willie reluctantly turned toward our bank. We watched with hearts pounding as Willie and Sherman carefully crossed the two unsteady, moving icebergs that separated them from our river bank.

We all thought Willie would get a terrible whipping, but Papa, who looked a little sick, just turned and walked to the house.

Later, I asked Mama why Papa had told Willie he would shoot him when we knew Papa would never shoot Willie.

"Your dad had to get Willie's attention immediately, and Willie is not inclined to listen. No, John would never have shot him. But, Willie would soon have been in the main current of the river, and he would never have lived to get out. He would have drowned.

"Your dad said when he went out and saw Willie and Sherman's dilemma, he thought he was going to watch two of his sons drown, and there was nothing he could do about it. If the current had caught the iceberg they were on, it would have been all over for them."

"I'm surprised," she added, "that Sherman followed Willie. Sherman is not a follower, but Nathan is."

Mama paused and shook her head, "Willie is so much like your Uncle Don. Your dad and I both fear he will come to a bad end. His daring greatly exceeds his judgment!" ∞

CHAPTER 14

POOR RICHARD

"Mrs. Clark bought a new car, and she is driving it from Minneapolis to Glasgow," Mama announced at supper. "She is going to buy a house, but she said she will rent an apartment until she finds the right one. She should be in Glasgow any day now. She said she wants a few days to get settled into her apartment, and she will drive out Sunday for dinner."

"But," Sherman protested, "She can't drive a car over our road. The truck can barely get through."

Springtime thawing of our river-bottom gumbo mud rendered our road without gravel almost impassable. Sometimes, even our truck would get mired down and Putt-Putt was engaged to pull the truck out.

"Well," Mama said, "You don't know Mrs. Clark. After she bought a car back in 1926 when she lived on the homestead she drove places men feared to drive. If she gets stuck, we'll just pull her out."

"Did she say anything about getting a job?" Papa asked.

"No," Mama shook her head, "I don't know if she plans to work. I don't know if she has enough money that she can afford not to work. I don't even know how old she is! Her age varies with her situations. She must be somewhere in her mid-sixties by now."

Sundays we attended church at Grace Bible Chapel in Glasgow. Mama attended with us most of the time, but, occasionally, she stayed home to prepare our big Sunday dinner. This Sunday, since Mrs. Clark would be at our house for dinner, Willie was allowed to stay home and help Mama. Willie's attitude about going to church was only slightly better than his attitude had been about attending school. Mama told Papa that Willie was a great help to her and she enjoyed her time spent visiting with him as they worked.

Reverend Wall, Cornelius Wall, was our preacher. Mama and Papa called him "Corny" when he was too full of himself. We all felt that his sermons were too long. This Sunday when we wanted to get home to see Mrs. Clark, it seemed he droned on forever. Mama had said that Reverend Wall saw the pulpit as his stage, and he was reluctant to relinquish the limelight by closing his sermons. One of his favorite topics was the perils of Hell and all the various things that either caused one to go there upon dying or things one could do to prevent going there. I wriggled on the hard bench as much as I dared. I agreed with Mama who often said that sometimes she felt as though she were sitting on broken glass before "Corny" ended his sermon.

Once he finished, we could not just hasten out. First we must sing another hymn while he implored us to give our hearts to Jesus. When finally he closed the service with a long prayer, the congregation stood and visited as they formed a line that inched to the door to shake hands with Reverend Wall before leaving. Mrs. Wall stood stout and dour beside her husband. He was reluctant to let his captive audience go, so he was in no hurry. We were.

Finally, Sherman and Nathan hurried into the back of the truck and we girls climbed in front with Papa. It seemed that Papa was driving too slowly, and I asked him if he was still driving the "victory speed." Papa laughed, "You're not in a hurry to get home are you?" We girls talked of seeing Mrs. Clark and what she might bring to us all the way home. When we drove through our railroad underpass and could see our house, there, parked in front of the house, was Mrs. Clark's new black car.

"I can't believe it!" said Papa in amazement, "How did she get through these roads?"

Our truck bucked, roared, and swerved back and forth as Papa charged through the muddy, rutted roads.

"I don't see any tractor tracks, so she did it by herself. Willie didn't tow her," Papa noted.

Nathan and Sherman stayed outside to look at Mrs. Clark's car, but we girls raced to the house and burst in, as Mrs. Clark said later, "Like wild men from Borneo!"

There in our crowded front room stood Mrs. Clark. She was smaller than I remembered her to be. Her glossy hair was waved and pulled back behind her ears into a long horizontal roll, she wore make-up, lots of jewelry, a beautiful dress, and high heels. This must be how city ladies looked.

Mrs. Clark laughed at our delight in seeing her and swept each of us girls into a hug and a kiss on the cheek. She gave Papa a warm hug.

Willie had gone out and he, Sherman, and Nathan were inspecting her mud-splattered car.

"It's a Tudor Sedan 1946 Ford," Mrs. Clark told Papa as she went out to join the boys.

We girls looked out the window at the new black car with the long nose.

"Well," Papa looked at Mama, "She won't be in until she tells them about every feature of the car. What can I do to help with dinner?"

"Did she bring any presents?" We girls asked as soon as Mrs. Clark was outside.

"Yes," Mama said, "but do not mention presents. You will see what she brought after dinner."

By the time Mrs. Clark and the boys came in, Mrs. Clark had learned that Willie was no longer attending school. Her comment to Mama was, "That is what happens when they ship all of those old maids out west to teach! Old maids know nothing about handling young men. Now he can't go to college."

Later I heard Mama tell Papa what Mrs. Clark had said about Willie, "It is interesting that her old maid sister, The Aunt Grace, was a high school English teacher! I didn't bother to tell her that Willie would never have gone to college, even if he had finished high school and we could have afforded it."

When we were seated for dinner, Mrs. Clark devoted attention to each of us children. She inquired of Willie how he was helping Papa instead of going to school. She wanted to hear about what Sherman, Nathan, and I were studying in school and what subjects were our favorites. She asked Dolly and Grace what their favorite books and stories were. Only then did she turn to Mama and Papa to catch up on their lives and homestead friends.

Dinner proceeded at a leisurely pace with as much talking as eating. When Mrs. Clark helped herself to another serving of Mama's chicken and dumplings, she laughed, "Helen, you are a great cook! You've come a long way. Do you remember our first summer on the homestead? Neither one of us knew a thing about cooking! We had a recipe book, poorly written, I might add."

Mama joined Mrs. Clark's laughter, "Maybe, the best stunt I pulled was when the recipe for muffins said to grease the muffin tin and fill two-thirds full. I filled it two-thirds full of lard!"

Mrs. Clark added, "My cooked dried beans were the consistency of gravel! And, our biscuits were as hard as brick-bats! I finally wound up piecing my piecrust together like a jigsaw puzzle."

Mama and Mrs. Clark continued recalling their cooking failures and laughing until tears filled their eyes.

"Thank God for Mrs. LaRoss at the LaRoss Road Ranch!" Mrs. Clark exclaimed, "As busy as she was, she took time to give us some basic cooking lessons. I asked her who told her that we couldn't cook. She never told, but I'll bet it was that stinking Henry Lick. She did tell me that he told her we would not last the winter, before high-tailing it back East. She said she told him that she was a better judge of character than he. She even bet him five dollars we would be there in the spring. That's probably the only five dollars of his own money that he ever lost! His specialty was losing mine."

Mrs. Clark paused for a moment. Her eyes misted, "That was my favorite summer, Helen."

"Mine too" added Mama.

When the dishes were cleared from the table Mrs. Clark asked Willie to bring the packages from The Old House. Her gifts to the boys were hunting knives with sheaths, so they could carry them on their belts. She gave Grace, Dolly, and me each a stuffed-cloth doll. Dolly's doll was a little Black girl. She wore a blue plaid dress and a crocheted cap that partially covered her black curls. Grace's doll was much like Dolly's, but with a white face and brown yarn braids tied with red ribbons. She wore a white ruffled apron over her red and white checked dress. My doll was different, because, although she was a cloth doll, she had a China face. Her real looking hair was blonde, her make-up was painted on, and she had real eye lashes. When I tilted her back her eyes closed. I had never hoped to own such a beautiful doll.

"Thank you, Grandma!" We could hardly breathe.

That night and many, many more nights thereafter we slept with our dolls. I named mine Susan, Grace named hers Alice, and Dolly named hers Judy.

Before Mrs. Clark left she told us about the cozy apartment she was living in until she could find a house to buy.

"And," she added, "After I am moved into my house we will celebrate with a girls' tea party."

↜·· o ··↝

Two years after WWII ended returning soldiers were still having trouble finding jobs. During the war America's economy had shifted its focus, and every factory possible was dedicated to mass production of supplies needed for soldiers and fighting the war. When the war ended those factories that could not be converted back to producing consumer goods, simply shut down. Unemployment soared. Six million women had joined the work force during the war. Now some of those were out of jobs, because their factories closed. Others simply chose to resume being housewives. Many women liked the independence making their own money gave them, and they did not feel like putting on an apron and staying home. They kept their jobs. This meant that returning G.I.s who were looking for work, found that the jobs were filled by women, as well as by men who had not served in the military. Papa said that it was tragic for returning soldiers to find that they had won the war, but lost out on the home front. Even though the overall economy was picking up, too many war-weary men could not find jobs to support themselves, let alone their families.

One summer day an old car drove up to our house. Papa, Willie, and Sherman were working in the hay field, Nathan was herding us girls, and Mama was in the house. Any company was an object of curiosity for us children. We girls raced to the car, Nathan followed at a dignified pace, and Mama came out of the house wiping her hands on her apron. Inside the car were a young couple in front and three blond children in the back. The young couple looked sad and tired.

The man told Mama that one of the neighbors told them to come to see us. The family was homeless; they lived and slept in their car. He had no job, and he could not find one. They could not keep their children, because they did not have enough money to take care of them. Could we please take their three-year-old boy? His name was Richard. They had been able to find homes for the other two, and they would go to their new homes tonight.

Mama sighed tearfully, "We can't take Richard. I wish to God we could. We are poor, have six children, and live in a small house. We would take Richard anyway, but social services would come to check us out. They have specific requirements that we can't meet. They would take him away. It is better that he settles in a home where they can keep him."

The man hung his head, "We just don't know where to turn."

Mama brightened, "We belong to the Grace Bible Chapel in Glasgow. One of the things our church does is to help people who are down on their luck. And, furthermore, Reverend Wall knows the Mennonites in Lustre. They are a prosperous community, and I'm sure he will have no problem placing Richard with a good family."

Mama asked Nathan to bring a pencil and paper. She wrote directions for the family to get to the Wall's house. She reassured them that they would get both help for themselves and a good home for Richard.

The couple thanked Mama several times. As they began to leave she called, "Be sure to tell Reverend Wall I sent you!"

ᴄ☺· · ·ᴏ· · ·☻ɔ

We could hardly wait to get to church on Sunday to hear about the young family and little blond Richard. Mama thought of different Mennonite families Richard could have been placed with to have a good home. When we arrived in church on Sunday, there sat Mrs. Wall with Richard! Of course, it had only been a few days, so maybe they hadn't had time to place Richard yet. After church we children went outside to play with other children from our church while Mama and Papa visited inside.

Once in the truck headed home, Mama turned to Papa, "If I had known the Walls would decide to keep Richard, we would have taken him to Lustre ourselves!"

Papa shook his head, "I have never known a couple so totally unsuited to raising a child. God knew what he was doing when they didn't have children!"

ᴄ☺· · ·ᴏ· · ·☻ɔ

I saw a glimpse into Richard's life with Wall's a few months later. I became ill at school, too ill to stay at school. There was no way to contact Mama and Papa, and we had no school nurse. Sherman was called from class to decide what to do about me. All Sherman could come up with was that he could walk me to Reverend Wall's home. They lived almost a mile from the school in an upstairs apartment. Perhaps, I could stay there until Sherman rode the bus home to tell Papa to come after me.

When Sherman and I finally reached Wall's home I was truly miserable. Yes, the Walls would take care of me until Papa could come to get me. Mrs. Wall made a bed for me on their sofa, and even though the Walls were kind and caring, I felt strange and uncomfortable at their home—I wanted our home and Mama. Richard was a sweet little boy who came to the sofa to look curiously at me and to show me some of his toys.

Their supper time came, and still Papa had not come to get me. I was sick and homesick. Before they sat down at the table Mrs. Wall gave me some hot tea and crackers, which was all I wanted. I watched as they ate at their table not far from the sofa; Mrs. Wall dished up Richard's plate with several foods including green beans. Richard ate all else, but the green beans. First Mrs. Wall and then Reverend Wall demanded that Richard eat the green beans, but he refused saying he did not like green beans. When Mrs. Wall decided to spoon the green beans into Richard's mouth he clamped his mouth shut; at this point Richard was taken from the table and soundly spanked. Their behavior regarding some uneaten food was new to me. By now I really wanted to leave!

Finally, we heard Papa's knock on the door. I thanked Walls, sent a sympathetic look to the teary Richard, and with new-found energy I hurried down the stairs with Papa. At home I told the story of Richard and the green beans. Mama had already named Richard "Spanky Wall" after seeing Mrs. Wall's big hand administer a severe spanking for a minor misbehavior at church. Mama always took what she considered abuse of Richard personally, because she recommended Richard be taken to them. "How could I have known they would keep him?" she reproached herself. ❧

CHAPTER 15

Mrs. Clark's Carpenter

Sunday when Mrs. Clark came for dinner the conversation turned to farming. Papa said that, although he much preferred that Willie had stayed in school, he could certainly accomplish more on the farm with Willie's help. One way Willie helped was that he drove Putt-Putt to Mr. Comb's farm when the tractor was needed. Papa had begun renting Mr. Combs' land that lay across Milk River from us in 1945 when he planted so much of our arable fields in sugar beets. Mr. Combs included a rowboat in the rent, so Papa could just walk down to the river and row across to his fields. The time-consuming part was that the only road to Mr. Combs' land was to and through Mr. Biddle's farm. It was a long drive on Putt-Putt.

Mrs. Clark suggested that, if Willie was indeed going to stay on the farm and work, then Papa needed another tractor. Shuttling one tractor back and forth was a waste of time. Papa replied that he had been thinking of getting another tractor.

The following week, based upon Willie's assurance that he would stay, Papa did, indeed, buy a new Ford tractor and necessary equipment to go with it. The new Ford tractor and equipment stayed on our farm, and Putt-Putt and its equipment stayed on Combs' farm. Now more crops could be planted and cared for, and more hay to feed more cattle could be harvested with this time-saving arrangement. Some of Mr. Combs' fields grew perennial mixtures of hay. Papa planted corn on Mr. Combs' other fields.

Papa had already planted several fields of alfalfa, a perennial, for hay on our farm. It was exceptionally high in nutrients, and it thrived in our farm's rich river-bottom soil. Irrigation of the alfalfa fields produced plants that were three feet tall. We girls played hide-and-seek in the tall alfalfa. Dolly was so short that we could only play when Nathan supervised. Mama said that we didn't want to lose Dolly to the alfalfa!

Papa planted another large crop of sugar beets. Summer of 1947 brought an end to sugar rationing, but demand for sugar beets was still high. German

POWs would not be working the sugar beet fields this year. Those held in the 700 German POW camps in America were released back to Germany. They were not all excited about returning. They knew of the devastation to their country and the economic deprivation to which they would return. There was definitely anti-German sentiment in America, but many American's did not hold the German people responsible for the war and its atrocities. Rather they blamed Hitler and the German government, so their interactions with the POWs were most often friendly. Papa's association with the POWs who came to our farm softened his anger toward the German soldiers for the heinous acts they committed in WWI.

He told Mama, "After being with these POWs, I believe most of the horrors I witnessed were the acts of a few depraved soldiers, rather than reflecting the typical German soldier."

The German prisoners had been well-treated in America, and less than one percent of the POWs had attempted to escape. Prisoners claimed they were never bored. POW camps were supplied with musical instruments, materials to pursue hobbies, and books, magazines, and newspapers. The Geneva Convention's mandate for treatment of prisoners was followed. They not only ate the same food as American soldiers, but they were paid by the American government the same as American G. I. Privates for their work. Those who were careful with their money returned to Germany with savings from their labor.

Mexicans had worked sugar beets before the war. After the German POWs left they were hired again to tend the sugar beets. Some of them came from permanent Mexican communities in Montana, and some were seasonal workers from Mexico. During the war the Mexican beet workers had found work in factories producing war materiel for better pay. Now that those factories slowed or shut down altogether, the Mexicans returned to the beet fields. This pleased Papa. He had found Mexican beet workers to be faster and better at working beets than the German prisoners had been. The long hours of bending over weeding and hoeing did not seem to bother them. Additionally, they appeared to have a hierarchy that allowed them to police their own ranks. They were dependable, hard workers. Papa highly respected them. They were there by choice, so all Papa needed to do was to be present in the field to supervise loosely.

A week day after the sugar beet weeding and thinning ended, Mrs. Clark drove out with a request. Would Mama and Papa come to town on Friday to look at two houses she was considering buying? She wanted Papa's opinion.

After Mrs. Clark left, Mama told Papa, "I don't know why she wants you to look at the house. She knows more about house construction than most men."

Mama went with Papa to look at the houses. Mrs. Clark settled on the house that Papa thought to be the better of the two. It was located on the south side of town near the Deaconess Hospital where Mama had attended nursing school.

That night at supper Mama and Papa talked about Mrs. Clark's house.

"She thinks it's small," Mama told us. "Well, her homestead house was a little bigger than this one, but not much. I guess it seems small to her, because when she returned to Minneapolis she lived in the Watts' house. It had ten spacious rooms. Two of the rooms had been for live-in servants.

"This house has four rooms and a bathroom—kitchen/dining room, living room/library, and two bedrooms," Papa added.

Our question was, "When could we go see it?"

"You'll have to wait until she has painted and remodeled," Mama told us, "She is going to invite you girls over for a tea party."

"She must have lost most of her money, or she would have bought a bigger house," Papa speculated. "But she must have investments to live on, because she said she does not plan to get a job. . . . just volunteer at the hospital."

"How could she afford her new car, if she isn't rich?" Willie wanted to know.

"Oh, that is Mrs. Clark!" Mama laughed, "She will have a really nice car, above all else."

"Painting and remodeling cost money," Papa shook his head, "Evidently, she can afford it. And she has to find a carpenter and painter to do the work."

"How long do you think it will be before her house will be ready for the tea party?" I asked.

Mama raised her eyebrows. "Don't hold your breath while you wait. It will take time to get the work done and for her to get moved in."

ᘓ· · · o · · ·ᘔ

A couple of weeks before school started, Mrs. Clark drove out for Sunday dinner with a man in her car. He came around to the driver's side and helped Mrs. Clark from the car. We flocked to meet him. He was a pleasant looking man a little shorter than Papa with dark hair parted in the middle. He was dressed up like he had come from church. Mrs. Clark introduced Bill Larson to Mama and Papa; then she introduced Mr. Larson to us children. His smile and his handshake were warm and friendly. Mr. Larson was a carpenter, painter, and decorator! He was also a magician, because he had already whipped her house into shape. We must see it! We all walked into the house. Mr. Larson held Mrs. Clark's arm and guided her.

During dinner Mr. Larson was quiet, but he followed the conversation closely. He laughed often at Mrs. Clark's witty remarks. As always, the conversation turned to the homestead. They spoke of old friends.

"We really lived, didn't we Helen?" Mrs. Clark smiled at Mama, "I think we can call ourselves frontiersmen!" She turned to Mr. Larson and covered his hand with hers, "Bill, you missed out on an exciting part of history. As far as people went, we could say homesteading 'separated the wheat from the chaff'! Helen, you know that to be true."

She turned to Papa, "What do you think, John?"

"Well," he said, "There will never be another time like it. It had some of the best of life, but there were hard times, too. Especially, for a family man. It either makes or breaks a man."

Talk came around to the Riggin family from the Barr Community where there was a store and post office. Mrs. Clark's mail had come to Barr when she lived on the homestead. Reverend Riggin and his three sons had homesteaded in the Barr community and bought the old Barr sheep ranch. Mama's friend Edna Johnson had married one of the Riggin sons, Harry. He died, Mrs. Clark said, of "questionable circumstances," and Edna married Charlie Rogers.

"I think Charlie had his eye on Edna and the homestead!" Mrs. Clark pronounced. "He sure hung around there a lot."

Grace and I looked at each other when we heard the name Charlie Rogers. Mama often told us homestead stories for our bedtime stories. She had told us that Charlie Rogers was her beau at one time. They became engaged—unbeknownst to Mrs. Clark. Mama said the engagement ended when she realized he was also trying to "make time" with Mrs. Clark. "He was a weasel!" Mama had told us. "He was small and not one bit good-looking, but he was a dapper dresser. He had very little feet, and he was so proud of it. I don't think he ever intended to do any real work. He specialized in running back and forth across the U.S./Canadian border. He fancied himself to be quite the lady's man. He was much too old for me! But," She had added, "I was very young, and I had read too many romance stories." We knew not to say anything about that story in front of Mrs. Clark.

Mama looked across the table at Mrs. Clark, "Did you ever learn why Charlie Rogers kept going back and forth from Montana to Saskatchewan?"

"No, I never knew. Was he running from something? Avoiding the draft? Was he a dual citizen? You know, he did come from England. I thought he might have been a remittance man."

"What," Sherman asked, "Is a remittance man?"

Mrs. Clark answered, "The homestead era had some remittance men. They were mostly from England. They were, for various reasons, an embarrassment to their family. Their families didn't want them around, so they paid them a remittance, money to go to another country and stay. As long as they stayed away they would receive a remittance at prearranged times." She paused, "He was getting money from somewhere, because he certainly wasn't doing enough work to support himself."

We wished Mrs. Clark would tell us more about Charlie Rogers, but she moved on to other neighbors. "Guy Riggin married Minnie Sorenson. What became of them?" She asked Mama.

"They had seven children. When Guy's health failed they moved to Hinsdale. He died a couple of years ago. I have seen Minnie a few times. She works at the Hinsdale School."

"What about Hans Sorenson? He married Grace Munger."

Mama replied, "They have five children, and they live near Hinsdale. We visit from time to time. Minnie and Grace were both girlhood chums. They were good friends and full of fun. Who would have thought Grace would marry Minnie's brother?"

Mama laughed and looked at Mrs. Clark. "Do you remember the time I went to a party and cut the sleeves out of a new black dress you had bought for me?"

"Do I!" Mrs. Clark looked at Bill. "When there was a party on the homestead the neighboring girls all spent the night at the home of one of the friends. This meant taking your party dress and overnight bag on your horse to her house. There they could all get dressed, fix their hair, and put on makeup together. I always made sure that Helen had a beautiful dress."

"Well," Mama continued, "I took my stylish new dress to Minnie's house. Grace and a few other girls were there. When we started showing each other the dress we would wear, mine was the only one with sleeves. The others were all sleeveless. Mine was very smart-looking, and the sleeves were sheer butterfly sleeves. Nonetheless, they were sleeves, and I wanted a sleeveless dress like the others. I asked Minnie for a pair of scissors."

Minnie was shocked, "You wouldn't!"

Finally, I coaxed her into bringing scissors to me. Minnie held up her hands. 'You tell your mother this had nothing to do with me!' Now that I look back, the girls were all horrified and protested that my dress was indeed beautiful. Still, I took the scissors, crossed myself, said, 'My mother will kill me!', and cut the sleeves out. It was a fantastic party, and we all danced until after midnight."

Mrs. Clark looked at Bill, "Obviously, I didn't kill her. Dances on the homestead meant there were lots of men and few women. All the men wanted to dance. Helen was always the prize!"

Mama asked Mrs. Clark, "Do you remember a pretty young Swedish girl, Olga, at the dances? She came with her brother. He danced every dance when he could find a partner, but she always sat and watched. I saw men ask her to dance, but she turned them down. Once when I was sitting out a dance, because my ankle hurt, I sat by Olga. We talked a bit. A young man stopped by and asked her to dance. In her strong Swedish accent she said, 'No thank you, I don't think so. When I dance I sweat so, and when I sweat I stink so. No thank you, I don't think so.' Mama laughed, I'm not sure he could understand what she said, but I did."

⋅⋅ ∘ ⋅⋅

Mama would not allow Mrs. Clark to help with the dinner dishes before she and Mr. Larson left. Again, Mr. Larson held Mrs. Clarks arm as they walked to the car. He opened the door and helped her into the car.

Once they had driven away, Willie said, "Since when has Mrs. Clark ever needed help getting to her car?"

Mama shook her head and fairly hissed, "I'll bet he isn't a day older than I am!"

"I think," Papa predicted, "That we will be seeing a lot of Mr. Larson!"

CHAPTER 16

"Hell is in the Heart"

Winds whipped yellowed cottonwood leaves from the trees. Flocks of geese migrating south called throughout the days and nights. Mexican beet workers harvested the sugar beets, then, they too, headed south. Sherman, Nathan, and I walked to the town road every day to catch the school bus. When Mama and Papa were out of earshot Willie joked about his getting to stay home while we had to suffer at school. Sherman and I both liked school, while Nathan was 'take it or leave it.' Mama said this was in part because Nathan wanted to imitate Willie.

After our farm was readied for winter, Willie made an announcement at suppertime. He had a winter job at LaFond's Packing Plant. It was located on a part of our land that lay across the railroad track from the rest of the farm. Papa had sold it to Mr. LaFond who built the meat packing plant. Later, Papa told Mama that Willie was 'champing at the bit' to get away from the farm and see the world. He evidently saw this as a step in that direction. The good thing about his working at the packing plant was that Willie would not have enough time on his hands to get into mischief.

Mrs. Clark, my mysterious grandmother, and Mr. Larson continued to be frequent Sunday dinner guests. Mrs. Clark always brought dessert. She and Mama still laughed about Mama's wedding cake. Mrs. Clark maintained that it would not have been quite as flat if Papa and Henry Lick hadn't been jarring the house as they fought. Sometime between then and now, Mrs. Clark had learned to turn out fantastic desserts. "The way to a man's heart is through his stomach." she had laughed when Mama asked why she spent so much time on cooking a dessert.

One Sunday Mrs. Clark extended an invitation to Mama and us girls for a tea party on Saturday.

She beamed at Mr. Larson, "Bill has worked wonders with my little house! Just wait until you see it!"

The week passed slowly. Saturday when Papa stopped the truck in front of Mrs. Clark's tidy white house, we girls skipped to the door. Mrs. Clark opened her door all smiles and loveliness. Papa walked with Mama to the door to say hello to Mrs. Clark, then returned to the truck to run errands. Mr. Larson was working, and he couldn't join us, "Besides," Mrs. Clark said, "This is a girls' party."

I knew her home would look nice, but I was unprepared for the richness of her decorating. Her living room/library floor was covered wall-to-wall with thick floral carpet. An elegant sofa, matching stuffed chair, and rocking chair were flanked by little glass-covered tables. A beautiful desk, chair, and shelves lined with books filled one corner. This part of her living room was her library. Ornately framed pictures hung on all walls. Her house even smelled good, like she did.

We moved slowly toward the kitchen as Mrs. Clark and Mama talked about some of her furniture pieces. They had belonged to Grandma Watts. Seated at her small kitchen table with white linen and fine china, she told us girls that it was time we learned some proper manners. We were to watch her and do as she did. She unfolded a white napkin and placed it on her lap. She stirred a sugar cube into her tea and, holding the cup with one hand, she sipped the tea. Mama suggested that, unless she wanted a tea cup broken, we should use both hands to hold the cup. "Oh, well," Mrs. Clark said, "This time." Next she nibbled on her cookie, much I thought as a mouse might have done, inviting us to follow her example.

Mama and Mrs. Clark visited, and all the time Mrs. Clark kept an eye on us girls correcting us as needed. Tea lasted a long time. After tea we were each to carry our cup and saucer to the sink. We took tiny steps and held on tightly, terrified that we might break her china. We then "retired" to the living room to wait for Papa to return. We girls sat stiffly on the sofa.

Mama had noticed one of Mr. Larson's pipes and a pouch of tobacco on a little table and his house slippers and one of his jackets by the door. Grace Bible Chapel, the church we attended, was very strict. The path down to hell was wide and slippery, but the path to heaven was a long, long ways up a very steep and very narrow stairway. Mama found some of the church rules to be ridiculous, but she took seriously the perils of "living in sin." She turned their conversation to church.

"Why don't you join us for church services tomorrow?" she asked Mrs. Clark.

"Because," Mrs. Clark replied, "God and I are doing very nicely as we are. Thank you for inviting me."

"But," Mama protested, "If you are living in sin, you are going to hell."

We girls heard a lot about hell in Reverend Wall's services. It was a frightening place, and we did not want to go there, nor did we want to think of Mrs. Clark's going there.

Mrs. Clark tightened her lips and raised her eyebrows. She fixed Mama with a steely-eyed look, "Helen, hell is in the heart!" She placed her hand over her heart. "This is the only hell there is."

We girls waited for a bolt of lightning to strike Mrs. Clark. None came. Mama was silenced.

Mrs. Clark laughed, "You can tell your church friends that Mr. Larson is boarding here. I have two bedrooms. One is his, and one is mine."

Just then we heard Papa drive up. We girls thanked Mrs. Clark and raced to the truck. Mama talked to Mrs. Clark a few more minutes as she stood in the doorway.

That night at supper Mama announced that Mrs. Clark was going to adopt Bill. He would be Mama's brother.

Sherman smirked; Willie snickered. Papa glared at both, and they straightened up.

"Since he is to be my adopted brother, I will call him 'Brother Bill'."

❧ · · ◦ · · ☙

Two of Nathan's friends that visited most often were Vernon Mattfeldt and Jackie Grandon. Both were "town boys," but they helped Nathan with his chores and included us girls in their activities when Nathan was supposed to be herding us.

With Nathan supervising me, so that I could learn to gather the eggs by myself, we all trooped through the snow to the chicken house. Gathering eggs would have been simple had all the hens either been off the nest, or graciously yielded to my hand as I reached under them to pick up the eggs. The hens shared the nests. Each hen only laid one egg per day, so the eggs under the hen on the nest did not all belong her. No matter, a hen on the nest was always ready to do battle to keep me from getting the eggs.

Nathan taught me to feint with my left hand, so the hen would turn her head toward my left. When she did this I was to dart out my right hand and hold onto her neck, so she could not peck me. While holding her neck with my right hand, I deftly reached under her with my left hand and picked up one egg at a time and placed it on a layer of straw in the basket. This procedure fascinated Vernon and Jackie. They both wanted to try. It looked easier to do than it was. Their apprenticeship resulted in some broken eggs.

Vernon declared that he always had a hard time eating eggs for the first couple of days after he went home from helping gather them. He said he just couldn't get over knowing where eggs came from!

⟋◉· · ◦ · · ◉⟍

None of us Sherwoods, nor Vernon or Jackie, owned skates, but a shallow pond past the pig pen was frozen as smooth as glass. We skated on it with our buckle overshoes. We played tag, dare base, and several other games on the ice. Nathan often skated while holding Dolly's hand, so she could participate.

One of the evenings when Jackie and Vernon had ridden the school bus home with Nathan, we all gathered at the skating pond. Jackie Grandon announced that he wanted to show us a new trick. He explained it to us before his demonstration. He was to run on the snow toward the pond to gather as much speed as possible by the time he hit the ice sliding. Once he was sliding he would squat down and wrap his arms around his knees as he sailed across the pond.

He said we could all skate a few minutes while he warmed up. When he announced it was time to clear the ice, we all stood in the snow by the pond watching. Jackie revved up and charged through the snow toward the ice. He hit the ice at high speed. He squatted down and leaned slightly forward to gather his knees in his arms. Instead of gliding serenely across the ice in a squatting position, his head kept going down. We heard a distinct smack as his face made contact with the ice.

We raced to Jackie. He howled and blood flew. Nathan and Vernon helped Jackie to the house with Grace, Dolly, and me tagging behind them. Mama cleaned up Jackie's face while Jackie stoically fought back tears. Mama said that while he did have a nose bleed, much of the blood flowed from where his teeth had cut the inside of his lip. She didn't believe that his nose was broken.

Mama suggested that we all take off our outdoor clothes and stay inside while she served hot cocoa and cookies to us. We sat at the big table in the front room and played cards until Vernon's mother came to pick up Vernon and Jackie.

As soon as they drove off, Nathan gave Mama a demonstration of what happened to Jackie on the ice. We children howled, but with laughter. Nathan demonstrated this again to Papa, Willie, and Sherman before supper. We children laughed again.

"It's only funny," Papa reminded us, "If you are not the one who's hurt."

Nathan quickly mastered what we dubbed as "The Jackie Grandon Slide." Grace and I practiced until we, too, could do it. Dolly insisted that she try. Nathan reasoned with her, but she was not to be dissuaded. She suffered the same fate as Jackie. We hurried her to the house with blood flying. Dolly was no stoic.

✑· · ◦ · ·✑

Willie stopped working at the packing plant in the springtime and began helping Papa on the farm. After the initial flurry of farm work was finished in June, Willie made another announcement at the supper table. He was going to work for Mr. Heisten in the Mennonite community of Lustre during the summer. Lustre was about fifty miles northeast of Glasgow. It was a prosperous German Mennonite community of dry land wheat farms. He had met Mr. Heisten at the packing plant during the winter, and he had made an agreement to work for him. Willie would return before our farm's harvest season to help Papa.

Papa reminded Willie that, based upon Willie's assurance of help on the farm, Papa had borrowed money to buy the ford tractor and equipment. Willie told Papa that he remembered his promise. He would help Papa make payments by giving Papa some of his pay every month. Willie was eighteen now, and, while Papa preferred Willie's help, he would settle for Willie's offer.

Papa told Willie that he was welcome to go to the job, but he was not going to find more freedom there. The Mennonites were hard-working, and they held narrow beliefs. If Willie thought Papa was too strict, wait until he lived with Mennonites. Willie did not seem to hear Papa, and during the few days before he left he was in high spirits.

✑· · ◦ · ·✑

On Fourth of July, 1947, as with every Fourth of July, work ceased after dinner. Papa and the boys drove to Glasgow to purchase ice and salt to make ice cream. Mama made the ice cream mixture while we girls hung around watching and waiting to taste it.

When Papa and the boys returned they brought surprises. Firecrackers and Bazooka Bubble Gum! Both were new to us girls. During the war, gum was unavailable to American citizens so that every soldier's rations could include chewing gum. Sherman and Nathan remembered chewing gum and Dubble Bubble gum. Bazooka Bubble Gum was new. They taught us how to chew the gum and make bubbles. First we chewed the sweet tasting gum until it was soft and pliable, then we worked it next to our front teeth, stuck our tongue into it between our teeth, and blew a bubble. This sounded simple, but mastering the technique, was not simple. Finally, we girls were all blowing bubbles. Bubble gum was a marvelous thing!

Manufacturing firecrackers had been suspended during the war. In fact, in honor of our troops who were fighting throughout Fourth of July, celebrations on the home front had been limited. Many workers, especially those with jobs associated with the war, worked straight through the holiday. Papa said those in town celebrating this Fourth of July seemed intent on making up for lost holidays.

While we ate strawberry ice cream Nathan wondered what Willie might be doing.

"Not much," Papa was certain. "In fact, I will bet that, even though the Mennonites came to America, they don't celebrate the Fourth of July."

"Working, I would be willing to bet." Mama said, "Just like he is working every day, but Sunday. And on Sunday he will go to church and not be allowed to do anything but necessary chores, like milking, all day. He won't be fishing. He won't be taking boat rides. He won't be playing games. He won't be happy!"

"And," Mama shook her head, "He certainly won't be eating ice cream and lighting fire crackers!"

ഐ· · o · · ·ൊ

Shortly, after the Fourth of July, a letter arrived from Willie. He wanted Papa to come pick him up, so he could come home. He did not like working for the Mennonites.

Papa said that the letter was not unexpected. "He wanted to leave the packing plant in the middle of their busy season. Now he wants to leave the Mennonites in the middle of wheat season. I could sure use his help here, but when you make a commitment, you have to follow through. Papa emphasized, "Willie needs to learn this. He will be finished by mid-September, and we will go get him then."

We were all quiet for a moment thinking that Willie wanted to come home, and we wanted him to come home, but we understood that Willie had made a deal, and he had to keep his end of it.

Even after his decision that Willie honor his commitment, Papa seemed worried, "Willie will only be satisfied for a short time when he gets home. He will soon be busy thinking about what to do next. I can only wonder that will be." ଭ

CHAPTER 17

HE'S IN THE ARMY NOW

School would begin soon, and again I needed new dresses. Mrs. Pratt, Virginia Pratt, sewed Mama's good dresses and the dresses I wore to church and school. In addition to dresses, Mama said I needed a new winter coat and bonnet. I hated bonnets! The only part of my winter clothes I hated more than bonnets were my sturdy buckle overshoes. I was ready for third grade, and third grade girls wore headscarves, not bonnets. And, most wore pull-on overshoes, not the ugly buckle ones like the boys wore.

Mama and Papa both agreed that my health was more important than my vanity. I would be dressing warmly. Although I would not have admitted it, there had been many cold days waiting for the school bus and on the playground when I was thankful for my warm clothes.

Grace was beginning first grade, but she, as always, inherited my outgrown clothes. When we were going to town to select patterns and materials for my clothes, Grace wanted to help with the selection, since she would wear them later. Dolly quickly picked up on this, and she, too, wanted her say. Papa dropped us off at the store, and Mama exhausted all of her patience as we girls tried to agree upon the materials to be purchased. The coat and bonnet material were last. Mama decisively chose a heavy Prussian blue wool fabric.

Sunday Mama and Mrs. Pratt agreed upon an evening when we would visit the Pratts and take my patterns and stacks of materials for sewing the clothes. The Pratts were younger than Mama, and they had no children. Mrs. Pratt was pretty and slender with an intriguing gold streak through one side of her glossy brown hair. Mr. Pratt, Conrad, was dark headed, swarthy complexioned, and very handsome. He always wore black, except, as Sherman said, "When he wore black and white stripes."

Mr. Pratt was in and out of prison. When he was in prison Mrs. Pratt euphemistically referred to his absence as being "away." Mrs. Pratt was a devout Christian, a staunch member of Grace Bible Chapel, and my Sunday school teacher. She prayed earnestly for Mr. Pratt's salvation, and sometimes when he was home, he came to church with her. Mama believed that Mrs. Pratt supported both of them as a nurse at the Deaconess Hospital and by taking in sewing. We weren't sure how Mr. Pratt earned money, aside from his petty thefts.

When we were driving home Papa said, "Trying to converse with Conrad is a little like having a tooth pulled slowly. I don't see what Virginia sees in him."

"Well," Mama laughed, "We know it isn't his I.Q., so" she hesitated and shot him a glance, "You guess!"

On a warm day in mid-August when Mrs. Pratt was not working at the hospital, Papa drove me to her house. Mr. Pratt was "away" again. Mrs. Pratt would begin sewing my clothes, and I would spend the day with her. My being alone with an adult, who was not my parent, felt strange. I looked out her windows. Houses were all around, making Mrs. Pratt's house seem closed in. I watched cars passing by and two children playing on the sidewalk. There was really nothing for me to do, except to stand still when Mrs. Pratt was fitting her sewing on me. I wanted to be home.

Mrs. Pratt stopped sewing to prepare lunch. She opened a can of soup and made a sandwich for each of us. I watched and set the table. I had never set a table for just two people, nor had I ever eaten soup from a can. The cheese bologna sandwiches were made with what we called "baker's bread." It came from the grocery store in cellophane bags, and I had only eaten "baker's bread" a few times. It was light and soft, like cake, and unlike Mama's coarse, heavier homemade bread. Dessert was a store-bought confection with coconut sprinkled on thick marshmallow-like covering. Inside was soft chocolate cake. Mrs. Pratt called it a snowball. It was the best dessert I had ever tasted.

The afternoon promised to drag more slowly than the morning. Mrs. Pratt noted my boredom.

"We rarely have children at our house. I sew mostly for adults." She walked to a trunk that was set against a wall in the living room and opened it. "I know you will be careful, so you can play with Conrad's toys." The trunk held amazing toys—toys we did not have at home. Jack-in-the-box, tops, kaleidoscopes, a few stuffed animals. . ... My afternoon passed quickly as I played with Conrad's toys.

When I was riding home with Papa, I told him about the trunk with Conrad's toys.

"So it is not just a rumor," Papa said, "Mrs. Lewis is a friend of Mrs. Pratt. She told us about his trunk of toys, but I didn't believe her."

When we arrived home, I told Mama about Mr. Pratt's toys. "There are some adults that are much like children. Conrad is one of them. He is actually a nice man. He grew up physically, but not mentally. He is in jail, because he isn't smart enough to be a thief. And, he is not smart enough to quit trying."

I told Mama about our lunch, and how when I grew up I would save time by buying soup in a can, "baker's bread," and snowballs. "That is not a healthy lunch," Mama responded, "I'm sure Mrs. Pratt only served it because she was too busy to cook."

Sherman, Nathan, Grace, and I started school in September. It was Grace's first year of school, and we all four attended North Side School that consisted of grades one through twelve. Last year I had attended second grade at the South Side Elementary school. Miss Westby was my teacher there. Mrs. Clark said she was another old maid. After my experience with Miss Shattuck in first grade, I thought Miss Westby was wonderful.

Miss Shattuck had been a "no nonsense" teacher who spanked readily. While I was not spanked, she had scolded me severely for minor infractions, and, worst of all, she used me for a bad example when I helped Bobby Westfall with his workbook. Well, more than helped. After our reading circle in the front of the room ended, we were sent to our desks with a workbook assignment. I quickly whipped through mine and, although it was forbidden, used my extra time to read ahead in our reading book. Bobby needed help with his workbook, so I helped him. Every time he needed help, my reading was interrupted. I thought of the perfect solution. I quickly filled in his workbook for him and handed it back.

When Miss Shattuck walked around checking workbooks, she noticed the Bobby's writing had changed. He told her whose handwriting it was. First I had to stand in front of the class for a humiliating lecture, and then she demanded I hold out my hands while she beat them with her heavy wooden ruler.

Miss Westby, on the other hand, rarely spanked anybody. Her classroom was filled with books and interesting activities available to all students when we finished our work. Best of all, she had a stereoscope and a schedule that allowed each of us to use it. The stereoscope, a device held up to the eyes to view stereo cards—picture cards placed several inches distant at the end of the stereoscope and viewed through the stereoscope to create three dimensional images. Miss

Westby had a seemingly endless collection of stereo cards with many showing far-away places and unfamiliar animals. It was wondrous!

My year in year in Miss Wesby's class passed pleasantly and quickly.

This year my third-grade teacher was Miss Hill who had grown up on a farm in Iowa. She was youthful with reddish hair and a sprinkling of freckles. I was the only student with red hair and lots of dark freckles. In first, second, and now third grade, I was teased because of it. While my siblings had freckles to some degree, I was the only one with red hair. I had complained about this to Mama. She said that the offending red hair and freckles were from Papa's side of the family.

My third-grade classroom had three girls named Ruth—Ruth Ming, Ruth Stensland, and me, Ruth Sherwood. I told Mama how the problem was solved. Ruth Ming was called Ruth Ann, Ruth Stensland was called Ruthie, and I was called Ruth. Ruth Stensland signed her name Ruth St. When I told Mama she said that I was never, ever to sign my name Ruth Sh. While I did not ask Mama why, I decided that it was because shit began with sh.

Some days after school Miss Hill asked me to stay and clean the blackboards. My school bus did not come until high school was dismissed, so I had extra time at the end of the day. I happily cleaned the blackboards. My reward was a nickel. I had seldom ever owned a coin other than a penny. With this vast amount of money, I had time to run down to Jon's Ice Cream Parlor and buy a large, translucent, aqua sucker.

⚬· · · o · · ·⚬

Now that Grace, too, was in school Dolly was alone at home with Mama and Papa for the first time. Mama said that with nobody to play with Dolly seemed at a loss as to what to do. She would go outside to play, but having never played alone she didn't know what to play by herself, so she came back into the house with Mama.

One afternoon when we hurried home from the bus Mama announced that Dolly's day was exciting. When we were all seated at the kitchen table for our after school snack of Mama's peanut butter cookies and milk, Mama said that before we told about our school days we would hear about Dolly's day first.

"Today, as usual, Dolly followed me around chattering until I told her she would have to think of some things she could do by herself," Mama said. "Your dad was working on Putt-Putt, so she went out and chattered to him."

Mama often said that Dolly was loquacious, and we all knew that Dolly's talking sometimes was too much for Mama. Papa not only tolerated her talking, it seemed to amuse him.

"I was helping him!" Dolly insisted, and we all knew Papa would have made Dolly feel that she was, indeed, helping him.

"Yes, you were," Mama placated her, "Unfortunately, I just didn't have anything that you could help me with."

Papa and Dolly heard a vehicle and looked up from Putt-Putt to see our neighbor Mr. Biddle driving on the road to our house. He stepped out and reached into his pickup for something that he held behind his back.

Mr. Biddle winked at Papa and smiled at Dolly. "You must be lonesome with everybody gone to school."

"Yes," Dolly had nodded.

"I think you need somebody to keep you company." Mr. Biddle brought his hands from behind him and held out a pure white pigeon. The pigeon hopped onto Mr. Biddle's shoulder and cooed in his sing-song up and down pigeon voice.

At dinner time Papa told Mama that Dolly's eyes were as big as saucers when she saw the pigeon.

"Hold out your hand," Mr. Biddle instructed Dolly.

Dolly held out her hand and the white pigeon landed on it, then hopped onto Dolly's shoulder and cooed.

"His name is Homer," Mr. Biddle told Dolly.

Mr. Biddle and Papa talked about caring for Homer and farm talk for a short time before Mr. Biddle was off.

Dolly had a pet—Homer Pigeon. He was her very first pet that was hers alone.

"Well! Well!" Papa smiled at Dolly. "I think old Putt-Putt can wait. Homer Pigeon needs a house."

Homer Pigeon rode on Dolly's shoulder as she and Papa went to the house to show Dolly's pet to Mama. Mama stroked the back of Homer Pigeon's neck, and he cooed for her.

The rest of the morning was spent making Homer Pigeon's house. Papa found a small wooden box big enough for Homer Pigeon and plenty of straw to keep him warm; then Papa covered the box with felt paper for extra warmth during Montana's cold winter. Next Papa made a shelf outside of our house on the east side of the front room that provided both a place for Homer Pigeon's house and a walkway for strutting and for food. Now Homer Pigeon could spend time in his house that Papa secured so it would not fall, or walk on his walkway where he could see into the east window of the front room. Last of all Papa and Dolly placed old towels inside the box and added clean straw.

Mr. Biddle said that Homer would need a nesting box in the house during very cold days and always at night, so a weasel would not kill him. Papa nailed another shelf inside the front room for a wooden box he found in Old House; once the box was on the shelf, he and Dolly put clean straw into the box and placed folded pages from the Glasgow Courier on the shelf where Homer walked. Mr. Biddle assured Papa that this was what Homer was accustomed to and that his droppings would be on the newspaper.

All the time Papa and Dolly worked on Homer Pigeon's houses Homer either rode on Dolly's shoulder or circled briefly in the air to return to Dolly's shoulder.

We all envied Dolly. Homer Pigeon became a favorite pet.

∙ ∙ ∙ o ∙ ∙ ∙

Willie returned home in time to help with the sugar beet harvest. He maintained that he was not ever going back to the Mennonite community again. Since he was not going to work again at the packing plant or the Mennonite community, Papa hoped he would stay on the farm and help. Fall harvest brought bumper crops. Papa told Willie that with a couple more harvests like this one, he would be able to pay a hired man and Willie would be free to leave. A hired man could live in the Old House with Sherman and Nathan.

Life settled back to its former routine. Willie's presence livened up our family. He told stories about the Mennonites and their way of life. One story Willie thought to be ridiculous was that when the Heisten parents returned home from town they sometimes brought bubble gum for their children. Before giving them the gum, the parents removed and discarded the little paper around the gum that portrayed some type of cartoon for children. "Too worldly," was Mr. Heisten's explanation to Willie.

He was puzzled about the Mennonites' clothes. They must have only buttons and no zippers. While the Mennonite women in Glasgow dressed much as other women, the Mennonite women in Lustre did not. Women and girls all wore long dresses with aprons over them. Women pulled their long hair up onto their heads and wore little white caps on their heads, even at home.

Men wore pants that had no zipper and buttoned up on both sides, and they wore suspenders instead of belts. They all worked hard, except on Sunday—Sundays consisted of long sermons, prayers, and reading the Bible and no chores other than milking cows and feeding livestock.

Now that Willie was home we children took more walks around our farm, and Willie again supervised and played games like darebase with us. At first Willie was happy to be home, but he soon became restless. He spent time looking at our big world atlas book finding places he would like to go.

One morning after harvest Willie was to disk the sugar beet field. We were in school, and Papa was cutting corn across the river on Combs' field. When Papa returned for dinner he found that the disk, unhooked from the tractor, was in the field, but Willie and the tractor were nowhere to be seen. Willie and the tractor returned in mid-afternoon.

"Where in the hell have you been?" Papa asked.

It seems that Willie had driven the tractor at top speed to Glasgow to sign up for the U. S. Air Force. He knew that with his being color-blind he could not be a pilot, but perhaps he could be assigned other duties. The air force recruiting office was closed for lunch. He had already scouted out the military recruiting offices, so he knew where to go. Next he found the marine recruiting office to be closed also. His last resort was the army recruiting office. It was open, and the recruiter told him the soldiers would wake up to music every morning. He signed up to join the U.S. Army.

Papa saw his dream of a hired man evaporate. Willie knew Papa would be keenly disappointed about his leaving. He told Papa he had arranged to have an allotment from his check sent home. This would help, but Willie's working on the farm would have helped much more.

Willie was leaving home forever, except that he would come home to visit. We all knew life would never be the same for our family. Although, none of us talked about our sadness from knowing he was leaving, a heaviness pervaded our home. Willie, though, was excited. He was finally going to get out into the world he was so anxious to see.

The Grace Bible Chapel congregation planned a farewell party for Willie at Anna and Jake Peters' home. The party was warm and light-hearted with much laughter. In addition to visiting, the adults played a variety of party games—church party games. Mama was the star of the competitive teams formed for answering questions about the Bible. She also won the game where competitors raced time to see how many words they could make from the names of books in the Bible. Mama may not have attended church every Sunday, but she soundly trounced those who did.

The last game played required Willie to come to the front to stand by Eunice Kjelman, an attractive single lady, as she told a story. Her story was about a man going fishing. Each time she mentioned what the fisherman saw, she touched a place near Willie's eyes; when the fisherman smiled or talked, she touched a place near Willie's mouth. . . . Soon everybody, but Willie, was laughing. What Willie did not see that everybody else could, was that Eunice was touching an ink pad with her fingers, so that each time she touched Willie's face she left an ink spot. When the story was finished, Eunice gave Willie a hand-mirror and he laughed, too. Eunice directed Willie to the bathroom where she washed the washable ink from his face.

A buffet meal of sandwiches and salads was eaten before a large cake was brought from the kitchen. It was decorated with stars and stripes and lettering that said, "Good luck, Willie." Last of all, Reverend Wall asked Willie to come and stand by him. He presented Willie with a Bible. He hoped the Bible would guide Willie through the difficulties he would encounter in the future. Reverend Wall ended the party with a prayer for Willie's safety.

On Sunday Willie and Mama stayed home from church to prepare dinner. Mrs. Clark and Mr. Larson arrived shortly after we returned home from church. She carried a small package for Willie. After dinner Willie opened his present. It was a pair of fur-lined leather dress gloves. It was his first pair of dress gloves, and he was rightfully proud of them. After dinner we six children took our last walk together around the farm through last night's fresh snowfall. Willie carried Dolly much of the way as we looked for animal tracks that the boys quickly identified.

All too soon it was Monday, November 8, 1948, the day Willie would leave. Sherman, Nathan, Grace, and I must go to school. Papa, Mama, and Dolly would take Willie to the train depot. We said our good-byes to Willie before walking over to the town road to catch the school bus. I snuffled along with my head down, hoping the others would not notice I was crying. They didn't notice, because they, too, seemed to be walking with their heads down. ༄

◆

CHAPTER 18

ELEANOR'S ELECTRICITY

One cold winter day Grace, Dolly, and I sat at the kitchen table while Mama baked bread—many loaves of bread for our family. When Mama baked bread, she made dough men for us. She shaped their round heads, round bodies, and fat arms and legs and put raisins down their front for buttons. When our dough men came out of the oven Mama gave one to each of us on a saucer. Dolly thought hers to be smaller than what Grace and I had, so she demanded that Grace or I trade with her.

"You are smaller, so yours should be smaller," I reasoned. This not only did not pacify her, but my reference to her size served to make her angry. She continued to demand that one of us trade with her, but now she was yelling. Grace and I were unyielding, and Mama continued working with the bread as though she heard nothing. Our non-compliance with her demands and Mama's ignoring her were too much.

I was skinny with red hair and freckles. Grace was sturdy with a touch of Mama's olive skin, a sprinkling of freckles and brown hair. But, Dolly was stocky with a round face, button nose, freckles, and a halo of very blonde tightly curled hair. She looked cherubic. Her actions were not always cherubic. Dolly had learned swear words from Mama who said she learned to use them while herding cattle on the ranch in baking sun in summer and bitter winds in winter. Mama's most frequently used swear word was, "scheisse" (German for shit, and rhymes with rice).

Dolly spoke volumes, but she did not speak clearly. Now she climbed down from her chair, and screamed at Grace and me. We ignored her.

Next she began stomping her feet up and down as she turned in a circle screaming and crying, "Chick, rice! Chick, rice! Chick rice!" We knew her intent was to say "Shit, Scheisse!" but she could not pronounce the words correctly.

Her behavior was so incongruous with her angelic appearance that Grace and I laughed and laughed while Dolly screamed, stomped, and swore.

Mama stopped, watched Dolly for a moment, and smiled, "Look," she said, "Dolly is doing the Naughty Waltz!"

Dolly's doing the Naughty Waltz was not a one-time thing.

◦ · · ◦ · · ◦

Some winter days Mama declared that it was too cold to play outside. When she had time she came from the kitchen to sit at the big table with us girls as we drew pictures or colored in our coloring books. Sometimes she would color a picture for one of us. As Mama sat down with us one afternoon Grace passed her coloring book to Mama. We each had our own box of 24 Crayola crayons, and we shared a big box of crayons that had 120 colors in it. Mama chose colors from the big box. While we colored I asked her to tell the story about Mrs. Pop-Eyes. Mama knew Mrs. Pop-Eyes when she and Papa lived on Papa's homestead on the prairie. Mama told her story as she colored.

Her real name was Ida, and Ida was a mail-order bride. Remember that these mail-order brides had never met their husbands before, and they left everything familiar behind to come out west to marry. All the brides knew about their husbands was what the husband chose to tell in his letters to her. What she told in her mail-order-bride ad and their letters to each other often painted a picture much better than reality.

Ida a skinny little woman about five feet tall—and that's shorter than I am—came out to marry Johann Heimer. He was a big ornery German bully. Well, when he wasn't drinking he could be a nice man, but he brewed his own beer and he drank too much of it. When he drank he grew ornery.

The only time I ever saw John when he drank too much was once when he came home from Johann's homestead. John rode over to talk to Johann about wheat harvest. When John arrived, Johann was sitting out in his barn in a chair by his store of beer. John said Johann was well on his way to being drunk and nothing would do, except for John to drink with him. John drank German beer when he stayed to occupy Germany after World War I, and he liked German beer. Johann brewed good German beer. They drank together until Johann started trying to pick a fight. Even though John used to box, he said he knew he was no match for a man the size of Johann, so John came home. John was tipsy and he laughed a lot.

Like most mail-order brides Ida was from a city and knew nothing about farming or ranching. I will say this for her, she worked very hard and did the best she could.

Mama's Family

Above: Caroline Watts Clark, Mama's mother, Glasgow, Montana, circa 1948.
Mama referred to her only as Mrs. Clark or The Anima. She is best described as "audacious."

Left: Grace Watts, circa 1890s,
Caroline's sister and a frequent
visitor in the Clark's home, The
Aunt Grace was a high school
English teacher in Minneapolis.
She was shocked by Caroline's
divorce and her move to Montana
to homestead.

PAPA'S FAMILY

Above: Papa treasured this plait of his mother's auburn hair.

Right: Arthusa Euphoria Bagby Sherwood, age 24. She died at 37 of childbed fever in 1890 after Papa was born.

Above: William Marshall Bagby, Papa's grandfather who raised him. He expected Papa to become a doctor. His sons, 4 doctors and 1 dentist, met his high expectations, but his Sherwood grandsons did not.

MAMA'S EARLY YEARS

Above: Mama, age 3,
St. Peter, Minnesota.

Left: Mama at nursing School,
Glasgow, Montana.

Above: Mama, lower right, and college friends. She loved going to college in St. Paul, Minnesota.

PAPA'S EARLY YEARS

Above: Papa, age 4, Plattsburg, Missouri.

Above: Papa, age 29, WWI in France.
He left his homestead to join the army.

Above: Papa, left, at William Jewell College, Liberty, Missouri.

Homesteading in the Barnard Community

Above: Picnic: Uncle Aub, left. Standing Uncle Ben,
Papa in cap. The Sherwoods reluctantly left their
Montana homesteads, but the drought necessitated it.

Above: Papa in hat.
Although he was in no way prepared
for farming, it was his first love.

Above: Sherwoods played
and worked together.

Above: Sherwood brothers' rodeo! Papa left his pre-
med studies in college in his last year to homestead
with his brothers. He did not want to be a doctor.

Above: Papa earned extra money by hauling wheat. As drought spread across the Great Plains,
making a living was harder. He must travel farther away in Montana and Canada to haul wheat.

HOMESTEADING IN THE GENEVIEVE COUNTRY

Above: Mrs. Clark's Homestead House. Mrs. Clark drew up the plans and helped build the house.
The pole is for the telephone line, not electricity.

Right: Henry Lick, lower left,
Mama (Helen) next to him.
Mrs. Clark, in white dress,
learned to cook, and she
loved to entertain.

Left: Mrs. Clark's
Team. Grandma Watts
holds the reins. She
overcame her shock of
Mrs. Clark's moving
to the "wild west."

IDAHO 1936

Above: Willie, Sherman, and Curly were a threesome until a mountain lion killed Curly.

Right: Mama, sickly Baby Nathan. Later goats' milk helped him. Idaho's damp weather exacerbated Mama's rheumatism.

HINSDALE 1941

Below: Ruth feeding chickens. Ruth was willful, spoiled, and naughty.

Above: Willie on Babe. Hinsdale was Willie's favorite place to live. We prospered on this farm, and left regretfully in 1943, so Papa could be near a skin cancer specialist in Spokane, Washington.

IDAHO 1943

Nathan   Sherman   Willie
Dolly   Grace   Ruth   In Idaho

Above: *Dolly and Nathan; Grace and Sherman; Ruth and Willie. The foothills of the Rocky Mountains are behind us, and a crystal clear mountain stream runs through the farm. Bears and mountain lions come down from the mountains. We were able to return to Montana when a new treatment for Papa's skin cancer was found.*

GLASGOW 1944–1951

Above: Mama, Ruth, Grace, and Dolly on the banks of Milk River. Mama sewed our home dresses.

Above: Nathan. His odious job was to "herd us girls," as Mama put it.

Right: Front: Ruth, Grace. Back: Willie, Nathan, Mama, Dolly, Papa. We are standing in front of our faithful tractor, Putt-Putt.

Above: Papa going to a funeral.

Above: Sherman, Papa, Nathan in orchard. Our orchards were mostly crabapples and a variety of plums.

GLASGOW 1944-1951

Above: Sherman, our dog Pinky, Ruth, Nathan, Grace, and Dolly with fish from Milk River.

Above: Dog Buck, Sherman, Willie, Nathan. Willie and Sherman helped Papa. Nathan helped Mama and "herded" us girls. A dastardly neighbor shot Buck.

Above: Grace, Ruth, Dolly, Nathan, Mama, Papa. One of our orchards in bloom. Mama canned both fruit from our orchards and vegetables from our gardens. Rows of canned goods lined the cellar shelves.

Above: Ruth, Grace, Dolly, Nathan. We are going to the Easter Sunday service at church. Milk River behind us is high and rising. Mr. Combs farm is in the background across the river. Every spring the possibility of a flood worried Mama and Papa.

Right: Papa, Dolly, Nathan. Truck: Old Shiny Eyes. A load of hay is hauled to be stacked on high ground.

GLASGOW 1944-1951

Above: Nathan, Grace, and Ruth with puppy and our dogs Rover and Pinky. Great Northern Railroad tracks and electric lines are in the background. The railroad bordered the south side of our farm. In summer the hobos who visited us traveled on the trains. Electricity did not come to our rural area until 1948.

Right: Papa on new Ford tractor, 1948. Having a second tractor significantly increased productivity. Later this tractor traveled in the back of our truck with us to Missouri.

Left: Geese on the main irrigation ditch in front of house. This ditch fed the smaller ditches throughout the farm. Scant rainfall made irrigation essential for success in farming.

GLASGOW FLOOD, 1950

Above: *Back to Front: Ruth, Nathan, Papa, Mama, Grace, our cat Eemy, and Dolly.*

Above: *Putt-Putt. Only a strip of dry land remains. All the buildings are on the dry land! Big Tree and Old House in background.*

Above: *New House, Old House. Papa hauled dirt so New House sat on higher ground. He long worried about a big flood happening.*

Glasgow, Sketches by Grace Sherwood

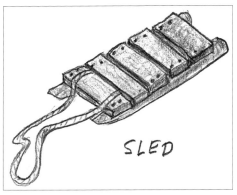

SLED

Above: Papa made our sturdy sleds that held up to "flying" down the banks of Milk River.

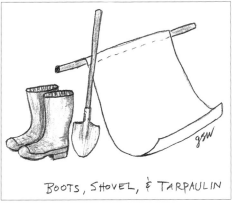

BOOTS, SHOVEL, & TARPAULIN

Above: Irrigation equipment. The tarpaulin was made from canvas to fit the size ditch where used.

STILTS

Above: Papa made our stilts.

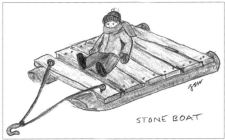

STONE BOAT

Right: Stone boat pulled by the tractor to haul hay, tools, etc. Originally used on the homesteads to haul rocks.

GLASGOW, SKETCHES BY GRACE SHERWOOD

Above: Papa made our sling shots from the forks of red willow branches.

SPLITTING WOOD WITH MAUL AND WEDGE

Above: Splitting wood with a maul and single-bit ax.

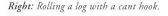

CROSSCUT SAW

Above: Crosscut saw. It is meant to have a person on each end. When Papa sawed by himself he took the handle off one end.

Right: Rolling a log with a cant hook.

ROLLING A LOG WITH A CANT HOOK

THE SHERWOODS

Top row: John Marvin Sherwood, Ruth Helen Clark;
Middle row: "Willie" Marvin William, Sherman Argonnne, Nathan Hale;
Bottom row: Ruth Marian, Grace Caroline, "Dolly" Mary Louise

SHERWOOD PARATROOPERS

All three Sherwood boys served in the military.

She was plain to the point of being unattractive, and she had a somewhat colorless personality. I suspect she became a mail order bride because she thought that was the only way she would get married. I hadn't moved to the Barnard community when she came out west to marry Johann. The neighbors told me they noticed that every time Johann would get drunk Ida would show up with bruises. Also, they said she wasn't pop-eyed when she first came to Montana. They believed he choked her so often she became pop-eyed. I'm not sure if I believe that was what happened. She may have had a goiter.

By the time I knew Ida she was somewhat pop-eyed. When she rode over to visit I did notice she sometimes had bruises. One day I decided to ask her about her bruises. At first she claimed she was just clumsy and bumped into things. When I told her I didn't buy that she started crying. Yes, Johann did beat her, but only when he was drunk. She would rather stay and be beaten from time to time than go back home in the East with her "tail between her legs."

I told her that it was obvious to others that Johann beat her and that John and some of the men had talked about getting together and giving Johann a taste of his own medicine. John said he and some other men planned first to go talk to Johann, and if that didn't work they would give him a good beating.

Ida seemed quite surprised people noticing her bruises might think Johann beat her, and she was even more surprised people cared enough to be willing to help her.

After she quit crying and drank another cup of good strong coffee, she pulled herself together.

'Helen,'" she said, 'This is my problem, and I am going to take care of it. John is right—Johann needs a taste of his own medicine!'

I asked her what on earth she could do about it. She just smiled at me and told me she might not be big or pretty, but she wasn't dumb. With that pronouncement, she road off at a gallop. She displayed more spirit than I thought she had in her.

A couple of weeks later it was Johann who was sporting some bruises, bad bruises. None of the neighbors could figure out who had even been in a fight with him, and Johann wasn't talking about it.

A few days later Ida came riding over to visit. She looked different. She had always seemed meek and mousy, but not today.

I brewed some strong coffee for her and fixed some tea for me. I made idle talk until we sat down at the table. I asked what had happened.

'Helen,' she said with her chin up, 'I will tell you on one condition. You are not to tell anybody, but John. He can know, because he came up with the solution. I gave Johann a taste of his own medicine!'

She was positively triumphant. She said that one night Johann went to the barn after supper to do some chores. This was Johann's pattern when he was going to get good and drunk. He would go out to the barn and drink and come back to the house during the night raging drunk and beat up on her.

This time, though, she was ready.

She claimed it sounded silly now, even to her, but when Johann would go to the barn to get drunk she would hide under the bed covers knowing full well that he was going to jerk her out and beat her. But where could you hide in a two room shack? This time she used some quilts to make it look like she was under the covers. She was hiding behind the bedroom door with a cast iron skillet in her hands.

When Johann went to the bed to jerk her out she came from behind him and hit him on the head with the skillet as hard as she could. He fell across the bed just as she had planned. Ida had ropes ready to tie him up and tie him to the bed. She did that before he came to.

Ida then proceeded to beat him with the frying pan from head to toe. She said she never heard so much screaming and hollering. She left him there until daylight when he could look her in the eye. She said she came up close and told him that if he ever beat her again, she would kill him the next time.

Ida told me that she could not believe how good Johann had been to her since his beating.

Ida straightened up, and looked at me with a hard, cold look totally unlike the Ida I had known before, 'And, I will kill him, if he ever beats me again.'

As far as I know Johann never drank again.

⚜ · · ◦ · · ⚜

On a cold windy day when the thermometer sank to ten below and Papa had declared at dinner that it felt like forty below, I asked Mama if we could look through the blue and black metal boxes that belonged to Papa and her. As soon as she found time she pulled the boxes from the closet. The boxes contained old pictures, newspaper clippings, letters, their college year books, and other mementos. She opened the boxes and I carefully touched a plait of auburn hair. Mama said that it was Papa's favorite keepsake. She told how his mother died of childbed fever shortly after he was born. She had long thick auburn hair, and after she died enough was cut off to make a plait for each of her ten living children. I never heard my father mention his mother. He often spoke of his Aunt Jenny and Grandfather Bagby who raised him. When Papa's mother died, his father had placed all ten of his children with her father and Aunt Jenny and left them there for them to raise. Papa did not mention his father either.

I looked through the boxes for a time, before I pulled out one of Mama's college year books. I asked Mama if she and I could look through it. Since this interested Grace and Dolly less, Mama settled Grace and Dolly with crayons and coloring books.

As Mama and I looked at the pictures of her classmates, she told me about them. We had looked at her year book so many times that I felt I knew her classmates, but I never tired of hearing about them. We looked at the picture of the girls' quartet. Mama was one of them. I asked what she liked best about college.

"Well, I liked making my own decisions. Mrs. Clark made decisions for me when I was with her. It was a pretty heady sense of freedom for me to make my own decisions.'

"As for college activities, I seemed to like them all. I was on the swim team. I was a good swimmer. After I had polio I walked with a limp, and my left arm was compromised also. Part of my physical therapy was swimming."

"What else did you like?" I prodded.

"Oh, I liked singing. But, my favorite was acting!" She turned to the page in her year book where she found a picture of the characters in a play. Mama wore a white dress. "I was the murderer in this play. That was fun! I wanted to be an actress, but Mrs. Clark wouldn't have it." "Tell us about the time you really did stab a man," I requested. Dolly and Grace stopped coloring to listen. This was one of the many stories Mama had told us at bedtime.

She looked at the clock. "This will have to be a short version, because I have much too much to do."

"That's all right." I just wanted to hear the story.

When I lived on the homestead with Mrs. Clark and Henry Lick they would sometimes go to Hinsdale and leave me at home to do the chores. This time I was seventeen. I was perfectly capable of milking, feeding the pigs, and taking care of the chickens. I wasn't afraid, and I rather liked time alone. The neighbors all knew I was alone, because when a homesteader went to Hinsdale, they checked with other neighbors to see if they needed anything.

On the second day when I was warming up some supper the dog started barking. That meant somebody was coming. Sure enough, when I looked out I saw Gunter Frieden riding up to the house. He often came over to visit Henry Lick. I didn't like Gunter. It wasn't because he was homely, pot-bellied, and shifty-eyed. It was because he stared at me too much. He wanted to be my beau. I had told him many times that he was much too old for me.

When I saw who it was I hooked the screen door. When he came to the door I asked what he wanted. He said he thought I must need help with chores and be lonely. I told him I had already finished the chores, and I certainly wasn't lonely. Then he said he would come in and have a cup of coffee. I told him that I didn't want him to come in.

He said I didn't need to be uppity with him. He jerked the screen door, the flimsy lock broke, and the door flung open. He came toward me and reached for me. I jumped back. I told him that Mrs. Clark would shoot him, if he didn't leave right now. As I kept backing up he kept coming toward me. I backed up until I reached the pie safe. I felt behind me for the drawer with the knives and picked up a big one. When he was close enough I stabbed him as hard as I could. He tried to get out of the way, so I only stuck the knife in his side, but he started bleeding. Before I could stab him again he ran out the door, jumped on his horse, and rode away.

When Mrs. Clark and Henry Lick came back the next afternoon I told them about Gunter. They were furious. Mrs. Clark said she was going over straight away and shoot him. Henry Lick insisted that it was his place to go. I don't know exactly what Henry Lick did, but Gunter never came over again.

Mama laughed, "When I saw him at dances after that he acted like he didn't know me."

Cold days and long dark winter nights meant keeping the wood stoves burning and kerosene lamps lighted. Mama and Papa looked upon both of these as fire hazards, no matter how careful they were. We children were warned repeatedly about fire dangers, and they reminded us of the tragedy of the Frisch family fire. The Frisch family had lived in the Hinsdale area, and they later moved to a farm on the Tampico road west of Glasgow. During the winter of 1944, only months before we moved to the McColley farm west of Glasgow, a house fire claimed the lives of Mrs. Frisch and two of their seven children.

One night when Nathan studied at the table in the front room, he scooted the lamp closer to him. Suddenly the flame leaped high into the lamp chimney. Papa was reading the newspaper in a nearby chair. He tossed the paper on the floor, jumped up, grabbed the lamp, raced to the door, and threw the lamp into the snow.

"If we had electricity, we wouldn't have to worry about the lamps." Papa often remarked to Mama.

Year after year in America, electricity had been brought to those in or near a city or large town. Electric companies did not believe it was profitable to bring electricity to rural areas. Eleanor Roosevelt, President Roosevelt's wife, had traveled widely throughout America when she was first lady. She was "the eyes and ears" for the president who was handicapped and not able to travel. She worked tirelessly for those in need. She informed President Roosevelt not only of the needs, but she suggested how needs could be met. Now Eleanor insisted that electricity must be brought to rural areas.

An executive order creating Rural Electrification Administration, or REA, as it came to be known, was signed in 1935. The purpose of REA was to loan money to cooperatives that would bring electricity to rural areas. Even with funding, electrification of rural America would take time.

We learned that REA was going to loan money to the cooperative in our area. Electricity was coming!

We watched the progress of electric lines as poles were set and wire strung along the town road. Finally, poles were set and wires were strung to our house. An electrician wired both houses for one outlet on a wall of Mama's choice and one light bulb for the ceiling of each room.

Mama warned us girls severely about the outlets. "Do not touch an outlet! Do not stick anything in it! If you do you will be electrocuted. A flash of fire, a poof, you will be a little pile of ashes!"

Not wishing to be a little pile of ashes, we didn't stick anything into an outlet. Mama and Papa had nothing to plug into the outlets, because they had no electrical appliances.

Papa bought light bulbs in town, so we no longer needed kerosene lamps. The old lamps were stored in The Old House in case of electrical failure. We could just pull a string hanging from the light socket in the ceiling and magical bulbs lit up. One bulb gave the room more light than several kerosene lamps.

Papa picked up a box at the post office that Uncle Don had sent to us from Idaho. We gathered around as he opened it. Uncle Don sent a pencil bag for each of us girls, a small pocket knife for Sherman and Nathan, and some hard candy for all of us. Best of all, Uncle Don had sent an electric radio for Mama and Papa. The old battery radio could be retired.

We no longer needed to worry about the life of the radio battery. This meant we could listen to all the programs we wished. Listening to the news and boxing matches had always been a priority. Now we could all listen to a variety of programs: *Amos and Andy, Fibber McGee and Molly, Mr. Keene, Tracer of Lost Persons, Dragnet. . ..* Mama began listening to daytime programs that included Ma Perkins and Pepper Young's Family. Some days after school we children listened to *The Lone Ranger.*

Papa bought a used cooler to keep in the kitchen/pantry in The Old House. It was a long, low red cooler with Coca Cola written in white across it. Mama stored the household milk and food items that must be kept cool in the cooler. It was colder than the cellar, and Mama or Nathan no longer needed to make the trips back and forth to the cellar. When the watermelons ripened, one of them was kept cold in the cooler. We all declared cold watermelon tasted better.

"How did we ever get along without electricity?" one of us would ask from time to time. ❧

CHAPTER 19

Polio, Spanish Flu, and Other Maladies

Mama feared illness. She often reminded us that she was able to walk without crutches, only because Mrs. Clark could afford physical therapy for her after she had polio. Her health would also have been much worse, if Mrs. Clark had not been able to provide the best of medical care for her when she had rheumatic fever. She warned us that we could not afford the kind of expensive care that she had received, so we must be extra careful.

We were frequent visitors to Dr. Agneberg's office. Augette Leone, a public health nurse, visited our farm to dispense cod liver oil capsules, to give us vaccinations, and to discuss our health with Mama. "An ounce of prevention is worth a pound of cure," Mama quoted.

She remembered the Idaho winter of January 1944 when all six of us children were in various stages of the measles at the same time. Measles is a respiratory virus that can cause pneumonia, for which the death rate was 30 percent. It brings a cough, rash, high fever, and red, irritated, watery eyes. She and Papa covered the windows with blankets, because it was believed that light in our eyes could cause blindness. Measles are highly contagious. A sign had been posted on our house warning all those who were not immune to stay away, and reminding us to stay home and not to have contact with other people. Neighbors were kind. We would hear the honking of a car horn and find that food had been left near the door.

Another illness Mama feared, but that we children did not contract, was scarlet fever. When I was in second grade I had come home with the report that Louise la Fournaise, a beautiful classmate who looked like an Indian princess, must stay home, because she had scarlet fever. Quarantine signs began to appear on houses in Glasgow as the scarlet fever spread. Mama had warned us over and over to wash our hands frequently and not to touch our faces. If one of us seemed to be catching a cold or the flu Mama checked our temperature. As a precaution, Mama looked at our tongue for the whitish tell-tale sign of scarlet fever and at the inside of our elbows for a rash. Much to Mama's relief winter passed with only the normal colds and flu.

The following winter when I was in third grade chicken pox seemed to be appearing more frequently than usual. This time we were not spared. Grace, Dolly, and I all contracted the chicken pox. While this was of concern to Mama, the fact that complications are not likely in those who are otherwise healthy, Mama was less stressed. While Grace and Dolly both did have a low fever and sore throat briefly, their longest lasting symptom was a moderate amount of the itchy blister-like rash. I was miserably sick with a higher fever and plagued with blisters, lesions, and scabs for what seemed to be weeks.

Finally, I was getting well and most of the lesions were either healed or covered with a scab. I wanted to return to school, but a few stubborn scabs refused to fall off. Then I learned about the missionaries.

Grace Bible Chapel sponsored missionaries in Africa. When missionaries returned to the states a special evening would be spent at church with the returning missionaries giving talks of Africa and showing pictures and movies. Missionary evenings were the highlight of my church life, because I was going to be a missionary in Africa when I grew up.

Papa returned from church Sunday with news that missionaries from Africa would be at church Wednesday evening. Wednesday evening was only three days away! Surely, my scabs would be gone by then—they must be. I had already learned that picking off a scab, before it was ready to come off, only resulted in another scab taking its place. When nobody was watching I began using my finger nail to lift the edges of each scab ever so lightly—just enough so it would not bleed and form a new scab. By Wednesday morning one big scab stubbornly remained on my forehead. I alternately begged to be allowed to go to church anyway and eased my fingernail beneath the scab edges. Mid-afternoon I could wait no longer and I simply pulled the scab off. A small amount of blood oozed for a short time, but I wiped it away with my handkerchief. I could go to see the missionaries!

Mama, Papa, Grace, Dolly, and I went to church without the boys who did not seem to have much interest in missionary evenings, but then none of them planned to be a missionary. The missionaries' presentation did not disappoint me. I was more certain than ever that being a missionary in Africa was my destiny.

Fascinated, I watched the missionaries' movies of African children in their school sitting on rows of benches in a building with no walls and a thatched roof while the missionaries taught them. I learned that the children with distended stomachs were not overeating, rather they suffered from malnutrition. In addition to teaching school, missionaries helped mothers to understand the kinds of food they could find and grow to help their children to be healthy. We watched Africans cook outside over open fires. The women wore colorful cloth skirts tied around their waists and nothing more. The missionaries explained that they had to choose the most important ways for the Africans to change little by little. Finding God, getting an education, and learning to take care of their health were priorities. Covered breasts were not.

⁊◌·•◦•·◌⁊

Yet, it was polio, or, as Mama referred to it, infantile paralysis, and not chicken pox that struck the worst fear. Hundreds of thousands of children world-wide were paralyzed every year. Unlike so many illnesses we knew, polio peaked in the summer months. Polio epidemics were common and fear enveloped the very word "polio." Pictures and articles about polio seemed to fill our magazines until I felt that the polio virus was everywhere waiting to infect me. Mama encouraged my fears. Her personal experience with having had polio caused her to be hyper-vigilant to be sure we children did not catch it.

Our newspaper, *The Glasgow Courier*, mentioned polio, but it did not focus on it as much as magazines did. Usually, the articles were accompanied by vivid pictures of polio victims, mostly children. More than one magazine showed long rows of children, each encased in an iron lung that was supported by a metal stand. The iron lung, a medical ventilator, helped those with partial paralysis of the chest muscles to breathe.

Looking at those pictures horrified me. They reminded me of pictures I had seen of coffins on biers. Each polio victim was fully encased in a rounded metal "box" with glass windows on the sides. The child's head rested on a support outside the "box" part of the iron lung. What looked to me like a lid with a mirror was at the front of the "box" above the child's head.

"Why would any child in an iron lung want to look at himself in a mirror?" I asked Mama.

Mama smiled at me, "Don't you think that the mirror is so the child can see what is going on around him?" This certainly made more sense.

She warned us that of those who developed polio some would die, some would never be able to live outside an iron lung, some would be left with mild to severe degree of paralysis, and the lucky ones would get back to normal. Even President Roosevelt had had polio, and he was left with partial paralysis. Fortunate were those who came through without lasting disabilities. So as not to be a casualty we were to wash our hands frequently and never touch our mouth or eyes unless our hands were freshly washed.

Sherman capitalized on the talk of polio to tease us. When we pestered him his hand would shoot out and grab our arm. Typically, we waited a bit to see if he would honor our request to let go. Next we tried to pull away. He held tightly enough to keep us from slipping his grasp. Finally, we would beg for him to let go.

"Oh, I do so want to," he would reply, "but you can see I have infantile paralysis, and I simply cannot let go. See, I am trying, but my hand refuses to open."

He went on to tell us he regretted having been seized with infantile paralysis at the very time he held onto us. This was a great inconvenience for both of us. The struggling and bargaining continued until we were on the verge of tears. Then the paralysis would leave as suddenly as it came. Still we did not have enough sense to leave him alone. Mama said she could not feel sorry for us.

Since polio was most commonly spread in crowds, our summers were spent on the farm, except for church, Vacation Bible School, special occasions, and buying our school supplies. The most exciting place I could think of to go was the Valley County Fair held each August. Every year I longed and begged to go, but I would not be going. Crowds, especially those with lots of children, provided the optimal place to be exposed to polio. After all, Mama reminded us, President Roosevelt had caught polio at a Boy Scout camp.

My consolation was that on the last night of the fair when the fireworks would be set off, Papa drove to Mr. Biddle's open field where we could watch the fireworks. We sat or stood in the back of the truck. We could hear the popping and see glorious patterns of fragmented colors filling the sky. Fireworks were wondrous—their beauty seemed other-worldly. And their trailing sparkles did not spread germs!

⁂

Colds and flu circulated regularly during the winter at school. I caught more than my share. Mama believed that it was because I was so skinny. Mama made certain that I took all the vitamins and cod liver oil recommended. When I was not in school she prepared a snack for me between meals. Now I was ten, still skinny, and suffered more bouts of the flu than anybody else in our family. Her new attempt to get me to gain weight was that I would drink a cup of cream every day. I thought it to be one of her better ideas, because I liked cream.

This was being discussed when Mrs. Clark and Mr. Larson came for Sunday dinner. Mama had attended eighteen months of nursing school and frequently checked out medical books at the library, so she had a good grasp of medical topics. Still, she often sought the advice of Mrs. Clark who read about the practice of medicine extensively. Mrs. Clark's keen interest in medicine may have been fostered by Mama's childhood illnesses and the fact that Mrs. Clark had spent much time volunteering in the hospital in St. Paul. Now Mama asked her opinion about my tendency to catch almost everything that came around.

Mrs. Clark looked at Papa. "You and your brothers all suffered from asthma, and you said that all of you seemed to have weak immune systems. I have read that when a parent has asthma their children often have weaker immune systems."

Sherman looked at Papa, "Did you get sick a lot as a kid?" he asked. "And you had Spanish Flu didn't you?"

"Yes," Papa remembered, "And that was the sickest I have ever been. The army doctors were so sure I would die that they sent telegram to Aunt Jenny telling her I did die. Perhaps, they had not reckoned on her direct line to god. She claimed it was prayer that kept me from dying. I'm sure that helped, but I also think that, when I was conscious, I thought of my obituary in the Plattsburg, Missouri newspaper saying I died in bed. After the horrific battles I'd fought in, I was not going to have my obituary saying I died in bed of the flu!"

"I read that more soldiers died of the Spanish Flu during WWI than died in battle," Sherman said.

Mama added, "People still die of the flu every year, but the Spanish Flu was different. It was a world-wide pandemic that killed fifty million people! Fifty million! A big difference was that with most flu types, it is the very old, the very young, or those who have poor health that die. With the Spanish Flu most of those who died were young and strong—like the soldiers."

"And," Mrs. Clark looked at Mama, "like those who died in the makeshift hospital in Saco where you and I worked." She turned to Mr. Larson. "Helen and I worked helping with the flu patients back in 1918. Even on the prairie where you would think we would be safe from an epidemic, so many were sick and dying that the hospitals and morgues were overflowing. Doctors and nurses were totally exhausted. They needed help.

"One day a car comes driving up to our homestead. A man gets out and tells me that the public health service had conscripted a dry goods store in Saco and turned it into a flu hospital. They needed staff to work, and they had heard I was a nurse. I didn't tell him I only had practical nursing experience, because I knew I could help. Then Helen came in from the barnyard to see who had come to visit. She was only fifteen, but she looked older. He saw her and said she must come too. We would be staying there for a while. A car would come the next morning to pick us up. That evening Henry Lick said he would take care of the homestead, so Helen and I packed to go."

Mama laughed, "Remember when we drove up to the store. A truck was backed up to the door and two men were carrying a stretcher with a sheet-covered body. The woman walking with them screamed as the wind blew the sheet off. The corpse lay there like a stuffed pig. I had never seen a naked man before!"

"Yes," Mrs. Clark said, "And as soon as we were in the building you ducked into the kitchen to see if you could help there."

"Well, I knew there wouldn't be any dead people in the kitchen! And, I hoped that I would be less apt to catch the flu. The cook was a man who had been conscripted from a ranch, and he was none too happy about it. He wanted to get back to his chuck wagon. He had dirty dishes stacked all over the kitchen. He told me he was happy that they had finally gotten more help for him. I thought about it and told him I was sent there to be his helper and, if anybody should ask, to tell them he required my help. I was able to stay in the kitchen all the time we were there. It was about a month."

Mrs. Clark looked at Mama, "I remember how red and chapped your hands were from having them in disinfected dish water for so long." She shook her head and looked around the table. "I walked into total chaos. It was truly a case of 'the right hand not knowing what the left hand was doing'. Too many of the kind people who had volunteered to help, had never worked in a hospital. There was a terrible shortage of nurses and experienced workers. My experience as a volunteer for several years in the hospital in St. Peter was invaluable to me in this situation."

Mama smiled at Mrs. Clark, "I did hear from the doctor and others that you were truly a godsend. Your being bossy and organized was never needed more!"

Mr. Larson beamed at Mrs. Clark, "You never cease to amaze me!"

She squeezed his hand and winked, "We've only just begun!"

"We both ended up seeing so many dead people there," Mama said. "One night a man had died in one of the upstairs beds. The women workers couldn't find any men to help move him, and his bed was needed. Two women decided that they could carry the man downstairs on a stretcher. It was getting late, but I was still in the kitchen washing dishes. I heard this yelling and thumping. When I looked out I saw two women with skirts flying, a dead man, and a stretcher tumbling down the stairs! The woman in front had tripped and turned her ankle. They were, as all of us were, totally exhausted. This was the last straw. They just sat on the floor at the bottom of the stairs and laughed until they cried."

"Physically and emotionally we were all stretched beyond our limits." Mrs. Clark shook her head. "We worked so hard, and we saw so much of death, suffering, and grieving. I think we were all numb. We had to be able to laugh once in a while to keep going day after day."

"Another night," Mama remembered, "I had finally finished the dishes after midnight, and I was so exhausted I had to lie down. I could have slept on the kitchen floor. I found an empty bed in one of the rooms and dropped down on it. No sooner had I closed my eyes than a woman was shaking my shoulder and telling me a man had just died in that bed, and they needed to change the linens!"

"I don't know how we ever kept from catching the flu," Mrs. Clark marveled.

She looked at us children. "You cannot imagine the panic the flu caused in every area of America. People were dying like flies, and doctors were unable to save them. Social gatherings of all kinds stopped. Schools, churches, bars, theaters, and even restaurants closed. When we first started hearing about it, we thought that the isolation of the prairie would prevent the flu from reaching us. Not so! I am still not sure how it spread so far and so fast."

"Let's pray nothing like this ever happens again!" Mama sighed. "With today's advancements in medicine, I don't think it could." ௸

CHAPTER 20

SCHOOL DAYS, SKUNKS, AND DRUNKS

I never understood how our school district officials decided which students who rode busses would attend South Side Elementary School or North Side High School that included all grades. What I did know is that I much preferred attending South Side. There were fewer students and the teachers supervised much more closely, so bullying and unpleasant incidents were rare. Attending Miss Westby's class in second grade was my favorite year.

Whether I would be going to North Side School or South Side School did not dampen my enthusiasm for beginning a school year. Mrs. Pratt's making new dresses and coats for me, choosing new school supplies, and getting to have new shoes were all wonderful preludes to the beginning of school. Grace and Dolly did not get new dresses and coats, because my outgrown ones were still perfectly good. But they did always get new shoes.

The night before we would go to town to buy school supplies and new shoes, we girls were too excited to go to sleep. We jumped up and down on the bed and horsed around until Mama told us that if we did not stop, she would ask Papa to come in with his razor strap.

We settled down, and Mama sat on the bed to tell us stories. We asked her to tell about when she and Papa went to school.

"I don't know much about your dad's going to school." Mama began. "He attended school in Plattsburg, Missouri, where he lived with his grandparents and Aunt Jenny. "What I do remember is his story about his encounter with a skunk on the way to school."

"A skunk in town on the way to school?" We were amazed.

"Oh, yes. This happened when he was in third grade. His home was on the edge of town, and he cut through some vacant lots for a shorter walk to school. One morning when he was walking through a brushy vacant lot he saw a skunk. Now you girls would know better than to do this, but your dad thought he would scare the skunk away if he threw a rock at it. He didn't hit the skunk, but he did hit close to it. The skunk took exception to this, and it responded by standing on its front feet, raising its tail, and spraying your dad liberally!

"He said the skunk smell was so awful that he coughed and choked, and finally vomited. Once he caught his breath, all he could think about was getting home and changing clothes. He was almost to school, but he turned around and started for home. He said that the further he went the less he smelled like skunk. Just before he reached home he decided he smelled good enough to go to school like he was, so he turned around and headed back to school.

"Classes were already in session, so he had to stop at the office for a late slip. The minute he walked in the principal and secretary made terrible faces. They told him to go home, bathe, and change clothes. Your dad didn't think he smelled that bad when he reached home, but Aunt Jenny wouldn't let him into the house. She made him go to the shed to take his clothes off. She brought out a tub and soap for him to bathe. She soaked his clothes in tomato juice and then buried them. She finally had to wash his hair in tomato juice, because the soap wouldn't get rid of the smell.

"John said the only good thing about his skunk encounter was that he was able to stay home the rest of the day."

"What about your dugout school?" I always liked to hear about Mama's going to school in a dugout.

"Barr School was about three miles from Mrs. Clark's homestead. Sometimes I walked to school, and sometimes I rode my horse, Teddy. Several of the children rode horses to school. Those who had siblings often rode two on a horse and sometimes three.

"It was one room with one teacher who taught grades one through seven. When I began the youngest child was four. The oldest boy was seventeen and in fourth grade!

"My desk was quite a surprise. It was made of two wooden soap boxes! There was not one real desk in the room, except for our teacher Miss Kingsley's desk. We had text books, but there were no library books. Fortunately, Mrs. Clark shipped a lot of books to Montana, so I had books at home, but many of the students did not.

"The school was strategically placed near a spring that never froze in the winter, so we could always get water. For drinking water and hand-washing each day two of the bigger boys would get two pails of water from the spring— one for drinking and one for washing. We all drank from the same dipper.

One day there was a drowned gopher in the spring. The boys all drank water anyway, but I didn't.

"Miss Kingsley would pour one of the buckets of water in a big pan on the stove. When it was lunch time, we all took turns washing in the same water. Miss Kingsley washed first and the youngest boy washed last. I was glad I was one of the older girls who washed after Miss Kingsley."

Mama looked at the clock, "Time for prayers and sleeping. Remember to pray for Willie!" We all said the Lord's Prayer together and asked God to keep Willie safe.

⋆⋆ · · ◦ · · ⋆⋆

We each owned two pairs of shoes—one pair for good and one pair for home. We were only allowed to purchase very sturdy brown leather shoes that laced, and our shoes were always purchased with room for us to grow. Papa kept our shoes in good condition by repairing them using a metal last, a foot-shaped form on a stand over which he placed a shoe upside down to repair or replace the sole. He owned different sizes of lasts, so he could repair all sizes of shoes. Additionally, he used a leather awl to stitch shoes that were coming apart. So, our getting new shoes was a very special occasion.

Grace and I climbed into the truck and Papa lifted Dolly onto Mama's lap. The boys would work at home while we were gone, because they would get shoes another time when just they and Papa went to town. We girls giggled and squirmed so much on the way to town that Papa finally told us sternly to settle down. Mama seemed to have a limitless number of poems that she could recite, and she told us that if we would settle down we could request poems. She began with our favorite, "The Highway Man," and proceeded through poem after poem until we reached town.

As we neared the downtown area we saw Joe Baker. We never saw Joe Baker's face; all we could see were his shoes and his floppy overalls, because a big box always covered his head and rested on his shoulders. His various boxes were large enough to afford him a view of what was on the sidewalks and streets directly below him, but he could not see ahead. Sometimes when a large box was available at home we girls practiced being Joe Baker.

Mama knew Joe Baker and his parents, and she had told us the sad story about him. She said that until Joe had the measles when he was seven years old he was just like any other child. Mama was in nurses' training at Deaconess

137

Hospital when Joe's mother and father brought in Joe who was dangerously ill with complications from the measles. Doctors diagnosed Joe with encephalitis, inflammation of the brain. One of Mama's responsibilities was to try to calm Mr. and Mrs. Baker. Mrs. Baker would not be calmed. She had miscarried many times, and Joe had been the perfectly healthy baby. Doctors did all they could do to save Joe, before telling Mr. and Mrs. Baker that Joe was dying. Mrs. Baker became hysterical, and she was given a sedative. Mr. Baker went crazy, but he would not let anybody close to give him a sedative. He cried great racking sobs. Mama said she was both heartbroken for them and scared of what Mr. Baker might do.

At one point Mr. Baker looked up at the ceiling, "God!" he yelled over and over, "You can't have my boy! I won't let him go! You can't have him!"

Mama said that when miraculously Joe slowly began to recover Mr. and Mrs. Baker were deliriously happy believing they could keep their boy. The medical staff soon saw what the Baker's did not. Physically Joe was recovering, but he was mentally impaired—encephalitis had damaged his brain.

"Joe still lives with his parents. We will remember them tonight when we say our prayers." Mama sounded sad.

Papa parked Shiny Eyes in the downtown area, and we girls scrambled from our truck. We were all getting new shoes! We bounced ahead of Mama and Papa into Spencer's store that smelled of all things new where we could admire the store's selection of children's shoes. I was drawn to shoes that were not sturdy, brown, lace-up shoes—they were shiny, black patent leather shoes that buckled instead of laced. I knew from school that these beautiful shoes were called Mary Jane's, and they were worn by some of the town girls. I longed for Mary Jane's, but I was not to have Mary Jane's.

We left Spencer's with each of us carrying a box of sturdy, brown, lace-up shoes. Mama announced we would go to Ben Franklin's next to buy some school supplies; this generated almost as much excitement as new shoes. Mama purchased Big Chief tablets, pencils, and crayons for home and school. We were all encouraged to write and draw at home. Grace was more artistic than I, but I felt I excelled at writing stories and poems.

When we reached home supper time was too near for us girls to take a nap, so we played happily with our shoes and school supplies. We could not wear our shoes yet, because we slept in them the first night before the soles were dirty, but once we were in our nightgowns and ready for bed we put on our new shoes and crawled awkwardly under the covers. Next morning not one of us had our shoes on even though we had laced and tied them. Neither Mama nor Papa seemed to know how they were taken off and put back into their boxes.

∽· · · ○ · · ·∼

My fourth grade teacher at North Side School, Miss Scotland, was beautiful! Her flawless ivory face was framed with dark hair, and her lips were red. She was my first teacher who wore bright red lipstick; in fact, she was one of the few women I saw who did wear bright red lipstick. Grace Bible Chapel forbade women to wear make-up—make-up was vain, and vanity was a sin. I knew that I would sin by wearing make-up like Miss Scotland when I grew up, but right now I would be happy with dark hair and a creamy complexion free of freckles.

I felt sure that Miss Scotland's clothes must be the latest fashion. She often touched and stroked her simple pearl necklace. Just like Mrs. Clark, Miss Scotland wore smart shoes and overshoes made to accommodate heels. Miss Scotland and Mrs. Clark both wore perfume and dressed in the nicest clothes of any women I had seen, but Miss Scotland's perfume was noticeable only when I stood very close to her. Not only would I wear red lipstick and perfume when I grew up, I would dress like Miss Scotland and Mrs. Clark.

When Valentine's Day neared Miss Scotland gave each of us students red, pink, and white construction paper to decorate brown paper bags for the Valentine's we would receive at our Valentine's party. Grace, Dolly, and I had already been making Valentines at home with Mama's help. Our home-made Valentines were made with flowered wallpaper, flower pictures from seed catalogs, colored paper, lace, buttons, and all the pretties Mama could gather, yet we would not take these lovely Valentines to school to give to others. All the children gave store-bought Valentines, and we did not want to be different.

Finally, Valentine's Day arrived. Staying in bed until seven seemed unnecessary, because we wanted so much to be getting ready for school. Finally, at seven, Mama brought our undershirts she had warmed in the oven into the bedroom as we girls dressed for school. Papa, Sherman, and Nathan were at the barn milking the cows. Mama warned us that two strange men came staggering to our house just before chore time and they were now warming themselves by the stove in our front room. When Papa saw they were much too drunk to drive for awhile, he decided he and the boys would do chores before pulling their car from the ditch.

Once in the front room we were temporarily diverted from our thoughts of Valentine's Day by our curiosity about the strange men sitting by our stove. We said hello as we passed by them on our way to the table. Mama brought our breakfast, and as we ate we watched the men in fascination. Their jackets hung on the backs of chairs near the stove to dry, and their field boots they had somehow managed to unlace were close to the stove. Their chairs were quite near the stove—too near, but they didn't seem to notice. Looking at their wet jackets and pants we knew they had fallen into the snow many times on their walk to the house. They clearly were not dressed warmly enough to be out in this weather, and Mama said even though they were half frozen when they reached our house they didn't seem to realize it. Now they were very, very happy, and they laughed a lot.

Without giving a glance our way as we ate breakfast, they discussed the Valentine's Day party they'd attended last night. They spoke of various people at the party; apparently, some women they thought to be pretty had attended and now they couldn't agree which were the prettiest. One of the men talked about what a horse's ass his boss was and that his boss's throwing a big party did not change the fact that he was still a horse's ass.

"Oh, speaking of my boss, I'd better get to work! Where's my car?" He wondered drunkenly.

"You won't be going to work," his friend explained. "You told off your boss and told him you quit!"

"Oh! No! Did I do that?" He put his head in his hands. "Well, where's my car? We better get going."

"Your car," his friend explained patiently, "is in the ditch. And these good people let us come in to get warm. They're even going to pull out your car."

"How did I get in the ditch?"

"I don't know how that happened. I just know that we drove a long time, before I realized we weren't going anywhere. I had you stop so I could get out and check. I couldn't even get my door open. You had to open your door. We both got out your door, and we were in the ditch. I don't know how long we were driving in the ditch."

Both men marveled they had been driving in the ditch without going anywhere. This seemed terribly funny to them, and they laughed and laughed.

Papa came in from milking and gave a disgusted look at the men.

"They won't be in need of their car any time soon." Papa told Mama. "They're still drunk."

We children all readied for school and set out walking to the town road to catch the bus. We could see the men's tracks; rather than walking in the ruts made by Shiny Eyes, they waded through the deep snow leaving a crooked trail with disturbed places in the snow showing where they fell and wallowed around trying to stand up.

While we waited for the bus we checked out the stranger's car that was mired deeply into the snow in the ditch. It had plowed through the snow berm on the side of the road and plowed a short ways through deep snow in the ditch before it stopped. Sure enough, snow was deeper than the bottom of the passenger door, no wonder he couldn't get out. Snow behind the car was blackened by exhaust as the driver had sat spinning his tires. No doubt Papa and Putt-Putt would have a big job pulling out the car.

Miss Scotland decorated our room by twisting red and white crepe paper and pinning it up in streamers, floating red and white balloons near the ceiling, and placing a big bouquet of red and white flowers on her desk—probably, courtesy of her boyfriend, I decided. Our room looked heavenly!

Our party was the last activity of our day. The lid came off our gorgeous Valentine Box, and students took turns reaching in and delivering Valentines to the recipients. Two of the students' mothers passed out pink punch and cupcakes frosted red. Some students received a big pile of Valentines while others received only a few; I assessed and decided my stack was middle-sized, and I felt sad for those who received only a few. It seemed cruel that on such a special day anybody should feel slighted, but those slighted pretended not to notice the difference. After playing a few games it was time to put our Valentines into the brown paper bags we decorated the day before with red and pink hearts, get bundled up, and go to the buses. Our Valentine's Day party was over.

When we arrived home Sherman asked Papa about getting the drunk's car out of the ditch. Papa admitted it had been quite a job when Papa had so much farm work to do. He did say they offered to pay him, but he didn't take their money, because his pulling their car out was the right thing to do. The knuckleheads had left the car running, and it ran out of gas, so Papa had to go back to our gas cans to get some gas for them. And they were even on the wrong road, because they missed their turn at the fork. Papa thought a minute and added, "Stone sober the two of them, collectively, could not make one idiot." ‿

CHAPTER 21

NEVER BORED

We looked forward to Willie's letters. He wrote that he had qualified to box in the Welterweight Division. Willie was 5' 10", but, unlike the rest of us siblings, he was of stocky build. Papa believed that with the army's rigorous training Willie must have lost some weight to qualify as a welterweight. He was pleased that Willie would be boxing, although he worried about Willie's success; not because, Willie was not capable, but that Willie wanted to win quickly. Boxing required patience and a studied, methodical approach.

Papa's favorite sport was boxing. He subscribed to the *The Ring* magazine, and he listened to every boxing match he could on the radio. Abby Addy's announcing boxing matches from Madison Square Garden commanded Papa's undivided attention. None of us would have thought of interrupting for any reason. Papa pulled his chair close to the radio and leaned toward it, so as not to miss one word. The boys joined him in listening to the boxing matches, and they sometimes read *The Ring* magazine, but they did not have Papa's dedication to boxing.

When Papa was living on his homestead and before he married Mama, he and his friend Bill Costin watched the already famous Jack Dempsey box on July 4th, 1923, in Shelby, Montana. Jack Dempsey was brought to the little oil boom town of Shelby in a misguided attempt to make a known name for Shelby and money for the promoters. Papa and Costin rode their horses to Hinsdale where they and their horses boarded the train to Shelby to see Jack Dempsey fight Tommy Gibbons. Papa and Costin thought the adventure to be a life highlight. Dempsey won the fifteen-round match.

Papa had boxed when he was young, and he considered the ability to box a necessity for every young man; busy though he was, he made time to teach Willie and Sherman as much about boxing as he could. We had a punching bag the boys used and two pairs of boxing gloves. Papa sparred with Willie and Sherman to teach them various techniques, and he watched them spar to give them guidance to improve their boxing. As soon as Papa felt Nathan was old enough he began to work with him.

We girls watched the boys spar and practice with the punching bag, but we weren't big enough to box. Sometimes we practiced using the punching bag or sparred with each other. After Papa began teaching Nathan to box, Nathan taught us what he learned. Most of the time we were careful not to hurt each other, but every once in awhile, one of us was too aggressive. There were tears and name calling and the boxing ended for the day.

Our learning to box and defend ourselves at home proved especially valuable at school. At the North Side School the lack of teacher supervision encouraged bullying, and every class seemed to have one or more bullies. Not only had we girls practiced boxing with each other and punching on our punching bag, but, additionally, we girls were out of Mama and Papas' proximity so much that we learned to settle big differences ourselves; this sometimes involved physical contact. We all knew how to fight.

The bully Dolly most often was tormented by was her classmate Johnny Stedfeldt, who especially disliked Dolly. During the first week of school in first grade Miss Shattock had placed the best readers, including Johnny, in the Blue Bird Reading Group. Dolly was placed with those who couldn't read in the Green Bird Reading Group. After a few days of reading classes Miss Shattock had Dolly and Johnny trade places, so that now Dolly was a Blue Bird and Johnny was a Green Bird. Johnny sought revenge on Dolly.

Mama and Papa knowing full-well that Dolly was a fluent reader were both unhappy that Dolly was placed in the non-reading group. Before they could go to see Miss Shattock, Dolly told them that now she was a Blue Bird and Johnny was a Green Bird.

"Glasgow schools favor students whose parents have money or importance," Mama told us. "Stedfeldt's have money, so Miss Shattock assumed Johnny could read. We don't have money, so she assumed Dolly couldn't read. She just had Ruth in her class three years ago. You'd think that since Ruth read well, she would assume Dolly could. Assuming is a poor way to place any child. I don't know where Miss Shattock learned how to teach."

At North Side School teachers were either absent from the playground, or they simply paid no attention to what was happening. Bullies had free reign, which meant Johnny had free reign to torment Dolly. One day when Dolly was swinging Johnny told her to get out of the swing, because he wanted it. Dolly refused. He then surprised her by slamming his hands against her chest and knocking her out of the swing and onto the ground, but before he could get into the swing Dolly was on her feet and socked him in the face with her fist. Johnny hit back hard. He was bigger and stronger than Dolly, and even though she was staggered, she came right back hitting. She told us over hot cocoa and cinnamon rolls that she was not going to let him know how much she hurt, and she was not going to let him see her cry. Fortunately for Dolly, the recess whistle blew, and it was time to go into the school.

Later Dolly reported that Johnny no longer picked on her.

Waiting for the bus to pick us up after school was a disorganized madness that brought out the worst in students. With no teacher supervision or organization all students in all grades left the building at the same time to wait for the same buses. One afternoon Dolly was one of the first students to gather where our bus would stop, and Grace stood close behind Dolly. A tall girl we called Daddy Long Legs stood by Dolly. As the bus approached she gave Dolly a shove, and Dolly fell into the street in front of the on-coming bus. Grace jumped forward and snatched Dolly up and back from the bus; then Grace turned to Daddy Long Legs, socked her in the chest hard enough to knock her down, jumped astraddle of her, and began pounding on her until she was pulled off by some older students. I was at the back of the group, and I had no idea what had happened until Dolly and Grace shared the story during our after school snack.

Mama told us to stand back from the bus stop hereafter.

৩৯৯· · ০ · · ৩৯৩

Papa made slingshots for each of us. We girls skipped along beside him going to the woods to find red willow bushes, because they provided the best material for slingshots. When Papa located a branch with just the right size handle and a perfect fork, he pulled out his hunting knife and cut it. Back at the house Papa smoothed the forked branches and cut a circular indentation near the end of each fork for attaching the straps, which were made from strips he cut from an old inner tube with just the right amount of stretchiness. He cut an oblong piece of leather from an old shoe tongue to hold the rock, and he poked a hole in each end with an awl. Last he used strong string to connect the leather to the straps and the straps to the forked stick. To use our slingshots we placed a rock on the leather, held the leather between our right thumb and forefinger, gripped the handle of the slingshot in our left hand, pulled the rock back, aimed, and let fly.

We needed rocks to shoot in our sling shots, but rocks were not to be found in the soil of our river bottom farm. We must walk over to the railroad tracks and collect gravel used in maintenance of the track bed or walk to the gravel road and choose rocks from it. This was another reason for my wearing Nathan's old jeans rather than my dresses around home— I needed big sturdy pockets to hold rocks for my sling shot. I sometimes still wore dresses at home, but my preferred clothes were those Nathan outgrew. When I first began wearing his old clothes he objected strenuously saying I looked ridiculous, and I did—even though the clothes did not fit Nathan, they were much too large for me. Now Grace and Dolly insisted on wearing pants instead of dresses at home some of the time. They needed to have big pockets, too.

We walked to the railroad tracks and filled our pockets with small rocks. Almost anything became a target, but fence posts were used most frequently, because we were near fences so much of the time. Our favorite targets were cows who did not step lively toward the barn when we went to get them in the evening; they were much easier to hit than fence posts. One evening as we brought the milk cows to the corral, one raised her tail to relieve herself. I pulled back on my sling shot and let go with a rock that disappeared up the cows behind! We were all amazed, but most of all me, because I was only aiming for the cow; not any specific place.

Money was short, but Papa was long on imagination, and he found many ways to create constructive activities. He hung a large rope swing for us on one of the sturdy limbs of a huge cottonwood tree between the river bank and New House. He bought a rope over two inches in diameter, cut a thick board ten by eighteen inches, and bored a hole in the middle of the board for the rope to fit through. Sherman climbed up the tree and out onto the limb to tie the rope Papa threw to him. Papa tested Sherman's knot to make sure it was secure. He slipped the swing's seat up the rope and tied another knot under the seat. Once Papa was certain the rope and seat were totally secure, we were ready to swing. We sat on the board straddling the rope.

At first we were content to take turns just swinging around in a large circle under the tree limb. As the swing approached the tree trunk we could look over the bank down to the cut bank and on down to the river. This view caused my stomach to lift up as I took a deep breath. Once the novelty wore off just swinging, Nathan thought it a good idea that we learn to perform tricks while swinging; in fact, once we perfected our tricks, we could hold a circus and the rest of the family could come to watch.

With practice we could hold tightly to the rope and put our head down and feet up. Nathan's next idea was that we needed a platform to stand on to jump and grab the swing as it came by, or to swing by and jump off onto the platform. Nathan, with our help, was able to drag a large wooden packing box from Old House out to our swing area. We turned it upside down to use for a platform to jump onto as we released the rope while swinging. Nathan, of course, mastered this trick immediately while Grace and I were having some difficulty. Dolly was not allowed to do it.

When we could perform several tricks and Nathan was confident that Grace and I would soon master the platform trick, he announced at supper one night that our circus would be ready to watch in three days. We busied ourselves finding circus clothes in the red trailer and practicing our tricks. The day before the circus I released the swing rope, leaped toward the platform and missed. I didn't miss entirely—I smacked my face, mostly my mouth, into the side of the box. I bellowed, blood flew, and Nathan rushed me in to see Mama.

No teeth were lost and my nose did not seem to be broken, but my bottom lip swelled and swelled. A man in town who worked at the grocery store, Mr. Langston, had a large protruding lower lip. Nathan and Grace promptly dubbed me "Liver-lipped Langston." Fat lip and all, we performed our circus next day.

Rare rainy days and days too cold to play outside we must stay inside. We played games, marbles, colored and painted in our coloring books, wrote stories, drew pictures, and put jigsaw puzzles together indoors.

Grace and Dolly enjoyed putting together jigsaw puzzles of which we had many. Some of their favorites were Norman Rockwell's charming pictures like we often saw on the front of *The Saturday Evening Post* magazine. I much preferred reading to jigsaw puzzles; however, both Mama and Sherman enjoyed jigsaw puzzles, and from time to time they helped Grace and Dolly. The only jigsaw puzzle I really liked and never tired of was our puzzle of the United States with pieces shaped like each state; each piece contained the name of the state, its capital, and its nickname as well as pictured the state flower and bird. Smaller state puzzle pieces had all this information on the side with an arrow pointing to the state.

We often used what we learned from our United States puzzle when we played hangman. The Art Swanson family gave us a large blackboard that brought us much entertainment, and our favorite game using the blackboard was hangman. One person is the player and the others are guessers. We called the player the hangman. Chalk in hand the hangman first drew a hanging scaffold with the rope to hang a person. The guesser's goal was to avoid being "hanged," so as to become the next hangman. There were a variety of objectives from which the hangman could choose, but the one most often chosen related to states. The hangman gave us clues about the state by drawing the shape of the state, or giving hints about the state's capital, bird, flower, nickname, or a fact about the state. The number of letters in the state was shown by the corresponding numbers of dashes at the bottom of the blackboard. Each wrong guess added a part of a stick person to the gallows; if a head, body, two legs, and two arms were all added, the person was hanged and another person was chosen to be the hangman. If on the other hand, the participant guessed before being hanged, then that person was the next hangman. The amount of help received depended upon the participant's age.

We all played chess, checkers, and Chinese checkers with emphasis on chess since Papa felt chess was a game we should all learn to play proficiently. I played these games only because that was what we all did. I much preferred one of our card games: Authors, Old Maid, and World War II Airplanes, my favorite being Authors where each card had the picture of a famous classic author with the author's name and a list of four of his most popular books. Nathan and Grace particularly liked the World War II Airplanes with each card having a picture of the plane that the player was to identify. This same card game was used by our military, because it was often a matter of survival for our soldiers to recognize both friendly and enemy planes. We did not have card decks that were used for gambling, because this would have been contrary to the practices of Grace Bible Chapel.

During extremely cold weather our windows frosted into exotic patterns of fern forests. We girls used bobby pins to scratch pictures in the frost, a thimble to make patterns, or a coin to press against the frost to leave an imprint.

Coloring and painting both on tablets and in our coloring books and drawing pictures provided entertainment.

"Remember when Willie used to color with us." Grace asked. We all missed Willie.

Willie was color-blind, and we had great fun when he colored dogs green and streets pink. He seemed to enjoy our laughing at his coloring.

Sometimes when Mama needed to sit down to rest her feet she would color with us. We each wanted her to color a picture in our coloring book, because her coloring was what we hoped ours to be. She often told us riddles, poems, or stories, all of which she seemed to have in endless supply, as we worked at the big round table in the front room. ৶

CHAPTER 22

ANGELS UNAWARE

The Great Northern Railroad fascinated us children. Trains roared past the entire length of our farm day and night. On rare still days we heard their whistle at Biddle's crossing east of us and at the railroad crossing at the west end of our farm. We marveled that the trains traveled with predictability. One train came by every day just before noon. Papa called it "The Gravy Train." Trains came from the east and from the west, yet, they never collided. Who was it that coordinated the travel for the trains? Who stayed awake all night working on the trains and who traveled on the passenger trains?

When we played near the railroad we hurried closer to the tracks to wave at the engineers and passengers. Most of the time, they waved back. We all knew that we wanted to travel on the trains when we grew up. Willie had left Glasgow on a train, and Mrs. Clark traveled by train when she returned to Minneapolis for a visit. Uncle Abby, Papa's brother in Missouri, worked for the Frisco Railway. Sometimes one of the cars on a freight train said, "Ship it on Frisco."

We thought it special to have a penny flattened by a train. Nathan would carry a penny for each of us and place in on a rail. We girls were strictly forbidden to get close to the tracks for any reason. After the train passed he collected our pennies. No two ever looked the same. We couldn't spend the penny now, but, none-the-less, it seemed more valuable.

We knew that "passengers" traveling on the freight trains did so illegally—in the eyes of the railroad companies. They were hobos, or as we children called them, "bums." Railroad boxcars were their homes, their only homes. Some still searched for jobs, some had given up searching for jobs, and some, misfits, had never collected themselves enough to search for jobs.

Mama and Papa thought it a travesty that some of the hobos were WWII veterans who had returned from the war and could not find jobs. Women and men who did not serve our country had acquired the jobs the veterans had held before the war. Out of options, they joined the hobos, and "riding the rails" became a new way of life for them. The railroad companies treated them cruelly, and did everything possible to discourage their traveling on their freight trains.

"How does it hurt the railroad, if hobos ride in the freight cars?" Papa wondered.

Hobos sometimes begged for food in towns and rummaged through trash. Other times they walked from town or bailed out of a boxcar before reaching town. Then they begged for food from farmers. They especially liked to find an underpass where they could spread out their hobo belongings, search for food, and, perhaps, build a fire and spend the night beneath an underpass such as the one that led from our farm to the road.

The divisions of our underpass, created by concrete supports, furnished a perfect place for hobos. We girls were never to go close to it in summer. By the time school started many of the hobos had already headed south, and they seldom returned before the school year ended.

Hobos wrote on the concrete supports often using symbols we could not understand. One symbol we did understand was a crude drawing of a cat. This meant that food could be found at our house. And the hobos came, always one at a time. Mama and Papa agreed that they should be treated with kindness and respect and fed a good meal. Mama had a standard meal she prepared for a hobo: milk, coffee, oatmeal, homemade bread, jam, eggs, and bacon or ham.

She seemed totally unafraid of the hobos. Perhaps it was her confidence in her ability to shoot the pistol that she kept in the cupboard, wield a knife, or use the hot water she kept on the stove in a teakettle. But more than that, she just believed hobos meant no harm. She called them "Angels Unawares" from the Bible verse, Hebrews 13: 2, "Be not forgetful to entertain strangers, for thereby some have entertained angels unawares."

Mama's work schedule was intensely busy, but she never seemed to resent fixing a meal for a hobo as an intrusion into her time. She was keenly interested in people, all people, whatever their station in life. She always said that every person had a story. Some told their stories enthusiastically, and others only with Mama's kind interest and respectful prodding. We could be sure that when a hobo called we would hear their story at supper.

The warning to us girls was that at the first sight of a hobo walking the quarter-mile road from the underpass to our house, we were to run to tell Mama and disappear completely until she told us he was gone. At times when Nathan was present, he would make sure we girls were hidden, and then go to the house from time to time to check on Mama and the hobo.

Once warned, Mama began the hobo's meal, then stepped out to watch him walk toward the house. She declared that she could tell by a hobo's walk whether or not he was crazy. One hot day a hobo wearing an overcoat walked toward our house. She watched for a moment. "He's crazy as a bedbug!" she pronounced before going into the house to prepare for him.

While we were eating supper, Mama told us about that day's hobo. Yes, he was crazy. The convoluted story he told about serving under General Patton in WWII was totally false. She believed that the hobo, who liked to call himself "Mr. Wizard," was crazy before the war, and he could never have passed a physical, even as desperate as they were for soldiers. The only part of his story she found credible was that he had escaped from the insane asylum in Deer Lodge.

Mama laughed, "It was in Deer Lodge that they installed wireless electricity in his head. Now he is able to intercept classified information going to and from the White House. He is off to confer with President Truman about world affairs."

He left with Mama's blessings for his mission.

$\cdots \circ \cdots$

Willie had not liked Montana winters, and Sherman referred to northeastern Montana as "the armpit of the world" without ever having seen the rest of the world. But, Lewis and Clark, during their exploration of the Louisiana Purchase, saw the area differently. They had camped about eighteen miles from present day Glasgow as they traveled west. They liked it so much that they returned to it as their party made their way back to Washington D.C. to report to President Thomas Jefferson. It was Lewis and Clark who named the Milk River. It looked to them to be "the color of a cup of tea admixture of a tablespoon of milk."

Prehistoric animals had roamed northeastern Montana millions of years ago. Much later buffalos and Indians inhabited the land, never imagining that one day life as they knew it would end. The end was brought about by strange looking men with white skin. Many of the white men were greedy and ruthless—they killed the buffalo and confiscated the land. Sherman said this was a big mistake. The white men should have let the Indians keep their land. Not because stealing their land was immoral, but because it was such a godforsaken place to live.

The ghosts of all previous life in this remote area could never have imagined what would take place in the 1930s. Ten thousand workers, most formerly unemployed, were hired to build the Fort Peck Dam. Service workers followed, as did the families of many workers. The population swelled to fifty thousand people. The Public Works Administration, part of President Roosevelt's New Deal, began construction on the world's largest hydraulic earth-filled dam.

The Missouri River winds around on its way southeast to the Mississippi River. Fort Peck Dam was built on the Missouri River at a place where it winds northward. The dam, located eighteen miles from Glasgow, faces northwest toward Glasgow and the Milk River, which flows into the Missouri River. Our farm was on the banks of the Milk River in the Missouri River and Milk River floodplain. Here, eighteen miles from Glasgow, the Missouri River flows from south to north, so the dam would face Glasgow and the Milk River Valley in the Missouri River flood plain.

This worried Mama and Papa, especially Mama. She knew that the construction of the dam had not been without problems and loss of life. If there were problems then, there could be problems now. Nothing could convince Mama that anything made by man was infallible. She lay awake at night with the knowledge that a man-made, earth-filled dam holding back a 135-mile-long lake was only eighteen miles away.

In the event that the dam should break, how would those of us in the flood plain be notified? The radio? Who sits by their radio all the time? The phone? For years we, like most of our neighbors, had no phone. This was a topic Mama often broached when visiting with neighbors. To her surprise most of the neighbors had never given a thought to the dam's breaking. Nor to how we would be notified in the event that it did break. She thought this to be very naïve.

We children believed, as Papa, that Mama spent far too much time worrying. By this time I had lived long enough to see that most of her worries had been for naught. Yet, the true story Sherman had read to us from his high school literature book about the 1889 Johnstown Flood, did weigh somewhat on my mind. The story told of a dam's failing and the wall of water that surged down river causing rapid destruction of everything in its path.

When Mama read an article about skywriting she felt sure that this was how we would be warned of the dam's breaking. Words were formed by smoke trails left by airplanes. A municipal airport used by wealthy ranchers and businessmen who owned small planes was located near Glasgow. Some of the pilots of these small planes appeared to fly for the sheer fun of it. They often flew over our house and performed aerobatics. When we saw that the plane was not just making a routine flight, we stopped what we were doing and watched.

The planes swerved and rolled; circled in graceful loop-the-loops; and sometimes, as we held our breath, plunged downward only to pull up sharply.

One summer day we heard an airplane. Papa and Sherman were irrigating the alfalfa field near the house, Nathan and we girls were weeding the garden, and Mama was cooking in the kitchen. When the airplane paused overhead we were sure we would get to see some aerobatics. Instead, white smoke emitted from the plane. It must be on fire!

We ran toward the house and yelled for Mama to come out. She ran out drying her hands on her apron. Papa and Sherman, still holding their shovels, hurried to the house.

"Pray for the pilot!" Mama directed.

The pilot, though, seemed to have control of the plane as he left a straight line of smoke against Montana's blue sky.

"Skywriting!" Mama told us.

We were awed as the pilot continued to maneuver his plane. He added a circle to the top half of the straight line to form the letter "P."

"Oh, my God!" Mama cried, "He is going to write "PECK DAM BROKE.""

"Just wait," Papa's voice was filled with concern. I imagined all of us, our buildings, and our animals pitching up and down in roiling water—just like the Johnstown Flood.

Next the pilot wrote "E."

"Pray!" Mama cried. I prayed, but I could not take my eyes off the plane.

We all stood and stared at the sky as the pilot wrote another "P."

"PEP!" We exclaimed weak with relief. The pilot was not writing PECK DAM.

We watched as he wrote, "PEPSI COLA."

We later learned that PEPSI COLA was being written in skies across America. Their business increased significantly, but not from us. Mama said that, because they scared us to death, we would never, ever buy Pepsi Cola again. We rarely bought pop, so the company didn't notice the loss of our business. ✍

CHAPTER 23

Two Mothers' Nightmares

Grace often suffered from what Mama called "school sickness." I loved going to school, Sherman seemed to like school, Nathan mildly disliked going to school, but Grace intensely disliked going to school. Grace often complained of an upset stomach, headache, or some other ailment on school mornings. Too many mornings when it was time to get up, Grace claimed to be sick. This was difficult for Mama. Was, or was not, Grace actually ill? We did not have a phone; therefore, Mama had no way of learning what was happening with Grace once she was at school. The result was she missed much school. When Grace perked up after we all left and she felt we were on the school bus, Mama knew Grace had "school sickness."

When any of us children became ill we knew we would get the castor oil treatment, unless we suffered from the stomach flu. Grace had "school sickness" so often that she was spared frequent doses of castor oil. The ill child would be lying abed after confessing to be sick to find Mama and Papa working as a team to deliver the castor oil treatment. First Papa came with a glass of too much clear, thick castor oil, and Mama came behind him with a chaser of orange juice. We were given the glass of castor oil and told that we would drink it, which we did with a display of terrible faces and retching to convey what we thought of such treatment. I was never sure if Mama actually thought the castor oil helped, or if its purpose was to deter our feigning illnesses. Mama also believed that bed rest was the best healer, and none of us liked to stay in bed when we were well, so this too made us think twice about making false claims.

One morning when Grace suffered what appeared to be one of her frequent bouts of "school sickness" Mama threatened her with castor oil, but Grace declared she really was sick this time; sure enough, her temperature was one hundred one degrees. Grace must have the flu. Throughout the day Grace worsened, her temperature shot up, and the inside of her throat was swollen. When she began talking about all the calendars she was seeing on the walls Mama realized she was delirious.

Mama held Grace as Papa drove Shiny Eyes to Dr. Agneberg's office. Dr. Agneberg was puzzled; although he did not think this to be a typical case of the flu, he prescribed medication and sent Grace home. When Grace failed to respond as expected to her medication, she was taken to see Dr. Agneberg again. Mama, who often read medical books, asked Dr. Agneberg if Grace might have leukemia, and Mama interpreted his being noncommittal and uncertain to mean he thought Grace might have leukemia. Blood tests were sent off, but the results would not be back for two weeks.

Mama was so sick with worry and fear that Papa kept Sherman home from school to help with farm work while Papa spent more time inside helping Mama with cooking and general housework. This gave Mama more time to devote to tending Grace, and it allowed Papa to keep a close eye on Mama's fragile emotional state. It did no good for Papa to remind Mama that Dr. Agneberg did not say he thought Grace had leukemia; all Dr. Agneberg said was that without tests he could not venture any diagnosis.

Before the two weeks passed when Mama and Papa could learn the results of Grace's tests they were both stretched thin. Their visit to Dr. Agneberg brought enormous relief. Tests showed that Grace did not have leukemia, but she did have infectious mononucleosis with which she was still quite ill. It was contagious and now Mama worried the rest of us might catch it; however, all but Grace stayed miraculously well.

Spring arrived while Grace lay abed inside, and now after a month of rest she was allowed to venture outside for short times on warm days. Much of summer passed before Grace seemed to have her strength back, so when Grace was out Dolly and I stayed close to the house and played gentle games in which Grace could participate. Grace felt the only good thing about her illness was that she missed so much school. Fortunately, Grace learned quickly and Mama helped her to catch up before school started again.

☙ • • ○ • • ❧

One evening while we were eating Mama's rice pudding for dessert, Mama and Papa were talking about a mystery book, *The Circular Staircase*, by Mary Roberts Rinehart. They both particularly enjoyed reading good mystery stories. Sherman had just finished reading Edgar Allan Poe's famous short story, "The Tell Tale Heart," and he had repeated the plot to us girls making it just as scary as he could with gestures and voice changes. Sherman, Mama, and Papa talked about "The Tell Tale Heart" and who the old man was that the narrator murdered.

"Tell us about the Missouri boy that was murdered on his homestead." Nathan requested of Papa.

I didn't know the boy, but I saw him at a couple of dances. His name was Jeff Potter. He was in his early twenties, and he had been on his homestead for about two years. I was never sure where he came from in Missouri, but most people just referred to him as the Missouri boy when they mentioned him. My friend Bill Costin became acquainted with the Missouri boy, and he wondered if he would be able to make it on the homestead. Potter came from Missouri with enough money to put up a homestead shack and a barn. He drove up from Missouri in a wagon pulled by a fine team of horses.

The next thing I heard about Potter was that he had a man from Canada living with him. Costin didn't know anything about the Canadian, but Costin said that with someone to help Potter he would be more apt to be able to make a go of it on the homestead.

About wheat harvest time Costin told me that the Missouri boy had left and gone back to Missouri. The Canadian who had been living with Potter was now living on Potter's place alone and driving Potter's team with the wagon hauling wheat. Potter had been gone now for some time, so he hadn't just gone for a short visit. Costin thought it strange that Potter left without his team and wagon and without telling anybody he was going. Potter made some money every year by hauling wheat, so we figured he would be here hauling wheat now, if he planned to stay.

"Maybe the Canadian bought him out," Costin suggested.

When I went over to help Costin with his wheat he had some surprising news. News spread fast on the prairie, because, even though it was a large area, there were few people. You knew about people a lot farther away than you would in other places.

Costin told me that Sheriff Benson from Glasgow and Potter's mother were going to everyone who knew Potter and asking a lot of questions. It seems Potter never made it back to Missouri. His mother hadn't heard from him for a long time, too long. Then she had a dream that her boy had been murdered. She came to Glasgow to find out what had happened to Jeff.

Sheriff Benson didn't want to go on a wild goose chase fifty miles away, because an old lady in Missouri had a dream, but Mrs. Potter was insistent.

In fact, Costin said that Mrs. Potter told Sheriff Benson she would be in his office every day until he agreed to take her to Potter's homestead. By the fourth day she wore him down.

The Canadian happened to be at home when they arrived at Potter's homestead, so he was questioned. He was certain Potter told him he was headed to Missouri. Maybe with the money Potter had from the sale of his team and wagon, he stopped for awhile to do some gambling. The Canadian winked at Sheriff Benson and added, 'or whatever young lads do with money in their pocket.'

When Sheriff Benson and Mrs. Potter got back into the car Mrs. Potter said, 'He killed Jeff!'

Sheriff Benson thought the Canadian's story seemed logical, and by now he was thinking Mrs. Potter might be a touch off.

When they returned to Glasgow, Sheriff Benson suggested Mrs. Potter return to Missouri. Jeff might already be there, or there might be a letter from him.

The next morning Mrs. Potter came to the sheriff's office again. She wanted an investigation of her son's murder. And again she brought her lunch and told Sheriff Benson she would be at his office every day, all day, until he investigated Jeff's murder. Nothing Sheriff Benson said dissuaded her. Finally, he agreed to go out one more time.

This time he and Mrs. Potter visited Potter's neighbors. None of them believed the Canadian had enough money to buy Potter's team and wagon. They were under the impression that the reason Jeff took the Canadian in was because the Canadian didn't have any money, and that the Canadian had agreed to help Potter in order to stay with him.

This gave Sheriff Benson something to chew on. They went back to Potter's homestead, and Sheriff Benson talked to the Canadian again. The Canadian claimed he came to stay with Potter only to help Potter. The Canadian had money, but, no, it hadn't been in a bank, because he didn't believe in banks. He carried is money with him in cash, and that was how he paid Potter. Sheriff Benson looked all around, but nothing seemed amiss. He looked in the barn and around the homestead. All seemed well. The Canadian was casual, but he was sorry Mrs. Potter was so worried.

Sheriff Benson and Mrs. Potter returned to Glasgow. A summer storm rolled in and welcome rain was falling. Sheriff Benson dropped Mrs. Potter at the hotel. Again, Mrs. Potter was urged to go back to Missouri and wait to see if Jeff had sent word or had come home.

The next morning Mrs. Potter came to Sheriff Benson's office with her lunch. Her son had been murdered by the Canadian, and until she felt his murder had been properly investigated, she would be here every day.

So Sheriff Benson and Mrs. Potter drove back to Potter's homestead. The Canadian reported a good rain mixed with hail had fallen during the night. The Canadian regretted giving a young lad so much cash. Now he worried that perhaps the lad had been robbed.

Sheriff Benson began another search of the homestead. He went through everything in the house including the Canadian's things. Mrs. Potter noticed a bundle of letters that had been sent to her son, including letters from his sweetheart. She did not believe Jeff would have left the letters, if he had not intended to return. The Canadian thought, perhaps, Potter had been in such a hurry to see his sweetheart that he had overlooked the letters as he left.

Sheriff Benson told the Canadian to stay in the house. First, Sheriff Benson went to the barn with Mrs. Potter stepping beside him. Her shrewd eyes watched every move Sheriff Benson made. Satisfied that nothing in the barn seemed amiss, Sheriff Benson followed by Mrs. Potter, who proved to be more lively than she looked, began walking back and forth across the yard, barnyard, and garden. Again, nothing seemed amiss.

Sheriff Benson expanded his search going carefully looking at the ground. Sheriff Benson now walked in ever widening circles beyond the area he had already searched. This brought Sheriff Benson and Mrs. Potter to a small, somewhat brushy gully south of the buildings. Sheriff Benson walked slowly looking at the ground. He spotted the end of a belt sticking up. He pulled the belt, but it did not budge. It must be attached to something heavy.

Sheriff Benson went back to the barn, picked up a shovel, and they returned to the belt. Sheriff Benson began digging. Jeff had been buried fully clothed in a shallow grave. Had the grave been deeper, or had it not rained, the Canadian would have gotten by with murder.

"I have always said dreams are more than 'just dreams,'" Mama definitely believed dreams have relevant meaning. She read many books about interpreting dreams and what dreams meant, and she often asked us to tell her our dreams so she could interpret them.

"Weren't there an unusual number of murders on the prairie?" Sherman asked.

"There were," Papa affirmed, "And I have wondered why. I concluded that, first of all, some of the people who came to homestead were simply no good and they hadn't been able to fit into the communities where they lived before coming west. Second, there was little law enforcement for large areas of land. Remember, most of us didn't even have cars. My homestead was fifty miles from Glasgow where the sheriff had his office. Valley County is a big county—too big for one sheriff. People who might not have committed a crime if they thought they would be caught, felt they would never be caught on the prairie. I have often wondered how many literally got away with murder."

"After such a sad story I think we need a little levity before the girls go to bed," Mama told us. "This is a story about pig rustling."

Back in Iowa where they raise lots of pigs they have pig rustlers. The sheriff's department was determined to stop the rustling, so they set up a roadblock from time to time. Well, Joe Smith owned a little farm with few pigs and his way of adding more pigs was to take them from a farm that raised lots of pigs near Des Moines. One night Joe Smith, his brother John, and his wife set out to steal a pig before the roadblock was set up. Once at the big pig farm they stole a little white pig, because it would fit into their car. Mrs. Smith sat in the back seat holding the pig, and Joe Smith and his brother John sat in the front seat.

They came to the roadblock that had been set up earlier than usual. They couldn't just let the pig out, because they would be seen doing so.

"Quick," Joe Smith told Mrs. Smith, "Do something with the pig."

Mrs. Smith grabbed some baby clothes that had been left in the car and quickly put them on the pig and held the pig on her lap.

A policeman shined a light into the car. He asked Joe Smith and John Smith their names. Then he shined his light into the back seat. He asked Mrs. Smith her name. Next, while all the Smiths held their breaths, he asked the pig its name. Just then the pig said, 'Oink!'

"All right go on," the policeman said.

After the Smith's drove off the policeman turned to the other policeman.

"I've seen a lot of ugly babies, but that Oink Smith is the ugliest baby I have ever seen!" ❧

CHAPTER 24

CYCLONE

Every spring we girls clamored to ride in the truck with Papa to the spillway on the canal. All winter the ditches throughout our farm stood empty of water. When spring crops required irrigation, the ditches must be filled. We girls thought little about the crops, as we focused on the endless amount of entertainment the ditches of water provided for us.

Papa drove to the canal road on the road bordering the west end of our farm. We girls sat in the truck while Papa pulled up the spillway boards. Cold water rushed with a whoosh from the canal toward the west end of The Big Ditch that carried water along the southern border of our farm to our farm's main ditch. The Big Ditch and the main ditch were kept full of water all summer. A network of smaller ditches would be filled from the main ditch only as water was needed for specific fields.

We returned home and waited and waited for the water to flow into the main ditch located next to our house and buildings. Weeks earlier Nathan had retrieved our jumping poles that had been stored for winter. Now that I was eight years old, my goal this summer was to do as Nathan did—jump with ease across the main ditch when it was filled with water.

Most days we had been practicing with our jumping poles. Nathan had again showed us how a part of jumping successfully with a pole was being able to determine where to hold onto it for the height or distance we wanted to jump. We began our practice with a rope. Two of us held the rope loosely at the desired height while one of us readied to jump. Pole in hand we raced toward the rope, placed the pole firmly on the ground, and leaped up and over it. Well, we didn't always leap over the rope. This resulted in falls, scrapes, bruises, and, sometimes blood, but no broken bones.

The week before Papa was to open the spillway, Nathan had declared that Grace and I had graduated to practicing jumping the empty ditch. Dolly would help Nathan give us helpful suggestions. Grace's determination to do what I did spurred her to success. I was taller than Grace, but skinny; Grace was slightly shorter than I, but she was huskier. And, she was willing to work relentlessly to reach her goals. This forced me to work harder than I wished to try to keep ahead of her.

Finally, the water arrived. Only a shallow amount of water covered the bottom of the ditch until water reached the end of it; then water started backing up until it was filled. Nathan jumped across the ditch with his jumping pole. The water was cold, and I didn't want to get soaked.

Jumping the ditch full of water proved more challenging than jumping it dry. Grace and I spent much of our first afternoon landing in the ditch with a big splash. Running and jumping in wet clothes made our task more difficult, but we did not give up, and within a week we successfully jumped the ditch most of the time.

Family friends drove out from town to visit. They parked their car across the ditch by the footbridge that led to the house. Mama stood visiting with them by their car before asking them to come into the house. An audience! After all of my hard work learning to jump across the ditch I was anxious to wow them with my new-found ability. I retrieved my jumping pole and raced toward them at high speed. I noticed the surprised look on their faces as I tore toward them with my pole in hand. In one smooth motion I set the pole in the middle of the five-foot-wide ditch as I had practiced; then vaulted into the air before their wide eyes. I rose to the middle of the ditch where, somehow, my momentum ceased. Hands holding tightly to the pole, I wavered as my body hovered around the jumping pole for what seemed a long time. Rather than landing triumphantly at their feet, I splashed down into the ditch. All that landed at their feet was water my fall had displaced from the ditch. I grabbed my pole, slogged from the ditch, and retreated faster than I had arrived. Later I heard Mama trying to tell Papa about the incident. She laughed so hard she could barely talk.

One hot summer day we girls talked about how good it would feel to go to The Big Ditch to swim in the cool water. Nathan was helping Papa and Sherman work on Combs' farm across the river, and we girls were not allowed to go close to The Big Ditch unless Nathan was with us. At noon when the men came to the house for dinner we begged for Nathan to be able to stay with us so we could go "swimming." None of us three could swim, but Nathan, who swam, could supervise us and give instructions. Papa relented. After dinner when

Papa and Sherman left to row across the river to work on Mr. Combs' farm, Nathan stayed with us.

We walked west along our farm road, and cut across a hay field to one of our favorite spots on our farm. Here The Big Ditch bank was wider and grassy. A young growth of gray-green willows lined its sides. We could smell the willows, water, and cattails. Soft green moss floated up from the ditch bottom and the cattails grew in shallow water. Sometimes garter snakes hurried away as we arrived, and always frogs moved away but kept an eye on us. Only the willows separated us from the trains traveling to and from Glasgow. We felt confident that nobody on the trains would ever guess that children played so near to the railroad tracks.

We girls laughed as we splashed and played in the water paying little attention to Nathan's directions for swimming. Clouds began filling the sky. Soon it looked as though it could rain any minute. We girls didn't care; we were already wet. Rather than swimming Nathan sat on the bank, and he had no intentions of getting wet. We begged to stay, but he insisted that we go. When we were in sight of the house and farm buildings the air seemed filled with an odd light. A white oblong cloud underneath the dark sky tumbled over and over rolling in the direction of the house. We had never seen this, and we were filled with apprehension. A sharp wind came. Nathan told us to run to the house.

Dolly refused to run. Grace and I started to run, but when we saw Dolly standing steadfast, we stopped. Nathan begged her to run, he tugged on her arm, but she resisted, and, as a last resort, he threatened to hit her. Nathan had never hit one of us—even when we deserved it. Grace and I started yelling at Dolly to run. She sat down. Nathan tried to get her up. She was too heavy for him. By now wind was whipping up dirt and lashing the trees. We knew something was terribly wrong.

We could hear Mama screaming from the yard for us to hurry home. Just then we saw Papa and Sherman racing up from the river bank behind the house. They both ran toward us as they yelled for us to run. Grace and I started toward the house, but Nathan stood helplessly beside Dolly as she sat. When Papa and Sherman reached us Sherman grabbed Grace's hand, Papa scooped up Dolly, and, catching up with me, Nathan grabbed my hand.

"Run to the cellar!" Mama commanded as we neared the house. Sherman let go of Grace's hand and ran ahead to open the heavy cellar door. The cellar was near the granary and chicken house. Most of the chickens that could always be found scratching and looking for food had disappeared. Only the goslings were visible. Seeing us run toward the cellar, they ran yeeping to us. They raced to the open door and tumbled down the steps ahead of us.

Sherman braced the cellar door with all his might until we were all safely down the steps. Papa helped hold the door until Sherman and he were safely down enough steps; then the cellar door slammed shut with a bang. We listened to the loud frightening roar of high winds above us.

When Papa lighted the lantern that he kept hanging from the ceiling I saw Mama's face. It was filled with fear.

"What's happening?" I cried.

"It's a cyclone," Mama's voice was subdued. "Pray that we don't lose everything we have."

We did each pray silently, but fervently. We knew about cyclones from Mama and Papa's stories of their earlier years on the prairie. Cyclone winds drove straw into boards; scattered barns, outbuildings, and houses across the prairie; killed people, poultry, and livestock. Cyclones even plucked chickens clean of their feathers.

We all sat silently in our quiet cellar listening to the roar overhead. We wondered what was happening, and we tried not to imagine what could be happening. The goslings felt safe enough to begin exploring. Our two resident lizards, Izzy and Lizzy, scurried out of reach of the gosling's pecking bills.

When the sound of the wind abated somewhat, Papa lifted the cellar door to look out. We hardly breathed fearful of what he might see.

"The house is there," he called down. We exhaled.

"Give thanks to God," Mama told us.

At last the sound of the wind stopped altogether and Papa opened the cellar door for us while we climbed up the steps. We and the goslings bounded out and looked around. Tree leaves plastered everything, many limbs lay scattered about, and some trees had been uprooted, yet all of the buildings stood firm! We offered prayers of thanks.

Once Mama recovered, she looked at Dolly. "Why didn't you come when you were called?"

"Because, Ruth and Grace were teasing me." Dolly was unrepentant.

"I don't care what is happening. When I call you, you come, and you come straightaway. Do you hear me? You could have been blown to the Bench!"

The Bench was prairie land up and out of Milk River Valley.

·⟨⟩· · · o · · ·⟨⟩·

We girls were still eating breakfast when Sherman returned to the house after working with the irrigation in the west alfalfa field. He carried a bundle wrapped in a colorful shawl.

"I found this under the west end bridge," Sherman told Mama.

The road to the spillway at the west end of our farm had a bridge over The Big Ditch. There was room for us children to get under the bridge on either side, if we scrunched down. A man could crawl under the bridge and be out of sight and out of the weather.

We watched as Sherman unrolled the bundle. In it were one pair of men's pants, two shirts, and two pairs of socks. In the middle of the clothes was a Bible. Mama looked at the Bible, and saw that it was printed in Spanish.

"It wasn't a hobo who left this. It was a Mexican beet worker." she told Sherman.

She looked for a name in the Bible, but there was none. Between two of the pages was a picture of a young Mexican woman and a little girl.

"This must be his wife and daughter," Mama assumed. "Now who would leave their clothes and Bible, unless, of course, they planned to return to get them?"

She directed Sherman to rewrap the bundle and take it back to exactly where he found it, so the owner could come and get it. Every day for the first week Sherman checked on the bundle under the bridge. Later he went less often to check it. The bundle was always there.

As time passed Mama and Papa discussed what they should do. They decided to tell the sheriff, but they did not want to move the bundle before the end of beet harvest, lest it would still be claimed. They never knew what action, if any, the sheriff took. Mama had decided that the owner of the bundle had been murdered. It was unlikely that any man having so little would not have come back to claim it, and no man would have willingly left his Bible with a picture of his wife and daughter. In fact, Mama concluded, it was probably not the man who owned the Bible and clothes who put them there, but rather the murderer who had put his victim's bundle under the bridge.

Mama and Papa returned to town so she could share her theory with the sheriff. She was disappointed when the sheriff agreed with Papa who suggested there could be other, less dire, happenings that prevented the man from returning to get his clothes and Bible. Mama held fast to her murder theory. She fretted about the young wife and mother who awaited the return of her husband in vain. ⟨⟩

◆

CHAPTER 25

PINKY, ROVER, AND BIDDLE THE BULL

Mr. Biddle drove up to our house just before milking time. Some inhumane, despicable person had dumped two pups near Mr. Biddle's railroad crossing. The pups had found their way across the railroad tracks and taken up residence under his granary.

"If I could catch the SOB low enough to dump animals, especially pups, out to starve, I'd kick his you-know-what all the way to California!" I had never seen Mr. Biddle angry before.

"I just wondered if you could take the pups?" he asked Papa.

Right now we only had one dog Lulu, but two dogs, if you counted Buck, Mr. Biddle's German shepherd, who spent most of his time at our house. Mama felt we girls were safer because Buck followed us everywhere.

Papa looked at us girls and Nathan. He half-way smiled, "Would you like to have the pups?"

The next morning after chores Sherman stayed home to irrigate, and we three girls, Nathan, and Papa drove to Mr. Biddle's farm to catch the pups. The granary rested on supports about eighteen inches off the ground. The pups hid under the granary too far back for us to reach them. Nathan and I lay on our stomachs and wriggled toward the pups as we talked our version of "puppy talk" to them. It took a long time, but gradually they moved toward us whimpering with fear and hope. Finally, we each held a puppy, and using our elbows we inched backwards until we were out from under the granary.

We brought the puppies into the house and Mama fed and examined them. She found them to be healthy. She declared they were a male and a female, part-collie mutts. Mama declared that since I was nine years old, I was old enough to be responsible for taking care of a puppy. The female would be my dog. The male would be Nathan's dog, but really both dogs belonged to all of us.

Mama told us to give them a name that had at least one long vowel sound, because dogs could recognize long vowel sounds more readily than other sounds. Nathan named his pup "Rover," while I sought for just the right name for mine. Her soft reddish colored fur reminded me of the librarian in Glasgow's Public Library—Pinky Putz. Her hair was the same color as my pup. The library was our favorite place in Glasgow, and we loved Mrs. Putz. My pup's name would be "Pinky." Mama said that the "y" on the end sounded like a long "e," so Pinky was a good name.

Buck quickly adopted Pinky and Rover, and now that the pups stayed with us girls wherever we went, Buck spent even more time at our house. Mama said that Buck had a strong maternal instinct. He would lie patiently while kittens climbed and played on him. Mama could even leave little chicks that had no mother with Buck. They peeped to him, hopped around and on him, and snuggled up against him to sleep.

We knew that Buck roamed freely around our neighborhood, but he came to our house often enough that we were alarmed when several days passed without our seeing him. We all worried that he might have been run over by a car or a train. When we learned that Mr. Biddle hadn't seen him either, Papa, Sherman, and Nathan searched for Buck, but without success.

Another week passed before Buck came limping and crawling to our house. He was badly injured. When Mama examined him she found that he had been shot in the head. We were all outraged! What dastardly person could have shot Buck? Buck who was the most gentle and loving of all dogs; Buck who would not harm anything, had been so terribly harmed.

Mama nursed Buck back to a measure of health over a period of time, but he was blind in one eye, and he never fully regained his strength.

෫෨· · · o · · ·෨෧

At first Pinky and Rover were afraid of our dozen or so cows, but soon the dogs followed us into the corral at milk time and made friends with the cows that we girls regarded as big pets. It was easy to tell the cows apart; they were of various breeds and dubious bloodlines and no two looked alike. Even their personalities were different. Mama referred to them as a "colorful herd of girls." What each cow had in common was that Papa only kept the ones that produced abundant milk with high cream content. We girls named them: Lady, Roany, Nancy, Martha ... .

Martha, who was the highest milk producer, was clearly the matriarch. She was smaller than most of them, but every cow deferred to sweet, gentle Martha.

When hay or corn stalks were fed to the cattle, Martha could displace any cow from her eating spot simply by walking to her and stepping into her place. The other cow would look at Martha and simply move away. It was Martha who led the cows to the barn when it was milking time.

One peculiar characteristic amused us. Before the cows came into the barn to go to the manger with stanchions, a fresh ration of dairy feed was poured into the manger. Cows loved the molasses smelling dairy feed! Each cow went to her own stanchion to begin eating. If a cow went to the wrong stanchion, she was quickly displaced by the owner; however, if the first cow had as much as stuck her nose in the dairy feed the second cow would throw up her head in indignation and refuse to touch it. It was necessary to place a layer of fresh dairy feed on the top. Only then would it be eaten.

Bulls on our farm must be changed out frequently so the cattle did not become inbred. Papa planned to sell our bull as soon as the bull he had purchased from Mr. Biddle was old enough to service our cows. The new bull was only a calf when Papa had brought him home—a beautiful pure white calf. We had named him Biddle, and he had quickly become our pet. Even though he was almost as big as Martha, we still brushed and petted him, and picked what we believed to be the best grass to feed to him. We sat on him as he lay down, just as we did the milk cows.

Nathan told us that if Papa had started picking up Biddle every day when he was a calf, he would still be able to pick up Biddle when he was full grown. When we asked Mama if this were true, she just laughed.

One late summer day Nathan was helping Papa and Sherman irrigate the east sugar beet field, and I was in charge of Grace and Dolly. Without asking Mama, or even telling her, I decided to take Grace and Dolly to a grove of box elder trees in the woods that we called the Pretty Trees. As usual Pinky and Rover walked with us as we followed the cow trail along the river bank leading east from the house.

All the cattle were near the Bee Tree. They were grazing, lying down, or just chewing their cuds in the warm afternoon sun. Biddle stood across our path blocking our way. Rather than walk around him, I shooshed him to get him to move off the trail. Biddle decided he did not want to be shooshed. He started shaking his head. My experience with animals told me that this was not good. Alarmed, Pinky and Rover barked at Biddle. Next he lowered his head and bellowed a low ugly bellow, unlike any I had ever heard from him. This was definitely a bad sign. Pinky and Rover barked aggressively. Trying to sound as though I were in charge, I stood my ground and calmly, but sternly, told Grace and Dolly to run to the fence—fast.

Next Biddle began throwing back dirt with his front feet as he bellowed and shook his head. He was getting ready to attack! Pinky and Rover beside me partially raised their front feet off the ground in a frenzy of barking. Grace and Dolly were still standing behind me.

"Run!" I screamed at them, "Run like hell!" Grace tore off running to the fence, but Dolly stood rooted to the spot.

Using my strongest language and loudest voice I screamed at Dolly, "Goddammit, Dolly! Run!" She did not move.

I knew that Biddle would charge any second, and he was going to kill us both. Pinky and Rover darted a short way toward Biddle, barking and springing sideways and back and forth. Only slightly distracted, Biddle bellowed and tossed his head at them, but his focus was on Dolly and me. I continued to scream at her. I was responsible for Dolly. She was too heavy for me to move, and I could not leave her.

Just then I looked up to see Papa flying over the fence with his irrigation shovel in hand. He was followed closely by Sherman and Nathan. Just as Papa reached Dolly, Nathan grabbed my hand and we and the dogs tore off to the fence and rolled under it. Papa and Sherman waved their irrigation shovels and faced Biddle as they backed to the fence with Dolly under Papa's arm. Papa placed Dolly safely on the other side of the fence and he and Sherman climbed over.

We all walked to the house. My legs were so weak they almost refused to support me, but I did not want anybody to see how shaken I was. When Papa told Mama what happened she blanched and sat down. She said it was providential the men were irrigating in a field near enough to the cow trail that they could hear Biddle bellowing, the dogs barking, and me screaming. She also believed it was providential that we had Pinky and Rover with us. She and Papa agreed that Pinky and Rover may have distracted Biddle just enough to save Dolly and me.

Papa told Sherman and Nathan to finish irrigating the field. He was going to town to buy a bullring and a chain. That evening when the cows and Biddle came to the corral, Biddle was put into a stanchion and tied off with ropes so he could not move. Papa inserted the bullring through Biddle's nostrils and attached the chain to the ring. The chain dragged on the ground, and Biddle must learn to walk without stepping on it. He would never run again.

Biddle, not yet full-grown, but very much a bull, was no longer our pet.

Mama said that she was definitely going to attend church that next Sunday to give thanks that Biddle did not kill Dolly and me. Grace Bible Chapel was a fundamentalist church with much emphasis on the perils of sin and going to hell. Papa had been raised in a very strict religious home, so much of what happened in Grace Bible Chapel may not have been new to him. Although Mama and Mrs. Clark had attended the Holy Communion Episcopal Church in St. Peter during Mama's childhood, Mrs. Clark was not of a religious nature. "Religion is a crutch," summed up her attitude. Grace Bible Chapel, then, was a radical departure from what Mama knew of church. She called it a "NO!" church. No makeup, no dancing, no movies, no Santa Claus, no Easter bunny. . . . Yet, she complied to a degree with what she considered to be their "outlandish" ideas.

Though the church's attitudes did not match theirs, Mama and Papa liked the people who made up the congregation. They had serious reservations about Reverend Wall and Mrs. Wall. The Walls' unreasonable expectations of poor Richard and their meting out physical punishment so freely had caused Mama to become almost hostile toward them. Mama nicknamed Richard, "Spanky" Wall, because Mrs. Wall spanked him so often. Mama could never forgive herself for having sent Richard's parents to the Wall's in the first place. "We should have driven him to Lustre ourselves," she often lamented. "Who could have thought they would keep Richard for themselves?"

One of the middle-aged couples from church with whom we visited was Anna and Jake Peters. Anna was the oldest child from a large Mennonite family in Lustre. Jake was not a Mennonite, but he attended Grace Bible Chapel faithfully with Anna. Jake was a nice-seeming, smallish man with a ruddy complexion and pop eyes. Anna was robust and very pleasant, but not pretty, while two of her younger sisters who often attended church with them were quite pretty. It was rumored that Jake had "made a pass" at each of Anna's sisters in turn as they matured. "Gossip!" Mama sniffed. Anna often drove the fifty miles to Lustre and spent lots of time with her family there. Perhaps Jake was lonely when Anna was in Lustre.

On the Sunday after God saved us from Biddle the bull, Reverend Wall stood and spoke on his favorite subject—transgressions and the need to confess our sins before God and man. He held up a stack of letters and looked meaningfully at Jake Peters. He announced that Jake wished to confess.

Jake rose slowly from Anna's side and walked up front mopping his eyes with his handkerchief. Awkwardly and painfully he divulged that he had written a love letter to Lola Penner. Miss Penner was single and beautiful. She was friends with Anna's sisters and as a nurse at the Deaconess Hospital, she worked with and was friends with Mrs. Pratt, my Sunday school teacher. All eyes turned to Miss Penner who sat serenely focusing straight ahead at Mr. Peters.

Reverend Wall shook the bundle of letters at Mr. Peters waiting for him to continue. "Well, it wasn't just one letter. I wrote a lot of love letters to Lola."

First he begged God's forgiveness and that of the congregation; then, tears streaming down his face he begged Anna's forgiveness. Anna shook her head in the affirmative. Jake was forgiven. Perdition had been staved off for the present. Once church ended, Sherman and Nathan climbed into the back of the truck, and the rest of us rode in front.

"To think," Mama said, "I might have stayed home today! I will be staying home next Sunday. I don't approve of offering human sacrifices, and that is what happened to Jake!"

"Well," Papa said, "Jake shouldn't have written the letters, but if Lola found them to be offensive, why did she wait until he wrote so many before she spoke up? She could have put an end to the letters in the beginning."

"I sympathize with Anna." Mama shook her head. "She should never have had to endure the humiliation of his public confession. And, why must he confess to all of us anyway? We're not God, and we're not married to Jake!"

From listening to Mama's stories, I fully understood why it was wrong for Jake to write love letters to Miss Penner, but Grace did not.

"Why shouldn't he write to Miss Penner?" Grace asked.

"He is married to Anna, and the love letters should have been written to Anna," Mama explained. ❧

CHAPTER 26

MAMA'S POINT OF VIEW

My days of endless play came to, what seemed to me, a rude ending. Mama's arthritis was worse, and she needed my help in the kitchen part of the time. Nathan spent most of his time helping Papa and Sherman. Grace and Dolly were old enough to no longer need my constant supervision, if they played near the house.

At first I was rebellious and surly. Mama ignored my unpleasant remarks that, while said in a low voice, were intended to let her know I was not happy about this new arrangement. The situation came to a head one day when she called me to come in and help her. Grace, Dolly, and I were building castles from the gumbo mud in the irrigation ditch that had been drained of most of its water. My castle was big and elaborate, and I wished to finish it.

I sulked into the kitchen. It was almost noon, dinner would soon be ready, and Papa and the boys would come in from the field. Mama continued with last minute dinner preparations while I fussed and complained about not getting to finish my castle. Appearing not to hear me, she pointed to the stack of plates on the counter and told me to set the table.

I would not be ignored. I grabbed too many of the fragile china plates for my small hands to hold.

"I feel like throwing these plates down and breaking them!" I almost shouted.

At that moment, to my horror, all seven of the plates flew from my hands and smashed onto the floor.

I had Mama's attention. She sailed across the kitchen and slapped me across the face. I stood stunned for a few seconds; she had never slapped my face before. Then I howled with indignation—the slap stung, and I had not really meant to throw the plates down.

"I didn't do it on purpose," I wailed.

Mama was unrepentant. "How many times have I told you not to pick up so many plates at one time? Wait until your dad sees this!"

I howled louder. Papa would spank me. How could he believe I did not break the plates intentionally after what I had said? And, worse, he would be disappointed in me.

By now Grace and Dolly, having heard the commotion, stood in the kitchen doorway looking at the broken plates with eyes agog and mouths agape. I began picking up the pieces dreading for Papa and the boys to return. I finished sweeping up the last of the pieces just as I heard them coming in. I continued crying loudly.

Mama told Papa what had happened. He was calm.

"Get out the rest of the plates and some bowls for dinner," he directed. I sobbed as I finished setting the table. Sherman and Nathan washed up for dinner as though this were a regular occurrence.

"I'll go to town and buy some more plates after we eat," was all Papa said. Everybody else visited during dinner while I snuffled waiting for my spanking that I was sure would happen. No spanking came. I needed no spanking to remind me of that day's events—or to stop my complaining about my new role as Mama's helper.

After dinner Papa drove to town and returned with one dozen sturdy metal pie plates. Much to Mama's dismay, that was the end of china plates on our table.

I continued helping Mama in the kitchen whenever I was not at school. I was not sweetness and light about it, but I was careful not to push Mama too far. I kneaded the family bread dough that she mixed, all the while letting her know that when I grew up I would be buying bread at the store. I washed the cream separator disks. The separator must be kept immaculately clean lest bacteria sour the cream we sold. I washed dishes and helped with the canning. Still, I had much time to supervise Grace and Dolly and play with them.

One of the advantages of my helping Mama in the kitchen, once I accepted that I would, indeed, be helping her from now on, was that she told me stories about her growing up time, life on the homestead, and her college years. I asked her so often about people on the prairie that I felt I had actually known them. Mama told these stories at bedtime, but she would tell me more details when I helped her in the kitchen. Details that she didn't feel would interest Grace and Dolly. This made me feel grown up.

I asked her what she thought about each of us children. I most reminded her of Mrs. Clark, who was bossy and intended to be in charge. She said that when I was four years old, I watched her in the kitchen and told her how to do things. She took this sort of behavior from Mrs. Clark, but she was not taking it from her daughter.

What about Willie? Well, he reminded her of Uncle Don. He needed excitement and he tested fate. If life was quiet, he would stir things up.

"Willie doesn't stir things up!" I defended him.

"No, he doesn't now, because he's in the army, and they know how to deal with him and others like him."

What about Sherman? Sherman did not move into the void that Willie had left. She wasn't sure if it was that Sherman had never had to be the big brother, or, perhaps it was just a personality difference. Willie was innately a natural leader and care-taker. Sherman was not. He created his own world and he was neither a leader nor a follower. Nathan tried to emulate Willie, but Sherman thought for himself and followed his own inner voice.

Sherman worked hard without complaint, and, unlike Willie, he followed Papa's instructions without resentment. Sherman most enjoyed reading. His reading preferences showed a wide range of interests, and he read every book and magazine that he could. Sherman, as did all of us except Willie, found going to the public library in Glasgow to be a favorite activity.

While we girls proved a nuisance to Sherman and often interrupted his reading, he seemed to enjoy reading to us. He read stories and poems that he found interesting, and he, like Mama, had an amazing repertoire of memorized poems.

Perhaps because we tormented Sherman when he was trying to read, or maybe he just found it entertaining to tease us, sometimes to the point of tears. When we took our tears to Mama, she said to just leave him alone. He needed his own space.

I reminded Mama of an evening when a few people from church were coming to eat supper with us. Sherman told me that he was preparing a picture of me to put up for their visit. I couldn't imagine what picture he could be thinking of, but I was pleased to be singled out for attention. When I entered the front room before the arrival of company, I looked around for my picture, but I couldn't see it. I asked Sherman if he was still going to put up my picture. "Oh," he replied innocently, "I already did. It's on the ceiling."

I looked up. There was a full page picture of a camel's face staring down at me. Few animals have an uglier face than a camel. I was certain our company would think the picture was of me. I demanded that he take the picture down right now.

Sherman laughed, "I wouldn't think of depriving our company the pleasure of seeing your picture!"

I raged at Sherman; he laughed. I tried to reach the picture from standing on a chair, but I could not. I begged; I cried. Mama was evidently listening from the kitchen, and now she came into the front room.

Hardly concealing a smile, she looked at Sherman, "You've had your fun. Take it down."

Now alone with Mama in the kitchen, I asked why Sherman would have done that.

"First of all, you girls buzz around him like mosquitoes. Maybe, he is getting even. Or," she looked at me, "Maybe he just gets a kick out of your totally ridiculous behavior when he teases you. Like the kick you and Grace get out of teasing Dolly."

"Which of us had the worst temper?" I expected Mama to say it was Dolly.

"Sherman," she replied. "True, he is mild mannered most of the time, but when he does throw a temper fit, it more than makes up for all the times he didn't.

"Who has the least temper?"

"You do. While you exhibit some ill-mannered, childish behavior at times, you are actually even-keeled."

I decided to ignore the negative part of Mama's statement and report my virtue to the other children.

"Mama said that I have the least temper of all of us."

My reward for bragging was that they immediately nicknamed me Temper Tootie.

"Who is the smartest?"

"Well, thank God, you are all smart! But, Sherman unquestionably has the highest I.Q. And to think, when he was a baby I feared he was not right-bright."

Why did she and Papa think that Willie would not turn out well? And, why did we have to pray for him every night after we said The Lord's Prayer?

"I told you that he was like your Uncle Don. Don spends his days working, but he spends his nights in a bar drinking and, until he was older, fighting. We are fearful that Willie, now that he is exposed to alcohol might have Don's predilection for drinking. Also, my father was an alcoholic.

"Don had a restless spirit. You remember how restless Willie is after he's home on furlough for a few days. Your dad and I always hope we can keep him constructively occupied until he goes back to the army."

I did remember. Nothing seemed to hold Willie's attention for long. It was as though he no longer seemed to fit in. Every night at seven Mama went to the bedroom with us girls to help us get ready for bed. Then she told us stories and quoted poems until prayer time. During that time Papa and the boys visited, played chess, listened to the radio, or read. Later, before the boys went to The Old House for the night, they sat at the table while Papa read to them from the Bible and finished by reading a prayer from his prayer book.

I had heard Papa tell Mama that Willie still participated, but his mind seemed elsewhere.

When the boys went to the Old House for the night, Nathan said that Willie told them wild stories about being in the army. After serving in the regular army in Fort Lewis, Washington, he had qualified to go through the United States Army Airborne School in Fort Benning, Georgia. Mama surmised that being at home on the farm was much too tame for Willie when he was accustomed to rigorous training and parachuting from airplanes.

Mama laughed, "When we lived on the prairie we rarely saw an airplane. One day when Willie was still a baby I thought I heard a plane. I ran out of the house. I saw that it was coming nearer. I raced back into the house and waked Willie. By the time I hurried outside with him the airplane was almost overhead. I kept pointing to the sky to get Willie to see it. When he was older I wanted him to be able to say he had seen an airplane." Mama laughed again, "Now he jumps out of airplanes!" ❧

CHAPTER 27

Gunny Sacks and Cow Chips

The early fall of 1949 found us without the necessary supply of wood for winter. Papa always hoped that he and the boys would find time during the busy summer to cut and haul winter's wood. True, they did have some ricks of wood ready, but more, much more, was needed. Before the bitter cold winds of winter swept down from Canada, Papa and the boys would spend Saturdays felling trees, cutting the limbs from them, and pulling them from the woods with the tractor. When the logs were near the house they must be sawed to stove lengths, split to the correct sizes, and stacked in ricks. Nathan, tired from helping with the wood all day, announced one Saturday night at supper that he preferred to do as Mama and Papa had done on the treeless prairie—gather cow chips.

"That," Papa laughed, "is because you have never had to gather enough cow chips to heat a house! You cannot imagine how many cow chips it takes to warm a small two-room homestead shack."

"What are cow chips?" Dolly wanted to know.

"They are dried cow piles," Mama answered.

Dolly made a face, "Yuck!"

Mama looked at Nathan, "It was drag the gunny sack and pick up cow chips, drag the gunny sack and pick up cow chips, throw the full gunny sack onto the wagon, grab another empty gunny sack day after day after day. You wouldn't have liked it."

"But you didn't just have cow chips for a fire?" Sherman asked.

"There were times when neighbor men would get together. Usually in spring or early summer when we had longer days and the wood had time to dry by winter. We would take our teams and wagons fifteen miles to cut small trees that grew along a creek. We limbed them and cut them into lengths that would fit into the wagons. It was a long hard day leaving at dawn and returning at dark. Our wives had to do all the farm chores," Papa remembered.

"And," Mama added, "sometimes your dad and I would take the team and wagon up north of us to hills that had a coal seam. The two-foot-wide seam was in the side of a hill. Dirt was above and below the seam. Lots of coal had been taken out already, so your dad had to lie on his side and scoot under a ledge with a pick. He would chip coal, and I would rake it out and put it into gunny sacks. It was too far to go all the time, so we only made a few trips a year. Besides, the coal was poor quality and stinky."

Papa shook his head, "I am so thankful to be able to take the tractor to our woods and cut trees!"

"How did you get heating fuel when you were growing up in Plattsburg, Missouri?" Sherman asked.

Papa smiled, "My grandpa paid a man to deliver wood that was already cut and split! That was the best way to get fuel!"

Mama said, "In St. Peter a truck delivered coal to the bins in our basement. The hired man filled the furnace and tended to it. Little did I know what a luxury that was!"

෫Ꮕ⊙· · ·o· · ·⊙Ꭶ෭

At bedtime I asked Mama to tell us the story of "The Ball Gown Lady" who gathered cow chips on the prairie when Mama lived in the Genevieve Country.

You already know about the catalogs advertising women who wanted to come out west and marry a cowboy. The ones like Lew Balky looked at. Many young women thought all men out west were cowboys! Those uninformed young, and some not so young, women had no idea of the reality of life out west.

This one poor soul, Marguerite, thought that living on a homestead must be a lot like living on a plantation in the South. Part of the fault lay with the men they wrote to. Men looked at life on the prairie much differently from women. Also, men were desperate to find a wife, so they often painted a glorified picture of life on the prairie.

Ole Swanson lived near Mrs. Clark's homestead in the Genevieve Country. He and Marguerite corresponded for a while before she took the train out to Hinsdale to meet Ole. They married the same day she arrived from the East. The next day Ole loaded trunk after trunk that Marguerite had brought with her into his wagon. They headed to his homestead. Marguerite was feeling ill so they stopped at La Ross's Road Ranch for the night instead of going all the way to Ole's homestead.

Mrs. La Ross told us later that Marguerite was almost in a catatonic state of shock. Everything from Hinsdale itself to the treeless prairie to the appearance of the little homestead shacks they passed was dramatically different from what she expected. Mrs. La Ross, who had been a mail-order bride herself, said that Marguerite absolutely was not homestead material. She tried to reason with Marguerite telling her that she should have Ole take her right back to the train headed east in the morning. All Marguerite could say between sobs was, "I can't. Returning would be too humiliating."

Marguerite stayed, but her mind did not. Children came, but the much needed rains did not. They were desperately poor. Marguerite wore out her every day dresses, and they couldn't afford to buy more. She opened the trunk of ball gowns she had brought to wear to the fancy balls they would attend on the prairie. They became her everyday dresses.

Often when I rode my horse on the prairie I would see Marguerite in a once beautiful ball gown with her long black hair whipped around her face by prairie winds. She dragged a gunny sack as she picked up cow chips. From time to time she would stop abruptly and raise her head to the sky and scream and scream. Then her screams would stop, and she would resume picking up cow chips.

Ole knew that she had lost her mind, but he could not persuade her to go Back East to her family. Finally, the doctor in Opheim said that she must go to the hospital at Warm Springs for psychiatric help. Marguerite's doctor wrote to Ole saying she was happy there. She thought she was on a plantation living the life she had imagined, before traveling to Montana.

Her doctor told Ole, "I would not restore her mind even if I could. Reality would destroy her."

"You can learn from the Ball Gown Lady," Mama would say after she finished the story. "Never perpetuate a mistake."

"Marguerite went crazy. Is it better to be crazy than real?" I would ask.

"Yes," Mama would answer sadly, "Sometimes it is."

ᘓ᙭ · · o · · ᙭ᘐ

Most of winter's wood was up before late fall when the weather turned suffi-ciently cold to butcher pigs. We looked forward to butchering time, because that meant we would be able to eat pork throughout the winter. During warm weather when Mama and Papa shopped for groceries at Buttrey's Grocery Store in Glasgow they occasionally bought some meat, but we mostly ate chicken we raised and fish we caught in Milk River.

I both dreaded and looked forward to butchering day. I dreaded it, because I knew all of our pigs by name, and Papa would kill one of them. I looked forward to it, because it was a family ritual where Papa, Mama, Sherman, and Nathan did the actual work. Grace, Dolly, and I alternately raced around playing in the snow, stood as close to the action as possible without being in the way, and warmed ourselves by the fire.

Butchering began immediately after breakfast was eaten and morning chores finished. The night before, Papa arranged wood for a fire under a metal framework that supported a large steel barrel. Nathan pumped and carried buckets of water to fill the barrel. The barrel was placed strategically under a sturdy almost horizontal cottonwood limb. Above the barrel Papa attached a block and tackle to the limb. The morning of the butchering Papa lighted the fire under the barrel so the water would be scalding hot by the time milking was finished. A second fire was laid nearby. A big black iron pot for heating the hog fat to make lard was suspended above this fire with two iron upright rods and a horizontal rod. Nathan was responsible for keeping the fires fed from the nearby stack of wood for that purpose.

A stout table made of boards laid across saw horses was placed near the barrel and scrubbed down with scalding water. Papa sharpened knives and placed them on one end of the table. Mama would test the knives' sharpness by flicking her thumb across the edge of the blade. If one was not as sharp as she wished, she would call to Papa, "Why, I could ride from here to California on this blade!"

I went to the house and stayed until after the pig was shot, had its throat slit to bleed it, and was dragged by the tractor to the butchering site. A gambrel stick between the pig's back leg tendons was attached to the hook on the block and tackle, so Papa could raise the pig by pulling a rope. When the pig was directly above the barrel of scalding water Papa carefully lowered it into the barrel. Once the pig was scalded, he lifted it above the barrel, so Sherman could help to swing it over and gut it. Then they moved it above the table and lowered it to begin scraping off the hair. Scalding the pig made the hair easier to scrape off.

A car drove out from the railroad underpass. Alma and John Franzen had come to help with the butchering and to get the pig's head, so Alma could make headcheese for them and for us. They lived in Glasgow, but they had been friends of Mama and Papa since homestead days. We girls ran ahead of Mama to greet them. Mr. Franzen was tall and thin. Mrs. Franzen was taller than Mama and wider—much, much wider. She was pretty with a merry laugh and easy manner.

Since it was time to begin dinner, Mama and Mrs. Franzen walked to the butchering site to take the liver back to the house to cook. I was torn—I loved to hear all the news of people as they visited, but I also did not want to miss the butchering itself. Already much of the fat had been trimmed off and tossed into the black iron pot. When the fat cooled it would solidify into white lard for cooking. But now, cracklings, pieces of tissue that were cut off with the fat, floated in the melted fat. They were almost ready to be dipped out, spread on a clean board, and salted. We could eat them then. I compromised by staying long enough to eat some cracklings, then skipped off to the house. I picked up a book and sat in the front room.

Mama and Mrs. Franzen were cooking and visiting about life on the homesteads. Mrs. Franzen asked Mama about Miss Willoughby. Mama had already told me the story when I was helping her in the kitchen one day, but Mrs. Franzen who only knew parts of it, begged Mama to tell her more. Miss Willoughby came from Back East to claim an abandoned homestead near Mrs. Clark's homestead. She seemed a most unlikely homesteader. Her flaming red hair that Mrs. Clark said was out of a bottle and her fancy, flashy clothes set her apart.

"I've seen women who looked like her," Mrs. Clark had said through tight lips, "But they lived in a section of Minneapolis where respectable people did not go."

Miss Willoughby had explained with a wave of her lacy handkerchief, that she was a writer of romance novels. She had come to the prairie to find the peace and quiet she needed to write.

"Well, you do know they called her the Pink Lady, don't you?" Mama asked Mrs. Franzen.

Mrs. Franzen looked puzzled, "No, I didn't. Why was that?"

Mama smiled, "It was said that when she arrived on the train in Hinsdale she was dressed in a fancy pink hat and a fancy pink dress. With her red hair and pink outfit she looked totally unlike anybody else getting off the train! So, she was called the Pink Lady."

Mama went on to tell Mrs. Franzen of a day when she and her friend Lars Johannsen were out riding. They were exploring the gulch on the other side of Miss Willoughby's homestead, because they were told you could find gold there. Too late they noticed a storm approaching. By the time they rode out of the gulch it was pouring rain. They must seek the nearest shelter, which was Miss Willoughby's homestead shack.

Miss Willoughby did not answer their knocking or shouting, so they went inside. She was gone. The inside of her shack was like no other they had seen. Red velvet draperies hung on the windows. Pictures of naked women hung on the walls. Her bed was covered by a red velvet spread and lots of lace trimmed pillows. A large gold-framed mirror hung above the bed.

"Lars could hardly blink his eyes, let alone close his mouth!" Mama laughed.

"I heard that she plied the world's oldest trade, but I had no idea she was so well out-fitted for it!" Mrs. Franzen shook her head in disbelief.

"Worst of all," Mama remembered, "Lars found his father's pocket watch on the dresser!

"He didn't understand what we were seeing, or what his father's pocket watch being on the dresser meant. And I did not tell him!

"After I told Mrs. Clark what Miss Willoughby's house looked like, Mrs. Clark said Miss Willoughby would be taking her writing back East very soon. And, she did."

Mama looked at the clock. "We have time for a cup of tea before everybody comes in to dinner. Ruth, since I am sure you have been listening instead of reading, do you want to join us?"

Mama and I sat down at the kitchen table with steaming cups of hot green tea and honey. Mrs. Franzen finished at the stove and pulled out a chair. As she sat down, the chair groaned slightly and gradually descended to the floor. Unharmed, Mrs. Franzen turned to get onto her hands and knees to get up. Mama, who had been completely silent as the chair sank, now made a strange noise. I looked at her. She was trying to keep from laughing. Mrs. Franzen heard her, and with her ample body on her hands and knees she began laughing. This meant I, too, could laugh. We all laughed until our sides hurt.

"Let me help you," Mama stood by her and helped, but Mrs. Franzen was a big woman, and it was a struggle for both of them to get her to her feet.

Once on her feet, though, they both laughed again until they wiped away tears.

When the others came in to dinner, Papa looked with curiosity at the broken chair, but said nothing.

Mrs. Franzen smiled at Papa, "I broke it, Mr. Sherwood!" Then she and Mama burst into laughter again.

That night at supper Mama told Papa, "When Alma sat in the chair it heaved a gentle sigh and sank slowly to the floor." ⌒

CHAPTER 28

CHRISTMAS MAGIC

Christmas season blew in on penetrating cold winds and more snow. Caring for the livestock and sawing and splitting wood for three stoves in the New House and one in the Old House kept Papa and the boys busy. We girls spent more time indoors reading, playing games, coloring, drawing, and gathering around the kitchen table to visit with Mama as she worked. Sometimes she made a cup of hot Postum for herself and hot chocolate for us girls. Then she would sit at the table and visit with us, or, if we could persuade her, color a picture in our coloring books. Our talk always turned to Christmas.

Some of the children in my third-grade class disputed the existence of Santa Claus. Somehow, I knew better than to tell Grace and Dolly. I struggled with it in my mind for a time, before telling Mama. She had laughed. "Do you like to believe Santa is real?" I did. "Then why worry about what others think?" The next time a student told me there was no Santa, I remembered what Mama had said, and I replied, "You think what you want to think, and I will think what I want to think."

Saturday before Christmas I was in the kitchen helping Mama with dinner, I asked her if she was excited to have Christmas coming. To my surprise she told me she had never liked Christmas. I had never heard her say that, and I pressed to know why she didn't like Christmas.

"It is because of my memories of Christmas in St. Peter."

I wondered how that could be. Mama had told us of magical Christmases in St. Peter: the wonderful gifts she had received, how elaborately their house was decorated, Mrs. Clark's Christmas parties in their beautiful home, how they traveled to Minneapolis and celebrated Christmas with the Watts family, and her shopping with Grandma Watts and The Aunt Grace. . . . What was not to like about that?

"But, you had wonderful Christmases in St. Peter!" I reminded her.

"I only told you about the good part of Christmas in St. Peter. There was a bad part. Mrs. Clark always spoiled Christmas."

I was bewildered by this. "How did she spoil Christmas?"

"As I have told you, my Papa was an alcoholic. When he was home during the holidays, he seemed to drink more. Part of the reason was that most nights of Christmas season Mrs. Clark was either having a party or dragging Papa off to parties. He was a traveling salesman, and he just wanted to enjoy quiet evenings at home. So he drank. Mrs. Clark despised weakness, and she would tell Papa that alcohol was his master and that he was weak and disgusting. She hid his alcohol, but he just bought more. Finally, she would taunt him to the point that he would hit her. They always had fights during the Christmas season.

"He hit her! Your Papa hit Mrs. Clark!" I could hardly believe it.

"Oh, yes, but she taunted him until he did. One night he was actually able to have a quiet evening at home. I must have been about five years old. He was sitting in the parlor between the Christmas tree and the fireplace. I had pulled my little chair up by him, and I asked him to read the story "The Little Match Girl" to me just before bedtime. He had a drink in his hand. I didn't know he was drunk until he began reading and slurring his words. But he wasn't causing any problem. Mrs. Clark came into the parlor. She was already in her dressing gown and had her hair down, because she was getting ready to go to bed. I didn't want her to see that he was drunk, so I told Papa that we could finish the story tomorrow. But, she had already noticed and she started mocking him and telling him he was a good for nothing drunk. He finally threw the book down, jumped up, and grabbed her by the hair. She started screaming. He told her he was going to stuff her into the fireplace, so he could have some peace. Elsie heard the commotion and ran in to hurry me upstairs."

"And that was Mrs. Clark's fault?" I questioned.

"Yes, if she had left him alone, he would have gone to sleep or quietly passed out. You don't taunt a drunk. Mrs. Clark knew that."

ভ৯· · · ০ · · ·৫৯

Saturday we girls rode with Mama and Papa into Glasgow to run errands. Part of our Christmas magic was seeing the decorations in town. Sturdy decorations that would withstand the whipping wind were secured to street lights, and stores decorated their windows with everything from a few Christmas lights to nativity scenes and Santa Clauses. Garlands shaped "Merry X-Mas" across the concrete of the railroad underpass. One of my school mates had said that it was unChristian to use the X instead of Christ.

I asked Mama about this.

"Hundreds of years ago the X was used in art to mean Christ. The Greek letter "Chi" that we call "X" began a word that translated to "Christ." There is absolutely nothing wrong with using the X. Besides," she laughed, "There isn't enough room on the underpass to spell "Christmas."

Papa's last errand in town was to go by the train depot. He was to pick up the evergreen tree that Uncle Henry had sent from Idaho. No evergreen trees grew in our northeastern Montana region, but vacant lots in Glasgow were stocked with evergreen trees shipped in from elsewhere. We believed that none could be as pretty as the fir trees Uncle Henry sent every Christmas.

Once home we girls hovered around as Papa made a tree stand and fastened the tree to it. When the tree was first brought into the house the branches still folded close to the trunk from having been wrapped securely in burlap for shipment. As the tree warmed the branches relaxed and a wonderful woodsy smell of fragrant evergreen slowly permeated our front room. Even without decorations we thought it to be enchantingly beautiful!

This year, in addition to our homemade decorations, we had store-bought decorations given to us by the Art Swanson family. Willie had worked for Mr. Swanson from time to time, and the Swansons sometimes drove out to see us. Their daughter, who was just older than I, passed down some of her beautiful outgrown clothes to me. Now they had contributed to our Christmas.

Mama lifted the Swanson's decorations carefully from the box: garlands, glass ornaments, strings of electric lights with reflectors around each colored bulb, and tinsel. When the tree was finally decorated and the lights were plugged in, we girls sat at the big table in our front room drinking cocoa. Mama allowed us to stay inside for the rest of the afternoon. We could not bear to be away from our magnificent tree.

Near Christmas Papa brought packages from the post office when he went to town. Uncle Don sent hard candy and small gifts from Idaho, Uncle Abby sent Russell Stover's candy from Missouri, and Mrs. Clark continued to have Harry and David's Riviera Pears shipped to us. Every mail day brought Christmas cards and letters.

A few nights before Christmas, I begged to sleep by the Christmas tree. I pushed three chairs together and turned the middle chair a different direction so I wouldn't roll off. Next, I brought quilts and a pillow to make my bed. I awoke in the night to singing. Mama and Papa had come into the front room, and they were standing at the south windows. Mama motioned for me to be quiet and come to them. Across the ditch almost a dozen people were standing in the snow holding flashlights to see their song sheets as they sang Christmas carols. Their singing in the cold, still night seemed heavenly, and I was sorry when they hurried toward their cars parked near the underpass.

"They were from church," Mama marveled, "And they drove all the way out here to walk through the snow to our house and sing for us on such a cold night. Why they must have been half-frozen!"

Our Grace Bible Chapel Christmas program was held on the Sunday night before Christmas. After an early supper we girls put on our best dresses, and Mama brushed and braided our hair again. My dress, given to me by the Swansons, had a black velveteen skirt with a silk-like butter-yellow top sprinkled with little red flowers. The jacket was black velveteen with fabric lining matching the dress top. If only I owned a pair of black Mary Jane shoes to go with my beautiful dress, but no, we would all wear our sturdy brown school-church shoes. At least Mama bought new white long-stockings for us to wear.

We children who attended church were ready to perform in the program we had practiced every Saturday after Thanksgiving. When we arrived at church it was dimly lighted with candles. Christmas carols were playing softly on the piano. Near the pulpit Mary sat on a stool by the manger; Joseph stood beside her. Neither moved. We, like the rest of the congregation, came in and sat silently and reverently.

Suddenly, our church blazed with light and the choir strode from the back of the church down the aisle toward the pulpit vigorously singing, "Noel." They lined up in front of Mary, Joseph, and Baby Jesus and sang a few Christmas carols before gesturing for the rest of us to stand and sing more with them. Mama singing in her wonderful clear, strong alto voice should have been in the choir, but she did not have time to come to town and practice with them.

When singing was finished we children who were participating in our part of the program left to go downstairs before Reverend Wall's short sermon; we considered that to be a benefit of being in the program. Mrs. Pratt and some other adults bustled around helping those who were wearing costumes. Two angels; three Wise Men with gold, frankincense, and myrrh; shepherds with their staffs; fat cottony sheep; a cow; and a donkey were finally outfitted and ready to go upstairs. Nathan was a shepherd, perhaps, because Papa made the staffs. Those of us, including Grace, Dolly, and I, with speaking or singing parts did not wear costumes.

We marched upstairs following Mrs. Pratt. Angels, Wise Men, shepherds, sheep, cow, and donkey would join Mary and Joseph at appropriate times during the program, but first the youngest children spoke their parts, so they could join their parents.

Dolly was third, and she was given a longer part, because she memorized so readily. Remembering last year, I held my breath as Dolly walked to the front to say her piece. Last year her first line was, "Christ the lord was born this day. . . ." She looked like an angel with her curly blonde hair and white fine-wale corduroy dress. When it was her turn to speak she walked to the front, stood looking out at the congregation, and opened her mouth without a sound emitting. Her big blue eyes grew bigger.

"Christ!" she finally spoke the first word forcefully; she stopped, looked at the congregation, and slowly pulled the skirt of her white dress over her head. Sherman dashed up, caught her in his arms, and carried her to Papa as Mama struggled to keep from laughing by holding her hand over her mouth.

Now Dolly stepped boldly to the front of the church and spoke her long part confidently and clearly. I wanted to clap like we did at school, but one did not clap in Grace Bible Chapel.

When the last prayer was said and the last song sung, we could visit. Two big boxes full of bags of candy, nuts, and an orange were placed on each side of the door leading to the entry for every person to take one. We knew we could not open them until we reached home.

When we were in the truck driving home Mama once again lamented the Wall's having Richard. Poor Richard—he would not know the joys of Christmas.

کی۔ · · o · · ۔یک

On Christmas Eve we girls selected one of our biggest everyday stockings to hang for Santa to fill. We each knew that when our stocking was filled he would lay additional presents near the stocking. Our dilemma every Christmas Eve was where to hang our stockings. I was still sleeping on my chair-bed in the living room, so I hung my stocking on the back of a chair. Papa read the Christmas story and prayed for Willie. We all missed him. He had not forgotten us. A box of gifts from him would be opened in the morning.

I vowed to myself that I would stay awake to see Santa. I turned on my side so I could see our Christmas tree. Sometime during the night I awakened.

The tree lights had been turned off, but the kitchen light sent a shaft of light into the front room. I could hear Putt-Putt driving away. Perhaps, as sometimes happened, Papa and the boys were going to pull a vehicle from the ditch. Then I saw him—a man was standing by our stove, and he was definitely not Santa Claus! This man weaved around by the stove holding his hands out to warm them. Occasionally, when his hands touched the stove he swore. No, this was not Santa Claus.

I lay perfectly still, so the man would not know I was awake. Mama came into the front room, approached my bed, and called my name softly.

"I thought if you woke up you might be scared. This is our neighbor Wayne Putz. He ran off the road and got stuck in the snow. Your dad and the boys went to pull out his pickup." I knew Mr. Putz. His wife Pinky was our librarian. I also knew that Mr. Putz had a drinking problem, and this was not the first night Papa had needed to pull him out of the ditch.

Next she walked to Mr. Putz and pulled up a chair for him. "Wayne," she demanded, "Sit in this chair, so you don't fall onto the stove." He mumbled and sat down.

When Mama left to go into the kitchen to make coffee for Mr. Putz I noticed my stocking was full. Clearly, Wayne was in no condition to tell that I had looked at my gifts early. Our gifts were not wrapped, and we were allowed to look at them when we woke up. I emptied my stocking of trinkets, hard candy, dried fruits, nuts, gum drops, and an orange. On the floor by my bed lay a thick coloring book and a red metal box of Copy Cat paints. I thought how good Santa Claus had been to me when I had not always been good.

Christmas day in the morning I found that Grace and Dolly had received much the same gifts as mine, but with different coloring books and paints. Sherman and Nathan's edible gifts were the same, but more of them. They also each received a new pocket knife. Willie had sent jigsaw puzzles, card games, candy, and gum.

I learned more about what happened when the boys had gone with Papa to pull out Mr. Putz's pickup. Mr. Putz had driven into the ditch, because he was too drunk to keep his truck in the road. Sherman told how Mr. Putz kept saying, "Don't let that little red-headed wife of mine know I was in the ditch!" Papa surmised this was because she might make contact with a skillet to his head.

Mrs. Clark and Mr. Larson were coming to Christmas dinner. When we finally heard her car we girls raced to the windows. Her big black car was charging through the snowy ruts left by our truck. Sherman said that she had to be driving, because nobody else could drive a car on our road and make it all the way to the house.

Mrs. Clark came in stomping snow from her stylish boots. She gave us girls all a hug while still wearing her big furry coat that smelled of perfume.

Mrs. Clark brought good news for us. They had seen Santa on their drive here and he was headed back to our house! But, he could not come unless we girls were in the cellar. We must not see him!

Sherman and Nathan put on their coats and boots and helped us into ours. Then we all trooped through the cold and snow to the root cellar. Our cellar stayed about fifty degrees all year, and now it felt warm. We looked around the cellar at rows and rows of canning jars full of fruits and vegetables. The bins were filled with potatoes, rutabagas, and carrots. It was enough food to last until next summer.

From time to time Sherman walked up the cellar stairs to see if Santa had left. He was almost a grownup, so he was allowed to see Santa. We clamored to peek, but Sherman declared Santa would leave and take our presents with him, if we dared to peek. Finally, Sherman reported that Santa had ridden away in his sleigh calling, "Merry Christmas!"

We raced to the house. Mrs. Clark told us that Santa had asked her to hand out our presents. She handed a beautifully wrapped gift to each of us, including Mama and Papa. Mr. Larson sat smiling as he watched Mrs. Clark. We unwrapped our gifts carefully, so we could save the paper and ribbon. Each of us held up a book that was to be ours forever. It would not need to go back to the library. My book was *Alice in Wonderland.*

We thanked Mrs. Clark for helping Santa, and she laughed in delight at our obvious pleasure with our gifts.

When dinner was ready we all sat down and Papa offered a prayer of thankfulness for our food and petitioned for Willie's safety. Yesterday Papa had killed and dressed one of our fat geese, and today Mama had roasted it with dressing. Our table was laden with our favorite foods, and Mrs. Clark's desserts awaited in the kitchen.

During the meal Mrs. Clark visited with Mama and Papa, frequently turning to Mr. Larson to include him. As usual he said little, but he often smiled at Mrs. Clark. Before dinner was over she engaged each of us children in conversation. She asked about school and our teachers. Which books we had read and which were our favorites.

I watched Mrs. Clark, all fragrant, smiling, and lovely, and I thought about Mama's story of Christmas at their house in St. Peter. Later I asked Mama if Mrs. Clark ever talked about that time when Mr. Clark was going to stuff her into the fireplace.

"No," Mama said, "Mrs. Clark believes in making the most of the present rather than spending time looking back." ❧

CHAPTER 29

MILK RIVER, HIGH AND RISING

The winter of 1949–50, as all winters, no matter how long or cold, passed. The coming of spring in northeastern Montana does not bring a rush of green grass and flowers; rather it brings Easter and a measure of warmth back to the sunshine. Long icicles hanging from our eaves dripped as they grew smaller. Snow melted during sunny days, then grew icy crusts that froze the day's melt during cold nights. Sometimes a warm Chinook wind, Snow Eater the American Indians called it, blew down the Rocky Mountain front and east across the prairie to speed up the melting process.

Easter comes in late March or early April as dictated by the moon and the church calendar. Papa helped make Easter special for us girls by encouraging our speculation about where we thought we should place our nests, and actually helping us with our nests. He found three wooden orange crates for us to use for our nests and forked clean fresh-smelling hay from a haystack for us to put into our boxes. We girls each carefully arranged a perfect nest, and Papa carried them to a snow drift we had scooped out near the trail we were sure the Easter bunny would travel.

Easter morning we grabbed our bags Mama gave us to put our Easter riches into and raced outside through the snow to our nests with our coats pulled hastily over our nightgowns and our bare feet clunking in our overshoes. We exclaimed excitedly over our now filled nests while Papa laughed at our delight. Hard boiled eggs of brilliant hues with flowers and designs on them, maple and divinity candy, pastel colored mints, and fluffy yellow toy chicks filled our nests. We carried our treasures in to show Mama, and she too was amazed at all the Easter bunny left for us.

The only flowers we would see on Easter were the lilies that flanked the pulpit of Grace Bible Chapel. Again, Reverend Wall warned us against the sins of celebrating Easter in any way that did not directly relate to the death and three days later the Resurrection of Christ. We girls sat unperturbed by the minister's serious demands, save for the sadness we felt for little Richard.

We knew that our Easter rabbit would always travel through snow or melt to fill our nests with candy, toy chicks, and artistically colored boiled eggs. Little Richard would never know the excitement and joy of our Easter season.

As days grew warmer our geese knew it was springtime. All night it seemed, they marched up and down in front of our house gabbling instead of going into their coops and sleeping like the respectable geese we knew.

"Somehow, they know it will soon be time for the migrating waterfowl to arrive," Papa answered when we asked him about the strange behavior of our geese.

"Or," Mama added, "Perhaps, this is just the goose way of celebrating the end of winter."

Yet, winter did not let go without trying to make a comeback. Spring snows fell, but melted almost as quickly as they arrived. We knew that spring held sway when we heard loud, sharp cracks, like rifle shots, coming from the river as ice began its first stages of breakup. The time between the beginning of breakup and the final clearing of snow seemed interminable. At last we shed our bulky winter coats and our hated buckle overshoes. Instead we wore jackets and breakup boots, smooth black rubber boots reaching to our knees

As the snow melted, gumbo mud became a menace. Milk River valley soil was gumbo—a clayey soil that became waxy, slick, and incredibly sticky when wet. It collected on our breakup boots with every step. Our boots became heavier and heavier until we stopped and knocked off some of the maddening mud.

Our road from the underpass to the house became mired with gumbo ruts. Our old Chevrolet truck bucked and roared as Papa shifted gears, stepped on the gas or eased up on the gas, and fought the steering wheel. Mud flew in every direction. Sometimes the truck admitted defeat; then Putt-Putt was brought chugging with the chains to pull the truck to solid ground.

Wild geese flying north called throughout the days and nights. Sometimes during daylight hours flocks of geese and ducks settled temporarily in the clear golden brown snow melt of our slough—a large, low area east toward the woods and the river. Nathan, Grace, Dolly, and I crept to the slough with Papa's binoculars to watch the waterfowl without being seen. The birds paddled around the slough slowly as though this were their final destination rather than a rest stop. All the while they visited incessantly. The colorful plumage of the male ducks was vivid and varied.

Melting snow pack in Canada, as well as Montana, determined the amount of water flowing into Milk River and the duration of the river's breakup. We children watched the breakup and rising water with curiosity and fascination. Mama and Papa watched with fear.

Papa frequently reminded us that our farm's proximity to the river meant its elevation was somewhat lower than that of farms that did not border the river. "One day," Papa predicted every spring, "Milk River will rise to such a high level that it will flood our farm."

When Papa had used his tractor and slip to move dirt to build high ground for The New House, he had also moved much dirt in order to build high ground south of the barn. Papa and the boys had built a pig pen containing a pig house and a log corral for the cattle in case of a flood. They also stacked the hay here. This, he believed, would be above flood waters. All of our buildings and the storm cellar were located along the main irrigation ditch on land that was somewhat higher than the rest of the farm, but not as high as the mounds Papa had built.

Roiling muddy water rose daily carrying icebergs, debris, and even bloated farm animals with legs sticking straight out. The swiftly moving water swirled against our river banks taking soil from the banks on its journey. The Dry Run, a low area between our fields and the railroad track, was dry only when Milk River was not high. As the river rose it filled the Dry Run with brown water, cutting off our road under the railroad underpass. Papa must now drive down our farm road to the west end of our property all the way to the spillway road in order to access the town road.

We children could not walk to the school bus, so we no longer attended school. We welcomed our unexpected holiday. Nathan thought it would be a surprise to those downstream from us if we were to stage an iceberg to look like somebody's home floating away. The flood water almost reached the top of the river bank, and a small iceberg lodged against the bank. Nathan carried a chair and an end table from The Old House and we girls carried outdated magazines and a Sears Roebuck catalog to place on the iceberg. After seeing there was nothing else we could spare he pushed the iceberg away from the bank with a long pole. We cheered as it floated away.

A few days later we children grasped the magnitude of the danger of our having been on the river bank when Mama told us about her experience when standing too near the edge of the bank. Mama stole the eggs from each goose every day. They were then placed under a setting hen that would hatch them, because chickens made much better mothers than geese. From time to time Mama checked the eggs to determine if they carried a live embryo. She placed each egg in warm water; if the egg wobbled it had a live embryo. If the egg was still, it had no embryo or a dead one.

She must dispose of the bad eggs where the dogs could not get them. If a dog gets a taste for sucking eggs, it will suck eggs in every nest it can get to. An egg-sucking dog is a liability on a farm—and a short timer. Mama solved her problem by carrying the bad eggs in a pan to the river. She was careful not to stand too close to the edge of the river bank that was now level with the water. But on this particular morning, just as she started to throw an egg she was seized with the impulse to drop the pan and jump backwards. When she did, she noticed a crack in the ground that was now before her, but had been behind her. At that instant the entire area where she had been standing to throw the eggs sank from sight into the flood water.

"I was so weak I could barely walk to the house." Mama told us at supper. "I would have been sucked under the water and drowned. Nobody would have known what happened. My body might never have been discovered."

We sat silently as our minds grappled with the horror of what could have happened to Mama.

"God spoke to me," Mama said in a voice filled with emotion.
Papa seemed shaken. He looked around the table, "Don't any of you for any reason whatsoever go near the river bank when the water is up."

I thought of Nathan's lugging the chair and table and our carrying magazines to the iceberg. We could have all disappeared under the water!

Sherman sought to relieve the tension, "Mama! Don't tell us you lost the pan!"

We all laughed, much more than the comment warranted.

৩৩· · ০ · · ৩৩

That spring of 1950, for the first time since our moving to McColly farm, the water began overflowing the river banks. Papa pounded a big stake into the ground in back of The Old House and another near the road to the underpass. Each stake had inch and foot measurements, so Papa could see how fast the water was rising. He needed to know from day to day whether the water was continuing to rise or beginning to recede.

Just before the water cut off Papa's exit from the farm at the west end, he drove the truck out our west farm road and parked it in front of the underpass by the town road. This way he could row the boat over to the truck.

The gravel road to town was built with foresight of a flood, and it was elevated to be passable during a flood. The Great Northern Railroad tracks alongside the town road were significantly higher. Both the train track bed and the bridge over Milk River had been engineered to withstand the worst of floods.

The rowboat, previously used to cross back and forth to Combs' farm and leisurely Sunday boat trips up and down the river, was now tethered where Papa could row it across the waters of Dry Run, under the underpass, and to the truck. Mama and Papa continued to go to town to sell our cream and to buy groceries. Papa noted each time he returned that our farm was one of the hardest hit by the flood; in fact, most farms he and Mama saw along the town road were not flooded.

Eventually, our farm, except for the area immediately around the buildings and the high ground Papa had built with his tractor and slip, was under water. Mama and Papa worried. Would even this elevated area stay above the water? Finally, with great relief, Papa noted from the stakes he had set that the daily rise of the river water had slowed.

"It may not be rising as fast," Mama noted, "But it is still rising. I don't know if I should send out a dove, or if you should begin building an ark."

"I did send out a dove, and it did not bring back an olive leaf," Papa laughed. "And I don't have enough cypress wood to build an ark." Then he added seriously, "All we can do is pray."

We took advantage of this normally busy time of preparing fields for crops and repairing irrigation ditches to take frequent boat rides. Papa rowed the boat right over fences bordering our fields. He said that one of the benefits of the flood was that it brought nutrients to the soil and new soil in the form of silt that would settle on the fields from the muddy flood water. This would make our crops more productive.

Finally, Papa reported that the flood waters were actually receding. Day by day we could almost see the water going down as more of our farm showed. Eventually, all that was left of the flood was the slough full of water and live fish and a layer of mud that covered everything that had been submerged.

My fourth-grade school year was not quite over, and we could walk to the bus again. My first day on the bus after the flood a friend told me that people were saying that flood water had come into our house and my parents were shoveling it out with scoop shovels. I laughed.

∼☙· · ◦ · · ·❧∽

We caught and ate fish trapped in the slough while there was still plenty of water to keep them fresh. When Mama and Papa were in town they asked friends if they too wished to come out to our farm to catch fish. Some did, and they were appreciative of the easy catches.

Alma and John Franzen came to dinner. Afterwards, Mr. Franzen, Papa, and the boys went to the slough to fish. Grace and Dolly tagged along. Mama and Mrs. Franzen cleaned up the kitchen. I feigned interest in finishing one of my Nancy Drew books before it was due at the library. Mama and Mrs. Franzen's talk was always much too interesting to miss.

After catching up on family, their talk turned to homestead people. Some of those they had known on the prairie lived in Hinsdale and others lived in Glasgow. Mrs. Franzen wondered if Mama had seen Agnes or Ray Schuler lately. Agnes had visited us just a few months ago. She came at about the time of my birthday, and she had brought a little red purse with a pretty handkerchief in it for me. I marveled that she would remember.

"You are one of very few people I know who was born during a blizzard," Agnes had laughed.

Mama and Mrs. Franzen spoke of Ray Schuler. Although, they were friendly, he and Agnes no longer lived together, but nobody seemed to know why.

"Maybe, it was his temper," Mama suggested. "Remember on the homestead when crops were dry and the rains refused to come, how he went outside and cursed God."

"I didn't know that!" Mrs. Franzen sounded shocked.

"Oh, yes," Mama assured her. "He would go outside and raise his fist to the sky. He would yell, 'You old Jew son-of-a-bitch! You could make it rain if you wanted to. We need rain. Send some!'

"Of course," Mama laughed. "It either rained or it didn't. If it did rain, Ray would say that God had just needed to be reminded that we were still here."

"And, if it didn't rain?" Mrs. Franzen wondered.

"Oh," Mama said, "He probably repeated his cursing!" ☙

CHAPTER 30

SILVER SPURS AND A GRAY PONY

Our seemingly short summer ended, and in the autumn of 1950, I began fifth grade at North Side High School. Sunday when Mrs. Clark and Mr. Larsen came to dinner, Mrs. Clark inquired about each of our teachers. She, like Mama had been, was particularly pleased to learn that Mrs. Adams would be my teacher. They had both known Mrs. Adams as Milena Keleshian when she was growing up on a neighboring homestead in the Genevieve Country. The Keleshians were an upstanding, hard-working family who had emigrated from the part of Russia that was formerly Lithuania.

While finishing dinner preparations, Mama and Mrs. Clark visited about people they had known in the Genevieve Country. I volunteered to wash and dry dishes, so I could listen to their conversation. The Keleshian family lived on a homestead bordering the Horvat's homestead. The Horvats were descendents of Lithuanian nobility who long ago were stripped of power and wealth by Russia. The Keleshian and Horvat families had met when they were crowded into the immigrant quarters on a ship bound for America. They had traveled together across America to Montana bringing little other than dreams of a better future and, for the Horvats, a piano stool.

Mama became friends with Eugenia Horvat at Barr School. Their family of fifteen lived in a two-room homestead shack to which they added a lean-to with floor-to-ceiling beds. Mama said they were good, hard-working people whose only material trace of former nobility was their elegant piano stool. They were not able to bring their prized possession, an heirloom piano, on the ship, but they could bring the stool.

Mama thought it was clever of Horvats to bring their piano stool even though they could not bring their piano. Mrs. Horvat fed thirteen children three times a day. The six older children sat at the table, but all seven of the younger children sat in a circle around Mrs. Horvat who was seated in the middle on her beautiful piano stool. Mrs. Horvat gave each of the seven a biscuit or piece of bread; then holding a big bowl of porridge or stew in her lap,

Mrs. Horvat turned on the piano stool going from child to child giving each a spoonful as she turned. This went on until the meal was finished.

Mrs. Clark opened the oven door to check the progress of the roast goose. Closing the oven she added more cook wood to the stove.

"Remember when you were riding with Eugenia and her sister Lavinia and they drank water from a contaminated well?"

"Oh, yes," Mama remembered, "One day when we rode around on the prairie it was hotter than usual and, as always, windy. We brought a lunch, but we didn't bring enough water for such a hot day. Finally, when we were totally parched from thirst we came to an old deserted school house that had a rusty pump nearby. Eugenia and Lavinia said they were going to pump some water to drink. Fortunately, you had warned me repeatedly to never ever drink water that might carry typhoid bacteria. An abandoned well seemed a likely source of typhoid bacteria to me. I tried to tell the girls that they should not drink the water, but they said they were so thirsty they didn't care. I think they really just didn't understand the danger.

"My mare I was riding had a colt at home that was still nursing. I told the girls we could each get a few swallows of mare's milk. They weren't having any part of it. While they were trying to pump some water, I pulled the mare over to the shade of the schoolhouse. I was able to get enough milk to hold me until we reached home. The girls managed to pump up some pretty bad tasting water. They drank some anyway.

"About two weeks later we learned that both Eugenia and Lavinia had typhoid fever.

"That was another time my having volunteered regularly at the hospital in St. Peter proved to be valuable," Mrs. Clark said. "Living on the prairie so far from medical help was certainly a liability. There were far too many unnecessary deaths."

"What happened to the girls?" I asked.

"Well," Mrs. Clark answered, "They were both very, very sick. I rode over almost every day to help Mrs. Horvak. Finally, a doctor came out, but Lavinia almost died. She did lose her hair, and it took a long time to grow back. She was just lucky it did grow back. Sometimes with typhoid it doesn't."

"And, that is why you all had typhoid shots." Mama concluded.

Just this spring Dr. Agneberg's nurse gave all of us typhoid shots at Mama's insistence. Mama declared that we drank well water and we were always playing in the irrigation water. It was far better to be vaccinated than to get typhoid. The typhoid shots hurt terribly when given, we were all sick with a slight fever for a few days, and my arm was swollen and sore for a week or more.

"You see," Mama had told me when I whined, "If the shot makes you sick, think how much more sick you would have been, if you had typhoid. You are lucky to have had the shot."

When we sat down to dinner Mrs. Clark looked at me, "You are fortunate to have a teacher who is married and who understands life in Montana. Coming from a large family, she will know how to handle children. All of you have had too many 'old maid imports'." It was true that many of our teachers were unmarried, recently out of college, and from another state.

Every day Mrs. Adams began the school day, just as our other teachers had, with our saying the Pledge of Allegiance and singing "The Star-Spangled Banner". Additionally, Mrs. Adams led us in singing "I Come from Montana."

> *I come from Montana*
> *I wear a bandana,*
> *My spurs are of silver*
> *My pony is gray . . .*

My favorite subject in fifth grade was our study of Montana. We each made a booklet from stories we wrote and pictures we drew as we learned about The Treasure State. For the cover of our booklets we drew our state flag with its blue background and "Montana" written in gold across the top. A circle in the center presented a picture of the mountains, the Great Falls of the Missouri River, a horse-pulled cultivator, and a pick and shovel. The cultivator represented farming and the pick and shovel represented mining. The state motto, "ORO-Y-PLATA," Spanish for gold and silver, was written on a ribbon across the bottom of the flag. After our interesting study of Montana, we students concluded that Montana was the best state of all!

⋅ ⋅ ⋅ ∘ ⋅ ⋅ ⋅

Winter's first snow in October brought joy to us girls and dread of the long, cold winter to the rest of our family—especially Mama. Mama's health, compromised from her childhood bouts of rheumatic fever and polio, continued to gradually decline. Papa worried about her health, and they talked more and more frequently about moving to a climate that would be better for her.

Sherman encouraged a move at every turn. "The only way a move would not be an improvement over northeastern Montana, would be if we moved farther north," he declared.

Most farm work in the winter involved caring for our livestock. After helping with the milking in the mornings, Papa helped Mama with breakfast while Sherman, 17, and Nathan, 15, hauled hay to the cattle from the haystacks. They forked hay onto the stone-boat, a large heavy-duty sled, like those built by homesteaders to haul stones from their fields. Sherman drove the Ford tractor pulling the stone-boat of hay across packed snow trails to the corral where the milk cows ate and to a large shed near the woods where the non-milking cattle ate.

One morning when Papa returned from milking, he announced that the mercury in the thermometer tacked to The Big Tree had shrunk into a small red ball at the bottom. The lowest reading on the thermometer was forty degrees below zero.

"The cottonwood trees are cracking and popping," he told Mama. We knew that meant the trees were not actually cracking open, just making the sounds.

"I'm not surprised in this bitter cold," Mama said, "The American Indians called winter's coldest months 'The Moon of the Popping Trees.'"

Extremely cold weather meant that Papa must always be prepared to get Shiny Eyes started, even in the coldest weather. Our food supply was plentiful, so no trips to town would be needed, except in case of emergency, and with five children at home one never knew when an emergency could arise. When the temperature required, Papa brought the battery into the house, drained the oil and brought it into the house, and drained the radiator; if the truck must be started shovels full of warm coals were brought from a heating stove and placed under the engine to warm it, boiling water was poured into the radiator, and the oil and battery were brought from the house. Papa took the same precautions with the tractor, for it too was important for feeding cattle.

In spite of Papa's precautions, Sherman came in to report that the tractor would not start. And furthermore, his efforts to start the engine had resulted in his breaking the key off in the tractor.

Papa thought a bit. "I'm going to help your ma with breakfast while you and Nathan fork hay into tubs and carry it to the corral. After breakfast I'll start the truck, and we'll haul hay to where the other cattle can get to it."

When Sherman and Nathan finally came into the house to warm up, Nathan moved stiffly. Papa helped Nathan get off his outdoor clothes and checked his feet. They weren't frozen, but they were too cold. Papa told him to sit by the front room stove. Mama brought hot cocoa to help Nathan warm up, and Papa brought a big pan of cool water for Nathan's feet. Warm water would have hurt his feet too much.

"How," Papa asked Sherman, "did Nathan get this cold and not come in to warm up?"

"I thought he had come in," Sherman reported. "He whined about the cold and disappeared. I thought he came to the house without telling me. I kept carrying hay. Nathan finally came out from behind a haystack where he had hidden to get out of the wind. By then he had been standing still too long, and I had to help him to the house."

We all knew that in frigid temperatures the first rule was to keep moving. When we waited in the cold for our late school bus we jumped up and down, stomped our feet, clapped our hands, and swung our arms around.

None of the burden of working outside in miserably cold temperatures fell to us girls. Our time outside was spent playing. When Sherman and Nathan weren't working they, too, enjoyed winter activities. A favorite activity was coasting down our river bank. Behind The Old House the bank sloped gradually downward for over one hundred feet to the cut-bank. The cut-bank was a clean, straight vertical cut approximately four feet high. Past the cut-bank the ground again sloped gently for about fifty feet to the river.

Papa made our rugged sleds and attached old car seat springs over the boards. The boys' sleds were larger and sturdier, and they could fly safely over the cut-bank, land on the lower slope, and coast all the way across the frozen river. We girls must turn and stop when we neared the end of the first slope. We could only go over the cut-bank if we rode with Sherman or Nathan.

Only one sled at a time left the launching site at the top of the bank. To avoid an accident another sled must wait until the first sled stopped. I climbed onto the sled with Sherman. Nathan shoved us off as hard as he could. We picked up speed all of the way to the cut-bank where we became airborne and my stomach lifted into my throat. The car seat springs helped to cushion our landing as we slammed down on the lower slope with enough momentum to sail all the way to and across the frozen river to the bank on Combs' side. Then we trudged the long way up to the top ready to go again. ☙

CHAPTER 31

SURVIVING A BLIZZARD

Winter waned; March arrived. The Swansons had given me a red jacket their daughter had outgrown, and now with warmer weather I was determined to wear it. Mama and Papa harbored less trust of the weather than I. Finally, on March 17, St. Patrick's Day, I was allowed to wear The Red Jacket over my green sweater.

Temperatures were moderate, the sun was shining, and I fairly skipped to the bus. I was free of my heavy winter gear. By mid-morning recess low gray clouds were spitting snow, winds arose, and the temperature dropped. By lunch recess it was snowing hard—tiny, icy flakes driven on an increasing wind. The Red Jacket lost its glory. I was cold! We gratefully entered our warm classroom as we stomped snow from our boots.

Unlike most of our teachers, Mrs. Adams grew up on the northern Montana prairie, and she knew the whims of weather here. She frequently stopped teaching and looked out the windows. By now the world outside was white with snow blown horizontally. Mrs. Adams seemed worried and distracted. I felt increasingly uneasy. I believed that this might be a blizzard.

Somebody knocked on our classroom door, and Mrs. Adams stepped out. We children were unusually quiet. When she stepped back inside she told us that school was being dismissed early, and she ordered us to put on all of our outdoor clothing. I was not the only one who had just worn a jacket to school, but that did not help me. We lined up in two lines as she directed. The town-student line left first. They were to walk directly home as fast as they could. The bus students were to board their buses.

Nathan made sure that we three girls were on the bus before he climbed aboard himself. Sherman had stayed home to help Papa move hay from Combs' farm to ours. Scotty, our bus driver, drove slowly out of town as the road became more difficult to see. Rather than the usual noisy visiting, teasing, and laughing, the bus was silent as we all strained to see the road. Scotty leaned toward the windshield and gripped the steering wheel tensely as the bus crept forward. Finally, we crossed the Milk River Bridge at the southeast corner of our farm.

We were almost home, but how could we see to get to our house? Scotty drove through the swirling whiteness inch by inch. Our mailbox became visible, but the nearby railroad was obliterated by the snow. Scotty turned into our driveway, stopped the bus, and stood up.

"We have to return to town," he announced. "Going on is too dangerous. Every one of you start thinking of some place in town where you can spend the night. It must be some place near our bus route. I can't drive all over town."

Nathan hurried to the front of the bus. "I'm getting off," he announced.

"I can't let you off in this blizzard!" Scotty objected.

"Let me off," Nathan demanded. "I need to help at home."

Scotty opened the door and Nathan hopped out. Scotty began backing the bus, so he could turn onto the town road and head back to town. A loud banging was heard on the door. When he opened the door, Nathan stepped onto the bus, but not far enough for Scotty to close the door. Nathan was totally covered in snow. "You girls stay together," he ordered looking at me, and, wiping snow from his face and eyes, he jumped back off the bus with Scotty telling him he could not get home in the blizzard. Nathan disappeared in the snow. I began praying for Nathan. Mama had told me many stories about people freezing to death after becoming lost in blizzards. If we couldn't even see the front end of the bus, how would Nathan ever get home? Fear clutched me.

We inched back to town through blinding snow and screaming winds. I had plenty of time to recall Mama's stories. Many homesteads had ropes tied to posts leading from the house to all outbuildings, so homesteaders could find their way back to the house during blizzards.

I most vividly remembered Mama's story about Emmett Averial, Mrs. Clark's hired man. One of his jobs was to ride his horse to Barr to the post office-store for mail and supplies. Emmett set out for town on a clear winter morning. By mid-afternoon the sky grew dark and a blizzard howled in. Emmett did not show up. Mrs. Clark stayed up all night with lamps burning near windows, in hopes Emmett would be guided home by the light. Morning came, the blizzard had blown out, but Emmett had not come home.

Henry Lick rode over to the neighbors, and they organized a search party. They found Emmett's horse not far from Mrs. Clark's homestead—it was frozen. This narrowed their search for him. At last they found him leaning against a haystack—also frozen. Unsure of what to do with him, they brought him to Mrs. Clark's yard. Mama said she could never get the picture of Emmett out of her mind. He had a rope of link sausages hanging around his neck like a scarf. Mrs. Clark concluded that he became too cold to reason coherently. Otherwise, he would have burrowed into the haystack to get out of the blizzard.

The bus trip back to town was silent except for the howling wind and the bus engine as it roared through drifts. The only people I could think of, who lived on the bus route were Anna and Jake Peters from our church. Once Scotty drove across The Dike, Peters' house was our first stop. I trudged through screaming, cutting winds; blinding, stinging snow; and growing dusk to ask if we girls could spend the night. Mr. Peters answered the door. "Yes, bring Grace and Dolly in."

Once we were in the house, Mr. Peters said that Anna was not there. It had looked to be such a beautiful day that she had driven to Lustre to see her family, and now she would not be able to return. The Peters did not have any children, and it was apparent to me that he had no idea what to do for three little girls. We were hungry, so I asked for bread, butter, and peanut butter, so I could fix sandwiches for us.

He volunteered that Anna's sisters made the sofa into a bed and slept there. He unfolded the sofa and brought some pillows and quilts. He said he must go to bed early, so he could get up early for his delivery route. I knew that he drove a bread delivery truck.

Once we said goodnight, we girls were more comfortable than when he was standing around watching helplessly. We knew of nothing else to do, so we pulled off our shoes and went to bed. I whispered to Grace and Dolly that they must pray for Nathan.

It was light when we woke up. Mr. Peters had set out some cereal and gone to work. Morning sun glittered off hard drifted snow outside. After we ate and washed a sink and counter full of dirty dishes we could not think of anything to do in a strange house not meant for children. Suddenly, I remembered! The Crane's house was just down the street. Wes Crane and Matie Crane, brother and sister, lived there. We sometimes visited them, because Mama and Papa knew them from homestead days.

I left a note for Mr. Peters that told him we were going to Cranes' house. Matie and Wes were surprised to see us. I explained our predicament. We were not the only ones stranded in town—the Askelson family from The Bench had spent the night at Crane's. Mr. Askelson was in town to pick up Mrs. Askelson and their son Tommy, who looked to be Dolly's age. Tommy had a tonsillectomy, and they were all to go home yesterday when the blizzard struck. They were thankful they had not left town yet, because they might well have frozen on the road. Their other children were home, but they were older and they would be all right.

When Matie Crane explained we were the children of Helen Clark Sherwood and John Sherwood, Mrs. Askelson smiled warmly at us.

"Your mother, Miss Clark, was my teacher when I was in eighth grade!"

We were more comfortable at Cranes, but I kept watching for Papa to come to get us. Wes said they would not have the road plowed as far as our house and nobody could get through the drifts.

Tommy Askelson played with his new top pumping the handle up and down to make the top spin around and around. We girls had never owned a top, so we were pleased when Tommy invited us to sit in a circle with him on the floor as he generously allowed each of us to have turns passing his top around the circle.

Mrs. Askelson visited with Matie near enough to us for us to hear what they said. They talked about homestead friends, and I listened attentively when they mentioned Mama. Eaves-dropping is not polite, so I tried hard to appear to be focusing on the top.

"I loved Miss Clark!" Mrs. Askelson told Matie. "I was in the eighth grade, and while I could read, I read very little. We didn't have books, except the Bible, in our home, and we only had our text books at school. Miss Clark brought the world of reading to us. Not only did she bring books from home to read to us, she could tell more stories and recite more poetry from memory than anybody I knew before or since. And her voice! What a voice she had! She should have been in theater."

"That was exactly what she really wanted to do," Matie told Mrs. Askelson, "but her mother wouldn't hear of it. I can't say I blame her mother. I don't have children, but if I did, theater is not what I would want them to do."

"She was pretty, fun, and lively. We girls all wanted to be like Miss Clark." Mrs. Askelson laughed, "I don't know if she beguiled the school board into buying some books for a small library, or if Miss Clark was just the first teacher to ask for the books."

"Helen and I palled around for several years." Matie smiled remembering, "She was laughing and spirited. Men like that. I remember when John came to the homestead after the war. We girls were all after him, but Helen got him."

Matie sighed, "After Helen lost her first two babies she changed. Her spirit was broken. Sometimes when we visit I see the old Helen, but not often."

I knew Mama did not lose her first two babies—it was the first and third babies. I didn't say anything, for fear they would stop talking about Mama.

Morning passed comfortably, and we ate our noon meal with them. Shortly after we ate a neighbor of theirs knocked on the door. She stepped in and looked at us girls. "Are you the Sherwood girls? There was an announcement on the radio asking everybody to go to their neighbors to see if they had seen the Sherwood girls. They are the only ones missing after the blizzard."

Word was sent to Papa who was standing by at LaFond's Packing Plant phone waiting for a call about us girls and for snow plows to clear the town road. When Papa picked us up at the Crane's he told us Nathan had found his way to the house and that his doing so was nothing short of a miracle. At home Mama reiterated that it was purely providential that Nathan had floundered through blinding snow close enough to the house to see the lights. She said he had stumbled in a veritable snowman and half frozen. Nathan said that he had thought he was going to freeze to death before he could find the house.

That night at supper Papa prayed a heartfelt prayer of thanks for our safety. ଈଓ

CHAPTER 32

LOOKING BACK AT MURDER

"I'm leaving Montana, I threw away my bandana," Sherman sang.

The final word on moving was left up to Mama. It was she whose health was most affected by the long, cold winters. The record setting cold of the previous winter followed by spring's stressful flood had pushed Mama nearer moving. But it was this spring's blizzard of '51, and Mama's awareness of how close Nathan had come to dying, that cinched her decision to move.

She and Papa had often discussed where they would move. They ordered books and checked out more books from the library. Going back to Idaho was out of the question. They narrowed the field to Missouri and Arizona. Mama's rheumatoid arthritis would be better in the arid climate of Arizona, but the vegetation there did not appeal to her. While she had learned to love the prairie, there were times she longed for the trees and green grass she had known when living in Minnesota. She chose the Missouri Ozarks.

When the snow melted and the rising river receded, Papa listed our farm for sale in the *Glasgow Courier*. Time was spent sorting our belongings as though we were moving and preparing the fields and garden as though we were staying. If the farm did not sell, we were prepared to stay, but we were also prepared to go. Each day we raced home from the bus to hear whether the farm had sold. Finally, one day Mama was able to tell us, "Yes, the farm has sold." We were elated! Moving seemed a grand adventure.

Papa set our moving date to be the first of June after the school year ended. He traded our 1937 Chevrolet truck for a gray-green 1948 Ford two-ton truck. We girls lost the only truck we had ever known. It had hauled German prisoners, hay, crops, cattle, and hundreds of tons of wheat to elevators. It had twice made the move to and from Idaho. Now this new truck would take us to Missouri.

"Will you miss Montana?" I asked Mama one day when I was helping her in the kitchen.

"Yes, I will miss our friends. Every time you move you leave a part of you behind. And moves are expensive. It is said that one move is as costly as having a fire burn you out. This move will be even more expensive, because we are going so far and we are leaving most of what we have behind.

"I'm forty-eight, and for some people who have good health, like Mrs. Clark, that's young. With my poor health I have aged faster than most people. Now I need to live where we have warmer winters. A pretty place where life will be easier."

⁂

Mrs. Clark and Mr. Larson came to dinner the first Sunday in May, as they did every Sunday now. Mrs. Clark brought most of the dinner, so Mama would not have so much to do. Once they arrived Mrs. Clark assumed responsibility in the kitchen and sent Mama to lie down and rest. She said that Mama was looking too tired. Mama was grateful for the rest, but later she complained to Papa that she was being treated like a child. With Mrs. Clark in the kitchen, the dinner process was speeded up. In her flurry of activity, she directed us children as to what we should be doing to help. And, she expected full compliance from us. Unlike Mama she tolerated no whining.

After one Sunday dinner and before we left the table, Mrs. Clark told Papa that she wanted to know the real story of Mrs. Kaderly's murder on Papa's homestead. She took out her cigarettes and silver cigarette holder. "May I?" she always asked before lighting up. At Mama's insistence, Papa had stopped smoking two years ago. She said that smoking was harmful to his health and holding a cigarette in his lips had to be harmful for his skin.

"We in the Genevieve Country heard rumor after rumor about the murder. It was amazing how far and fast, without drums or smoke signals, news traveled on the prairie—rather like wildfire. And, the more salacious the story the faster it traveled." She looked expectantly at Papa.

Papa tilted back in his chair.

The Kaderlys, a young couple with two small daughters had lost their homestead after he was injured and unable to work. When my brother Henry moved to Idaho I rented and farmed his homestead, because it bordered mine. I didn't use the house, so I let Kaderlys live there rent free. The wife let it be known around the community that she was willing to cook and clean house to earn some money. Besides feeling sorry for them, I had way more than I could do on two homesteads, so I hired her to come over to clean and cook dinner three days a week. Two or three other days she went to a different homestead.

Bill Costin and I traded work when we needed an extra hand. One day I was putting up hay, and Costin came to help. Mrs. Kaderly was already there by the time he showed up. She made a fresh pot of coffee and we three visited a short time before we left for the hayfield.

Costin and I worked in the hay until dinner time. When we went to my house to eat we saw that Mrs. Kaderly had obviously started dinner, but she was nowhere to be seen. We called and called and checked the out-buildings with no success. Then we looked in the garden. There she lay all puffed up and dead. We believed she had been bitten by a rattlesnake, even though I had never seen one near the house.

Costin had a car that he had driven over to help me. He left immediately to go to Opheim to get Dr. Rosak and call the sheriff in Glasgow. I really stewed. Here I was a bachelor and this young woman is dead at my house. Clearly, she died of poisoning—either a rattlesnake or other means. Dr. Rosak checked her over in the garden when he arrived. He saw no sign of snakebite. We waited and waited for Sheriff Benson. The three of us kept going over the things we could imagine as possibilities of her being poisoned.

Finally, Sheriff Benson came. He had us move her to the bed, so Dr. Rosak could give her a thorough check for snakebite. In the meantime, Sheriff Benson took notes from Costin and me. He then went over everything outside and inside, repeatedly. Especially, the dishes and food items. Dr. Rosak reported that there was no snakebite. She had been poisoned. But, how and by whom?

We thought of her husband, but he had to be at home watching the little girls. Somebody must have known Costin and I would be putting up hay in a field out of sight of the house. Sheriff Benson speculated that somebody she knew came to the house and had coffee with her, poisoned her coffee, washed the cups, and left. But, who would want to kill Mrs. Kaderly?

We loaded Mrs. Kaderly's body into Dr. Rosak's car. Before Sheriff Benson left for the day, he looked at me. 'Sherwood, you are one damn lucky man that Costin was here this morning!'

Sheriff Benson was back and forth for two weeks checking with all the neighbors and looking for clues. He was told what I had heard—that Mrs. Kaderly was having an affair with Gordon Hulme who was also married. And, Hulme, other than Marie Costin, was the only person who knew that Costin and I were putting up hay in the north field that day. But, he came up with an ironclad alibi. Marie Costin would never have done such a thing. Anyway, Bill Costin had their car. I always suspected Hulme, but it was an unsolved murder—like too many on the prairie.

Mama had met and visited with the Hulmes after she and Papa married.

"All of you forgot one person," Mama said, "Julia Hulme. If Gordon knew where you would be putting up hay, he probably mentioned it to her."

Mrs. Clark flicked ash from her cigarette. "What was Julia like?"

Mama was ready with an answer, "Let's just say that if I were having an affair with her husband, I would not have been having coffee with her!"

༄· · o · ·༅

After Mrs. Clark and Mr. Larsen had left, we children coaxed more prairie stories from Mama and Papa.

Papa turned to Mama, "The children have never seen our Barnard homestead, and wouldn't you like to see it one last time? Our truck has low mileage, but it is used, and it needs to be driven a distance to check it out before we start on our twelve-hundred-mile move. What do you think about driving up there Sunday, if the weather is good?"

Mama was wistful, "Sometimes I dream I am back on the prairie. When I first saw it I was disappointed, but I grew to love it. The prairie has a beauty all its own—it gets in your blood. Yes! Let's go."

Papa looked at us children, "You will appreciate our river bottom farm once you see the homestead, but we knew good years and good times there." Papa was quiet a moment, "In fact," he added, "Some of the best years of my life were spent on the homestead. After the Great War all I wanted and needed to do was to get away from the world." He laughed. "When you see the homestead you will see that it is definitely away from the world!"

A short drive up from the Milk River valley lay The Bench, the beginning of the high prairie land of the Great Plains. We had sometimes driven up to The Bench and the prairie. I fully suspected the rest of the prairie would be the same—not much to see. Yet, it would be interesting to see where Mama and Papa had lived; we had heard so much about it. A trip was rare and welcome.

Saturday after supper Mama and I packed a picnic lunch. We prepared chicken sandwiches, boiled eggs, oatmeal cookies, and jars of water. Sunday morning there was no church for us. Barnard was far away, and we needed to get an early start.

Papa drove, and drove, and drove. This was our longest trip since moving to Glasgow. Soft gray-green tufts of spring grass covered the prairie, except for wheat fields. The fields of winter wheat were somewhat greener and taller than the more recently sprouted fields of spring wheat. Only an occasional small creek with scrubby shrubs and, sometimes, gnarled cottonwood trees relieved the monotony of low rolling hill after low rolling hill. They all looked alike. Now I understood Mama's stories about people getting lost on the prairie.

"This," declared Sherman, "Must be the most god-forsaken place in the world!"

At long last, after only one stop en route, Papa parked the truck. We scrambled to get out. Prairie winds whipped us as we children looked around with deep disappointment.

"Where are your buildings?" Nathan asked Papa.

"After the government relocated farmers from their homesteads during the thirties, all buildings were bulldozed down."

We followed Papa around as he showed us where his buildings had been. All that remained was a large white rock slab he had brought from the field on his stone-boat. It had served as a step to his homestead shack.

"Where did you get water?" Sherman looked around for a pump.

"I was lucky. See that gully." Papa pointed to a small brushy gully downhill from his house site. "A spring trickled from this upper end of the gully all year. I made a dam, and the spring was sufficient to fill a small pond for the cows. I was even able to water some cottonwood trees I planted."

We looked at the two remaining scraggly cottonwood trees. Compared to those on Milk River they looked pathetic.

Mama called us to the lunch she had set out on blankets. "Well, what do you think?"

We didn't know what to say. I thought it to be an awful place to live. I was sure the others thought the same.

Finally, Sherman spoke, "All I can say is that I'm sure glad we aren't moving back here."

Papa looked around. "It does look rather grim now. I see it as it looked in the good years when rain was adequate." He motioned southward. "Looking south from the house I could see the sweep of the large valley with hills on the horizon. The time of day and weather determined the ever-changing color of the hills." He pointed east. "That big field rippled sky-blue when the flax was in bloom. And over there," he pointed west, "That field undulated like liquid gold when the wheat was ripe."

"So many different kinds of wildflowers bloomed on the prairie," Mama remembered. "It took me a long time to stop comparing the prairie to the lush green fields and vibrant colored flowers of Minnesota. Beauty here is softer, more subtle. But beauty is here once your eyes are trained to see it."

I knew with a certainty that I didn't want to spend enough time on the prairie to learn to appreciate the beauty Mama saw.

"I prefer the green of our farm," I announced.

"The Milk River valley is like a narrow green ribbon threaded through the muted colors of the vast prairie," she informed me.

We children ran off to explore when we finished eating. Papa helped Mama put away the lunch items and blankets; then they walked hand in hand around where the buildings had been.

"Give me Idaho," Nathan said as soon as were at some distance.

"Amen!" echoed Sherman, "Thank God we are moving to Missouri!" Knowing there was a place like Idaho, I could not see how anybody would settle here intentionally.

Soon it was time for the long trip home. When we arrived, Papa pronounced the Ford truck to be everything he hoped it would be. He was confident it would carry us safely to Missouri with no maintenance problems. ⁊

CHAPTER 33

THE PROMISED LAND

Mama insisted we make one more trip before moving to Missouri, this time to Opheim. She wanted to see her babies' graves. I heard Papa tell Sherman that he didn't know what to do. He feared going to the cemetery would give her an emotional setback.

Mrs. Clark was also worried, and she tried to discourage Mama's going. "Helen, you are too fragile emotionally to allow yourself to get worked up over the past. You are beginning a new chapter of your life. Just look forward."

But, Mama had never seen her babies' graves, and she was determined to go. "I always knew I could go when I wanted to," Mama told Mrs. Clark, "That will no longer be the case. I am strong enough to go, and this will be my last chance."

Papa set aside a sunny day in late May for the trip. Sherman and Nathan stayed home to work.

Mama and Papa had talked fondly of Opheim as far back as I could remember, but we girls had never seen the place. Once there, I concluded that we had not missed anything. It was a small, raw, bare, unattractive western town whipped by grit carried on an eternal prairie wind.

Papa drove to the cemetery that was surprisingly well-cared for and attractive. Mama told us the beautiful bushes with little yellow flowers surrounding the cemetery were caragana, or, as some people called them, Siberian pea shrubs. We girls followed as Papa searched for John and Mabel's grave markers. He stopped in an area near the border of shrubs where many small white crosses stood.

"I know it was in this area, and the crosses I placed here had their names on them. That was twenty years ago, and the crosses have been replaced. They have added more crosses since then."

"You have to find John and Mabel's graves," Mama's voice rose.

Papa sighed and looked around. "We'll have to drive to the café and see if anybody knows who has a plat map of the cemetery." He was directed to see Mrs. Walstad.

When Papa knocked on her door a lady about Mama's age answered. After Papa told her who he was and what he wanted, she opened her door and beckoned for Mama to come in. We girls scooted out of the truck and followed, before we could be told not to.

Mama and Papa told their story about John and Mabel.

"I remember them!" she exclaimed. "Mr. Walstad and I owned the lumber yard, and we also made coffins. Everett made your babies' coffins and I lined them."

Mama began to cry. Mrs. Walstad patted her shoulder. "Your babies have lovely coffins. They are softly lined with thick cotton padding covered by rosebud fabric. I kept it on hand for babies."

Mrs. Walstad grew teary, "There were so many babies. And, your losing two babies in such a short time would have been so very, very hard."

She turned to Papa, "I don't have a plat map of the cemetery, but I know who does. You and I can just walk over to his house."

When they returned Papa reported that the man was not at home. He told Mrs. Walstad that we must find the graves today, because we were moving next week.

Mrs. Walstad frowned and thought. Suddenly, she brightened. "I believe I can find the graves! I attended graveside services for both babies."

She went on to explain to Mama, "We formed a volunteer group at church of those willing to attend services for the deceased on short notice. Many of the homestead families who have a member die must get back to their homesteads. Often other family and neighbors didn't even know who died until after the burial. We didn't want any family to attend the services alone, so we went to be with them."

"I know," Mama replied in a shaky voice, "John said it was such a comfort." We girls climbed into the back of the truck and Mrs. Walstad rode in the cab by Mama. Once at the cemetery, Mrs. Walstad walked decisively to two of the little white crosses.

"I remember. These are your babies' graves. She then turned to us girls. "Let's take a little walk and give your parents time together."

When we returned Papa was helping Mama into the truck. The day was beautiful, warm, and sunny. We girls chose to ride in back.

Mrs. Walstad said good-bye to Mama and walked with Papa around to his side of the cab. Just as he was climbing in Mrs. Walstad called to him.

"Oh, Mr. Sherwood, this back tire looks low."

Papa came back and bent down to check the tire. Mrs. Walstad leaned over. "God forgive me. I didn't know which graves were right, but Helen needed to know."

Papa rose, looked at her, and shook her hand, "God will bless you."

"I'll put a little air in the tire when we get home." He announced to all of us as he climbed back into the truck cab.

Once home, Mama went to bed. Papa tossed a dish towel over his shoulder and cooked his favorite breakfast for our supper: ham, eggs, and his original honey buns.

The next morning Mama came into the bedroom to get us up as usual. She never mentioned the Opheim trip, nor did any of the rest of us.

She reminded us that today was the neighborhood picnic for us at Preston Meyers' farm. The Meyers family lived across the town road from the Biddles family. Neighborhood picnics were always anticipated with excitement, this one even more so, because it was for us. But it was also sobering. We had known most of these people for six years, and now we were leaving.

When we arrived, tables had been set up outside, and women were filling two of them with food. After everyone had eaten as much of the delicious food as we could hold, the women and big girls cleaned up; then settled down to visit.

Two of the teen-aged girls came out to organize games for us children. We played red rover, drop the handkerchief, tug of war, and darebase. Later, left to our own devices, we visited, played marbles, jumped rope, and played tag.

The men and big boys played horse shoes, baseball, and a football game called 500. Mr. Meyers let some of the older boys take turns riding his horse. When it was Nathan's turn he rode under a low branch, and it swept him off the horse. Mama was called to check him, but he was unhurt—except for his ego.

As we drove home Mama said that life was like a picnic. No matter how much you like it, the time comes when you are ready to go home.

⁊⊙· · ◦ · ·⊙ᴦ

Our church congregation held a party for us at Anna and Jake Peters' house. From time to time friends drove out to our farm to bring food, to help Mama and Papa with last minute jobs, or just to visit and say good-bye. We girls mostly stayed out of the way.

A few days before we were to leave Nathan was given a reprieve from work to go with us girls so we could walk around the farm and say good-bye to our favorite places. A rancher had wanted to take Rover, so now just Lulu and

Pinky walked with us. We went to The Big Ditch and smelled the water, cattails, and willows one last time. We walked past The Bee Tree to the woods to visit a group of box elder trees we called The Pretty Trees. We had spent many, many hours climbing them and playing on them.

Our farm did not seem quite like our farm with so many of the animals gone. I alternately felt sad about missing a familiar way of life and excited about a new life ahead of me. We only saw a few cows on our walk, because Papa had sold most of the milking cows and all of the non-milking livestock. Gone were the pigs from the pigpen. No geese announced a car driving up, because they too had been sold. Only a few chickens remained. The new owners would not sell eggs or cream. Mr. Kountz was a mechanic in town, and he had limited time to work on the farm.

As the time for our move grew closer Mrs. Clark and Mr. Larson had visited more and more often; Mr. Larson helped Papa, and Mrs. Clark bustled about helping Mama and giving her directions. The rest of the packing moved along so smoothly that Mama overlooked Mrs. Clark's bossiness. The day before moving day they came one last time to help and to say good-bye.

Papa drove the Ford tractor onto the truck bed leaving enough room in front of the tractor for us children and our pets. Our dogs Pinky and Lulu, our cat Eemy, and Homer Pigeon were moving with us. The tractor was secured so it could not move, and all else was tightly packed around and under the tractor and two pieces of tractor equipment. Sorting had been a difficult process, because if it did not fit, it did not go. We left almost everything. That which we thought the Kountzes could not use, we burned. When the men finished loading the truck they wrapped tarps around all that must not get wet.

By evening the truck was ready to go. Sherman and Nathan wanted to spend the night sleeping in the truck bed, because they would be doing so on our trip to Missouri. Papa would park our truck in front of a motel room where he, Mama, and we girls would stay each night. Sherman and Nathan would sleep in the truck, so they would be with the pets and also on the lookout, if anybody tried to steal from the truck.

Mrs. Clark had brought a picnic supper with her when she came. Now we all sat down together for one last time. As always, the talk turned to the Genevieve Country and the Barnard Community and the people they knew there. They talked of the intervening years and how quickly time had passed. Mama laughed, "Remember Bachelor Limberg on the prairie. I saw him in

Glasgow yesterday. We were reminiscing, and he told me that time passed so fast now, because the earth is spinning faster!"

Talk shifted to Missouri and our expectations there. Everybody agreed that they looked forward to less brutal winters. When Sherman said that Missouri sounded like the Promised Land, Papa laughed, "That is exactly what I said about Montana when I left Missouri. Always remember, every Promised Land comes with its own set of trials and tribulations."

When Mrs. Clark hugged us all for the last time, she and Mama both cried. They had been through so very much together.

After they left Mama told Papa that Mr. Larson had found an opportunity to talk to her. He assured Mama he would always take care of Mrs. Clark, and Mama need not worry about her.

Mama looked puzzled, "It never occurred to me that Mrs. Clark might need to be cared for. She was always in charge, and, somehow, I assumed she always would be."

∾෨· · · ○ · · ·෨∾

June 1st we woke up early. Shortly after sunrise Nathan, Grace, Dolly, and I donned jackets to walk to the west end of our farm where Papa, Mama, and Sherman would meet us. The truck load was too high to go under the underpass, and Papa would drive out the farm road. It would do us children good to stretch our legs before the long day's ride. We girls had been much too excited to eat breakfast, so Nathan carried a paper bag with sandwiches in it. When we had walked for a way, we turned to look back at the Old House, the New House, and all the buildings one last time.

We heard the Ford truck coming just as we reached the spillway road. Sherman helped us into the truck. He and Papa would take turns driving and navigating with the maps. Nathan would stay in back with us girls.

Nathan climbed onto the tractor seat. "I'm going to be able to say I rode a tractor all the way from Montana to Missouri!"

We rode through Glasgow in the early morning hours. Few people were about. We children startled those that were by yelling "Missouri or bust!"

Papa drove our Ford truck into the sun and headed up out of the green ribbon of the Milk River Valley across northeastern Montana's windswept high plains for the last time. ෨∾

ACKNOWLEDGMENTS

The value of the gift of encouragement cannot be measured."
—RMS

The completion of this book would not have been realized without much encouragement and help. My heartfelt appreciation goes to the following and any others whose names I've missed.

Linda Peavy, my mentor, my friend—and an accomplished author in her own right—shared her expertise and offered on-going encouragement as I worked to transform a book of family memories into a memoir that would appeal to a wider audience. And, as she has done for other fledgling writers, she helped me find the right publisher for this book.

Linda directed me to Erin Turner, Editor and Director of Publications at Farcountry Press. Erin read my collection of family stories and gave me suggestions for restructuring and refocusing my stories to create a book of wider interest. Erin's belief in my book and my ability to revise it gave me confidence.

Valerie and Laurel are the pillars of my support system.

Brittany's interest in these stories and my desire for Michael to know them were my inspiration for writing them.

Michael missed hearing the stories, and I wrote them so he too would know family history.

Nancy B's interest in my stories led me to believe that others who are not family would enjoy them, also.

Bob offered computer assistance and patiently shared my attention.

Eleanor H. and Carol M. edited for clarity and orthography.

Jeff, Missy, Doris, and Olaf assisted with family historical information.

David H. gave invaluable technology for my research.

Grace and Dolly gave family reality checks and generous encouragement.

Nancy R. and Jack read and gave feedback about the farm activities.

Grace was a consistent, willing source of information for me. Her vast general knowledge plus her scientific, geological, and computer expertise proved to be invaluable.

About the
Sherwood Siblings

The Sherwood siblings in 1967 after Papa's funeral. Front: Grace, Ruth, Dolly; Back: Nathan, Sherman, Willie

Marvin **(Willie) Sherwood**, born 1930, joined the army when he was eighteen. He proudly served his four years of military service as a paratrooper in the 82nd Airborne Division, with multiple jumps from fixed wing and glider planes. After discharge he became a merchant mariner on ore ships on the Great Lakes, training that served him well when he later sailed on ships that delivered military matériel to our troops in Viet Nam as well as on ocean drilling ships, and a military reconnaissance ship in the Mediterranean Sea during the Desert Storm Campaign. He worked in the oil fields of Texas for years, finally returning to Missouri to live after retirement.

Sherman Sherwood, born 1932, served as a paratrooper in the 11th Airborne Division of the U.S. Army. Later he worked as a merchant mariner on ore ships sailing the Great Lakes. Sherman, like Papa, wanted only to farm. He bought land near family in Missouri where he lived the rest of his life. On his beloved farm, Sherman built up a herd of registered Limousin cattle, in which he took great pride.

ભ⊙· · · o · · ·⊙જ

Nathan Sherwood, born 1935, was stationed in Germany part of the time when he served as a U.S. Army paratrooper with the 82nd Airborne Division. He visited every place in Europe where his father had been during WWI. After leaving the military Nathan worked for various companies in oil fields. Most of his career was spent as an oil field consultant. He worked in countries in Central America, South America, Europe, Africa, and many western states in the United States. Nathan spoke fluent Spanish from working in Spanish-speaking countries and with Spanish-speaking employees. His favorite quote was, "A rolling stone gathers no moss."

ભ⊙· · · o · · ·⊙જ

When **Ruth Sherwood**, born in 1940, was 31 years old, she bought a like-new Catalina Pontiac and a small travel trailer. She and her two daughters packed some necessities into the travel trailer and drove from Missouri to Fairbanks, Alaska. In 1971, the Alaska Highway had only 300 of its 1500 miles paved. Moving to Alaska was the best decision she ever made, and she stayed for 28 years. She taught in public schools around the state. Her favorite place to live was Homer, and her favorite place to teach was on the Pribilof Islands in the Bering Sea. Her master's degree focused on reading and qualified Ruth to certify as a Reading Specialist. Believing that reading is the most important subject taught in school, she wrote a successful beginning reading program.

ભ⊙· · · o · · ·⊙જ

Grace Sherwood, born in 1941, grew up loving the outdoors, nature, and rocks. After high school she became a registered nurse. As a young nurse she studied midwifery in London, England. Back in the United States, she served as an officer in the USAF Nurse Corps during the Vietnam War. In a major career change, Grace then attended Montana State University, where she majored in geology. She obtained a Master of Science in Earth Sciences, studying basaltic volcanism in the Pribilof Islands in the Bering Sea on a grant from the National Geographic Society. This led to teaching geology for several years.

Grace still loves the outdoors, nature, and rocks, and now works as a geologist and naturalist on National Geographic expedition ships.

Mary (Dolly) Sherwood, born in 1943, has always prioritized faith and family. She still attends the same church her family began attending when they moved to Missouri in 1951. When Mary's children were almost grown, she enrolled in Missouri State University and graduated cum laude in three and a half years while commuting 100 miles round trip and never missing any of her son's basketball games. She loved teaching school and the students. While still teaching full time she earned a master's degree in education, and traveled to beautiful San Andres Island off the coast of Nicaragua in the Caribbean Sea, assisting a Christian college with their education program. She retired from teaching full time after 21 years, but continued to work as a substitute teacher for 5 more years. ৶

About the Author

Ruth Sherwood

A blizzard howled across Montana's high plains, down the Milk River Valley, and into the small railroad town of Hinsdale the day Ruth Sherwood was born in 1940. Her parents, no stranger to blizzards, had both homesteaded in different areas to the north. Many of Ruth's early years were spent along the Milk River and Great Northern Railway. She grew up with rich stories of homesteading from her parents and family friends from their homesteading days.

Once grown, Ruth sought her own adventures. Her example was her colorful grandmother, Mrs. Caroline Clark, who left high society life in Minnesota in 1915, and with her daughter, Helen, Ruth's mother, claimed a homestead in the Genevieve Country of northern Valley County, Montana. Here she succeeded where many men failed.

In 1971 Ruth left her old life, taking her two young daughters to Alaska to build a new life. She purchased a like-new Pontiac and a small travel trailer. They packed some necessities and drove north to Alaska; she never looked back. Ruth carried with her a solitary silver fork that belonged to the set Mrs. Clark had shipped from Minnesota to Montana.

Towing her small trailer over the Alaska Highway, when only 300 miles of the 1,500 miles of the road were paved, was the beginning of an exciting adventure. Once settled in Fairbanks Ruth worked as an educator for the Alaska Public Schools System. She taught in many areas of the state. Every area held its own beauty and interests. Ruth and her family made the most of Alaska's magnificent outdoors. They hiked, backpacked, camped, fished, hunted, and snow- machined.

When Ruth's girls were older, she spent three summers in Seattle earning her master's degree from Seattle Pacific University. Raised in a home where reading was valued and trips to the public library were always enjoyed, Ruth focused on reading. She developed a successful beginning reading program that she employed in her job as a reading specialist. She also produced a manual and taught her reading program to other teachers.

Retired from teaching, Ruth had time to reflect upon her unique past. The story of her family's farm life and her parent's homesteading lives in Montana are retold in her book, *Where the Wind Never Sleeps, A Memoir from the High Plains of Montana.* ⁐